FORBIDDEN THINGS: BOOK THREE

APOSTATE

NIKKI McCORMACK

ISBN-13: 978-0-9963196-6-9
First Edition 2016

Published by
Elysium Books
Seattle, WA

Written by Nikki McCormack
(https://nikkimccormack.com/)
Cover Design by Robert Crescenzio
(https://robertcrescenzio.artstation.com/)
Spot Illustration by Raquel Neira
(http://kellieart.deviantart.com/)
Layout & Typesetting by Brian C. Short

•

*To Uncle Greg
for your love, enthusiastic encouragement,
and fantastic editing.*

•

Indigo moved her mount out at a swift trot to keep pace with the jogging Kudaness. Their stamina in the sand was an impressive thing, but it meant she had to harden the ground under her horse with every stride to keep up his pace without injuring him. That effort required significant energy expenditure, though it didn't seem to be wearing her down as fast as it had the night she left Yiloch and the others to seek out Suac Chozai. Once she recovered from the side effects of the drug the suac had given her to enable a walk with his gods, her ascard connection was crisp and strong, almost more so than it had been before.

Since the Kudaness looked on deliberate use of ascard as a form of blasphemy, it had already become a source of friction between her and Chozai. Their initial confrontation on the matter was still fresh in her mind. Chozai had stopped them perhaps an hour outside of the Murak village and led her away from the warriors.

"You must stop your use of ascard. Your use of it is an affront to our gods and consequently an affront to us. I cannot allow it to continue and expect to retain the respect of my warriors."

She'd swept the group with her gaze, noting the dark looks they gave her, then met his copper eyes. "Those gods you speak of have already confirmed my path. I cannot keep up the pace you set on foot and I will not injure this horse. If you take issue with my methods, I suggest you discuss it with your gods."

Chozai's answering scowl had chilled her blood, but he had turned away and ordered them to continue their journey. Her refusal to be cowed by him had earned her his grudging respect and they had both shared the vision that sent them on this journey. He was unwilling to argue against the will of the gods

Before leaving his home village, the suac sent messengers out to several Murak villages to request that they ready their warriors and send them to the northernmost village. Along the way, they stopped at two other Murak villages so Chozai could give them the same message. From there, they continued into the Farid tribal lands, resting during the hottest part of the day and traveling through most of the night.

She felt the press of time, knowing the Grey Army had a considerable lead over them. If this journey were successful, would the Kudaness gather only to arrive in Yiroth and find it destroyed? They might still defeat the Grey Army in that case, but it mattered little to her if Lyra was already defeated. Yiloch would try to save his empire at any cost. That was who he was, and she shared his desire to protect that empire even if she no longer held his love.

They came upon the first Farid village midmorning on the third day, a collection of huts gaining form on the horizon. When they were close enough to make out villagers among the huts, a flood of armed warriors surged out to intercept them and she gathered ascard to her as a precaution. Chozai signaled their group to stop. She brought her horse up beside him as the Murak warriors moved in close, weapons ready and eyes full of grim determination.

"They don't look that pleased to see us," she commented, trying not to let the tremor of fear in her chest pass her lips.

Chozai's sour grimace wasn't reassuring. "Murak and Farid have long been rivals. If they can be turned to your cause, the rest will be easy."

"If they can't?"

Chozai said nothing.

She watched the approaching warriors, calming her mount with ascard so her fear wouldn't panic the animal. When they were close enough, she realized that the man in the lead bore no weapons and, like Suac Chozai, tattoos covered most of his visible flesh. Another Kudaness high priest.

"He is their suac?"

Chozai nodded. "He is why we come to this village first. With your power and the aid of a second suac, the suacs of the other tribes can be contacted through a walk with the gods."

She shuddered, recalling the vile taste of the liquid he'd given her to initiate the previous walk with the gods and how sick it made her. "You would use my power for this? I thought you considered it blasphemous."

Chozai narrowed his eyes at her, muscles in his jaw twitching. "You are a fractious woman. If you would rather travel to all the tribes on foot, I can oblige you. By then, Lyra will have certainly fallen."

"My apologies." She lowered her gaze hoping he would accept it as a show of deference and sincerity. "What must I do?"

"You will feed power into me to amplify the call," he replied. There was a catch in his voice and bitterness in his eyes when she met them again that helped her realize what it must cost him to ask such a thing of her.

"As you wish." She bowed her head again, this time in respect and gratitude for his efforts.

"I do not wish it," he growled under his breath.

Since the subject was upsetting him, she let the conversation end there and watched the approaching warriors close the distance until they came to a stop a few yards from the Murak group. The warriors on both sides seemed to grow larger, bristling like angry dogs, ready to attack at any provocation. She wondered if they would make it long enough to discuss their proposal before someone lost control and attacked the other side. The opposing suac barked a sharp order and the Farid warriors lowered their weapons. Suac Chozai did the same. The two suacs stepped up to one another and began to converse in their native tongue. Indigo caught a few words she had picked up in her short time among them, but she learned far more following the discussion by reading their emotions with her power.

For a few delicate minutes, the discussion was calm, then it grew heated, both men exuding hatred born of a long rivalry. Careful to keep her activities well masked, she pushed a slow stream of calm over them the same way she would with an agitated patient. Both men would turn on her in an instant if they had any idea that she was manipulating them, but she counted on their lack of conscious ascard control to keep her actions secret. The heated exchange mellowed and she smiled to herself. Eventually, the other suac gave a gruff nod and they turned to her.

She caught her breath. *He has copper eyes too.*

Did every suac have such eyes? What would cause such a thing?

"Suac Therah has agreed to walk with the gods. We shall go to his temple."

Doubt swept through her then. She had no desire to experience the side effects of the drug he had given her again, let alone try to choke it down. She didn't belong here. Nor did she belong in Caithin anymore, not after setting free the man accused of having the Caithin royal family assassinated. Along with her place in Caithin, she'd also lost Yiloch's love and the possibility of a place in Lyra. Still, she refused to see him or his country destroyed. There were people she cared for there. It wasn't only about Yiloch anymore. Ian and Cadmar had become dear to her as well. Adran also, for the love and loyalty he gave to Yiloch and for his practicality that balanced Yiloch's passion. If this was the price she had to pay to get Kudan to help Lyra, then she would do it.

She nodded and Suac Therah answered with a curt nod of his own, giving her a suspicious glower before turning to lead them back to the village. Their destination, Therah's temple, was a long hut similar to the one Chozai lived in. Warriors from both tribes escorted them to the door.

Before they could enter, the door flaps opened from within and a group of warriors emerged, carrying a body between them. Indigo stepped back, bumping into one of the Murak warriors. The man glared at her and she inched forward, trying to stay back from the emerging group without touching anyone else. She felt small and conspicuous among the tall, dark skinned Kudaness men.

The body was that of a young man. A reddish foam bubbled from his mouth and nose. His dark eyes stared at the sky, devoid of that distinctive spark of life. Indigo dared a quick inspection with ascard. He had died only moments ago. There was something in his system, a poison of some kind that was uncomfortably familiar. None of the others appeared bothered by the death, though Suac Therah inclined his head, closing his eyes for a quick moment, and she sensed a hint of disappointment in him.

When the group was clear of the door, Therah entered. Indigo followed, staying respectfully behind Chozai. One warrior from each tribe entered with them. Both of the suacs sat, one on each side of a ring of pillows, staring at one another with dislike so intense it charged the air around them. When no one offered any guidance, she sat on another edge of the ring halfway between the two men. At least they had the good sense to start seated this time. After falling the last time, she felt this was a much safer option.

The Farid warrior walked to a cabinet almost identical to the one in Suac Chozai's hut and retrieved a water skin. This he carried over and handed to Suac Therah.

Therah offered it to Chozai first. She struggled not to fidget as the Murak lifted the water skin, his eyes never leaving the other man. She hoped their standing rivalry wouldn't come into play here. How easy would it be for the Farid suac to eliminate his rival with a touch of poison? She inspected the substance in the skin with ascard and panic made her breath catch, tightening her chest when she realized it was the same substance she had detected in the dead man's body. Before she could move to intervene, Chozai took a deep drink from the skin. When Therah accepted the water skin back, he too drank deep and passed it to her.

She hesitated, remembering the dead man's face, and gave the liquid a tentative sniff. It was the same thing Suac Chozai had given her before. If she refused to drink it now, would he abandon the journey? It hadn't killed her the last time, though it had made her violently ill. Pushing aside fear, she brought the skin to her lips and made herself drink. She drank less deep than the two suacs had on the reasoning that the two men might have developed a tolerance for the substance.

The Farid warrior snatched the water skin from her and returned it to the cabinet. She was barely aware of the two warriors leaving the hut. Both suacs were swaying now, their eyes losing focus and glazing over. They both began to hum and, as her vision started to blur, she began to sway with them, trying not to fight the drug as she had the last time. This time, the pain that radiated out from her stomach was less severe and the transition less jarring. The hut vanished and there was only a brief instant of blackness. Then she was sitting under a star filled sky in the desert. Chozai and Therah sat across from one another in the same positions they occupied within the hut. A pale, glowing orb appeared in the center of the circle, illuminating the tattooed faces of the suacs.

Reminding herself of their purpose, Indigo focused, drawing on ascard and feeding her power into Suac Chozai. The other man did nothing to indicate that he was aware of the offering, but the orb glowed brighter. Chozai's lips moved as if he spoke, but no sound came out.

She waited, keeping the feed of power open so Chozai could take in as much as he needed.

Another suac emerged from the darkness beyond the circle and sat across from her. This man appeared older than the other two and was missing his left arm below the elbow. Neither Chozai nor Therah made any move to acknowledge the newcomer, so she followed their example, focusing on the orb. They sat in silence, all of them gazing into the pale orb at the center. The desert pulsated around the edges of her vision, stars flickering and dancing in the sky above. More Kudaness, tattooed with the elaborate designs of their priesthood and the varied facial tattoos that declared their tribes, came into the circle from the darkness and sat. The orb glowed brighter with each new arrival.

She dared to glance around, taking quick inventory of the men joining them. Suac Chozai's hair was longer and woven with more beads than that of any of the others. She wondered if that was significant or if it might merely be a tribal difference.

Now that she had a better idea of what to expect from a walk with the gods, she felt less out of control. The lingering image of the dead man, killed, as best she could tell from her cursory examination, by the poison they had consumed to get here, kept her nerves on edge, but the experience itself was less terrifying this time. Each suac swayed with the pulsing of the desert, and she did so too, understanding now that it helped ward off the nausea the vile drink caused.

When a twelfth suac joined the circle, they all looked up. Most glanced at her first, their scrutinizing looks like a collection of daggers waiting to be thrown. The notorious prejudice of her people did her no favors here. Then they turned their attention to Suac Chozai. Somehow, they appeared to know that he was the one who called them together.

"I have called upon you to initiate a Dursik un Kar," Chozai stated. Two of the others began to speak in Kudaness, but Chozai held up a hand to silence them. He nodded to Indigo. "The Unseen Woman has been brought to us by the gods. She does not speak Kudaness. I ask that you speak the trade tongue."

There was a flurry of discussion around the circle. When it stopped, all eyes turned to Indigo. She struggled to focus past the dizzying influence of the drug and figure out what they expected of her.

Chozai stepped in to spare her embarrassment. "This is your journey. It falls to you to explain why the Kudaness should initiate a Dursik un Kar." She looked askance at him and he frowned, perhaps searching for the right words. He finally said, "Gathering of blades."

She nodded and looked around the circle, noticing as she did so that they all had those odd, dark copper eyes. Was it a sign somehow of their being chosen by the gods or could it be a side effect of using the drug? Her gut twisted at the latter possibility. If it was the drug, how long did it take to develop? She had no interest in copper eyes.

There was growing impatience in the eyes of the suacs. She forced her fears aside.

"Some of you have already encountered the Grey Army that swept up eastern Kudan to Lyra. The Silik," she said, remembering Yiloch's description of the army's destructive path. She received a confirming nod from one suac and did her best not to glare at him. Did he have anything to do with Ferin's death? Glancing away from those cold eyes, she continued, "…and possibly the Denilik…" the elder suac with the partial arm gave a quick nod, "…have felt the power of that army. The Grey Army now travels through Lyra toward the capital. Should they defeat Lyra, they will not leave the Kudaness in peace. The tribes of Kudan must join against this foe." Several expressions tightened with disapproval and she plunged ahead before they could put voice to their disagreements. "Now is the time to attack. If the Kudaness join together in a rear attack on the Grey Army while they are engaged with the Lyran army, the Grey Army *will* fall." She said the last with an assurance that surprised even her, but it felt right and she needed them to feel it to.

"And what if they take Lyra before we reach them," one suac argued, glancing at Suac Chozai as he spoke.

"Then they will be weakened by the battle and vulnerable to attack," she countered.

"Who are they?" another Suac asked.

Before she could come up with an answer to that, the suac from the Silik tribe spoke up.

"They came from beyond the Rhuakine. Two of our villages were completely destroyed, no one left alive." As he spoke, the short, powerful warriors of the Grey Army on their stout horses appeared around the perimeter of the circle. She had to struggle not to react to their presence, but none of the suacs responded, though several glanced up at the Grey warriors, acknowledging this new component of the group hallucination. "I do not know how they defeated our warriors, but none of the Grey warriors left their lives there."

"I came upon them on my journey to Kudan. They have strong adepts creating protective barriers around their warriors," she explained. It was a little simpler than the truth, but the truth frightened her and she didn't want to share that. One adept controlled the power of every adept in the army. That made him more powerful than she cared to consider now. For now, she needed to focus only on convincing the Kudaness to act.

"Then how can we hope to defeat them?" Suac Therah demanded.

She met his eyes, holding up a hand when several of the others started to speak into the moment of silence. Whatever they thought about her for her race and gender they still respected the gesture, falling silent.

"I can destroy their barriers," she said, hoping that she wasn't promising more than she could deliver.

The suacs turned on Chozai, slinging outraged objections at him for bringing an ascard user among them and several reverted back to their native tongue. She kept her silence, refraining from commenting about the way they used ascard themselves, for she was certain that power was involved in this in some way. If not, how could her power have been of any use in calling the other suacs together?

Once more, she waited.

The Grey warriors around them vanished, replaced by scenes of Lyran adepts wielding ascard in various destructive ways and the grim outcomes. Fire, ascard enhanced speed, weapons made of power all wielded by Lyran adepts with bloody results. Among those images, she was certain she spotted Yiloch at least once, or perhaps she wanted to see him bad enough to impose his image upon the memories of the suacs.

"The gods support her words," Chozai defended. "Look."

Around them, the images changed. Grey warriors fought Kudaness, and not just from a single tribe, but from many different tribes judging by their varied tattoos. Indigo wondered if Suac Chozai somehow controlled the images though she could find no evidence that he was consciously controlling ascard in any way. Blood spattered Kudaness warriors cried out in victory around the perimeter of the circle, raising spears and curved blades in celebration. Then the image of the Grey Army's leader appeared among them. He stared at her and smiled and she sucked in a breath, terror coursing through her.

Blackness fell around the circle, the glowing orb no longer penetrating beyond those gathered. She was trembling. Whether from fear this time or from the effects of the drug she couldn't tell.

"I, Suac Chozai Galal of Murak un Ani, pledge the warriors of Murak to the Dursik un Kar," Suac Chozai declared, his strong voice echoing in the emptiness around them.

After him, silence reigned for several minutes and Indigo, her head spinning now, wondered if she would manage to avoid passing out before the others gave their answers.

The Denilik suac pounded his knee with a fist and swept the circle with a challenging glare. "I, Suac Kipith Denilik of Denilik un Ani, pledge the warriors of Denilik to the Dursik un Kar."

Chozai offered a nod of appreciation to the crippled elder. The silence held even longer this time then the Farid suac sat up straighter.

"I, Suac Therah Hesik of Farid un Ani, pledge the warriors of Farid to the Dursik un Kar."

This time there was no pause. The rest of the prophets spoke in turn, pledging the warriors of their respective tribes to the Dursik un Kar. As they spoke, she realized tears were tracking down her cheeks. She made no move to stop them, feeling the gesture would be somehow inappropriate in this setting. They should know she felt the weight of their decision in her heart. When the last suac pledged his warriors, Suac Chozai met and held her eyes. He nodded once and she felt he did it in approval of her emotion. The gratitude her tears represented was not lost on him, though the deeper sadness, the sense that even this would not earn her a place in life, evaded him.

"The Dursik un Kar will gather on the northern border where Murak lands meet Lyra."

The other suacs nodded and lowered their gazes to the glowing orb. One by one, they vanished, the orb fading more with each departure, until only the original three remained. Suac Therah nodded to Suac Chozai and vanished. Chozai turned to her and reached a hand out. She took the offered hand and blackness fell.

When she woke, she was alone. She threw up again, emptying her stomach, but she recovered faster than she had the first time. Once she'd composed herself, she got up from the pillows and stepped outside. Chozai waited there with his warriors and Suac Therah. They both acknowledged her with a nod and a warrior held the reins of her mount out to her.

"We will meet again, Unseen Woman," Suac Therah said. "The gods have a purpose in bringing you to us. Never before has anyone from outside the Kudan brought about a Dursik un Kar. But remember, having the attention of the gods is not the same as having their favor."

She nodded, too tired to worry over his words, and the suac turned away, exchanging a few words in Kudaness with Chozai. Then she mounted and followed the Murak suac and warriors away from the Farid village.

Screams echoed through the night. Screams of terror, of pain. The screams of the dying. The intense heat of the inferno that engulfed houses and other buildings throughout AhnSegys had become almost too much for Yiloch and his soldiers, but they pressed on. Adepts scanned for life, sending soldiers after survivors when they sensed them. Yiloch's need for vengeance burned as hot as the fires around them. Most of the soldiers and adepts acted out of obedience to their emperor, but a few, like Adran and his sister Eris who had grown up with Yiloch, acted out of love for their Prince. Those few would always support him, even in this grisly deed.

A young woman bolted from one of the houses, an infant in her arms. Yiloch moved to go after her, but one of the soldiers came around the side of the burning house into her path and thrust his blade with enough force that it passed through the child into the woman's chest. She shrieked as he ripped the blade free and the infant slumped in her arms. It was a sound of complete despair. A second strike cut off her screams. Yiloch stared, wishing he could erase from his mind the memory of his mother falling from her mount, a crossbow bolt through her throat. These people harbored her killer. Every one of them would pay.

Someone touched his arm. He turned to Adran.

"Have they not suffered enough?"

"Father offered to forgive if they gave up mother's killer. They chose this," Yiloch shouted over the din of the fires.

Above the trees, he could see flames rising up from the neighboring village, Segys, settled less than a quarter mile away from this one. Another band of soldiers and adepts were busy wiping it out of existence as well.

Upon receiving word that the man who killed the empress, Yiloch's mother, was hiding in one of the two villages, Emperor Rylan sent a contingent led by Yiloch to teach them a lesson. The villagers refused to give up the murderer, insisting he had never been there. Yiloch was more than willing to mete out his father's justice.

He turned away from those flames and spotted another woman stepping out of her burning home. She peered up and down the street for an escape route. Drawing on his power, he swapped himself with ascard in the air beside her and swept his elegant blade, the one his mother had commissioned for him, in a deadly arc. The flame reflecting on the blade left a trail of orange light in its wake. Her head flew, striking the ground some distance away and rolled to a stop like a child's ball. Her body, slow to acknowledge its fate, remained standing for several seconds, as though propped up by unseen hands, then crumbled to the ground.

Looking past that lifeless figure, Yiloch spotted a young boy standing in the doorway of the house. His eyes were wide with horror and the anguish of loss twisted his pale features. It struck Yiloch that the devastated expression on the youth's face was probably much like that on his own face when the crossbow bolt had punched through his mother's throat in front of him. He stepped toward the boy, not certain whether he meant to kill him or try to help him. The boy shrank back into the burning house, his pale eyes filling with tears. There followed a crack like thunder and the structure gave, collapsing on the youth.

Yiloch stared at the collapse for several minutes, frozen in place by the remorse that welled up in him until someone touched his arm again. Adran. It was always Adran in his worst moments, regarding him with eyes full of sympathy and adoration. Never judgment, not even when he needed to be judged.

They deserved it though, didn't they? The villagers deserved this for harboring the man who had killed his mother. They all deserved it.

•

But they didn't deserve it. They never had.

Standing here now, with the pungent smells of burnt wood and flesh stinging his nostrils, he felt that old guilt twisting within him. This village, built on the site of the old AhnSegys, he himself had destroyed almost ten years ago. They had suffered the same fate again, but at the hands of the Grey Army this time.

Back then, he had led the warriors and adepts of Yiroth against the villagers on his father, Emperor Rylan's, orders. He was young then, and full of blind rage at the loss of his mother. Later he learned that his father had sent him to destroy the villages not because they harbored his mother's killer—that man was never found—but because he promised the land around the river to an old friend. That friend died of illness before he ever got around to building there and the people eventually came back to rebuild AhnSegys.

Rylan had used him, stoking his rage until it burned out of control then setting him lose with a target on which to vent that rage. That was why Rylan was dead now, by Yiloch's own hand, but his death didn't undo this wrong. Why, of all the villages the Grey Army slaughtered, had they chosen to burn this one? They couldn't know the history of the area, but that only made it seem like more of a dark portent.

"My Lord," Ian approached cautiously, sensing the volatility of Yiloch's mood.

Neither of his current companions, the young creator Ian or the warrior Cadmar, were part of that original misguided campaign. Like everyone, they knew the stories of the massacre that had earned him the nickname, The Blood Prince, but they would never understand the reality of that night and the events leading up to it. They would certainly never understand the unending torment of those memories.

Yiloch scowled at the destruction, the churned mud colored deep red in places with the blood of villagers, the blackened wood of the still-smoking buildings. "The Grey Army will pay for this," he snarled.

His dappled grey stallion, Tantrum, snorted at the sting of smoke in his nostrils and stomped a foot in response to Yiloch's upset. He patted the stallion's shoulder, feeling his own head begin to ache from the acrid smell. Rather than depart, as he wanted to, he urged the stallion into the village. Tantrum tossed his head, displeased with the choice, but did as directed.

Every village they'd passed through to this point had been the same. All the people slaughtered and homes ransacked for useful supplies. He had learned next to nothing new from poking around the remains. Still, it would be foolish to assume there would never be anything to learn, especially here where the fires already made the attack unusual. For some reason, the efficient slaughter had gone differently in AhnSegys.

In the heart of the village, his efforts finally reaped rewards. With a squeeze of his legs, he drove the stallion toward the remains of a larger building, an inn judging by the size. Near the debris of the inn lay three bodies, not burned or damaged beyond the large wounds in their chests. They were the first Grey warriors Yiloch had seen and he finally understood the name the Kudaness had given them. The cast of their skin wasn't bronze or pale or black like any of the races he knew. There was a distinct Grey cast to the skin that had nothing to do with their recent death. The hair and unseeing eyes of the dead men were as black as soot. They were stocky and muscular, broad across the chest, and they wore a flexible leather armor woven with small plates of some unfamiliar hardwood in the more vulnerable areas.

Yiloch dismounted and examined the armor. The plates were woven on with perfect symmetry and, despite the thinness of those plates, the wood was extremely strong. Whatever these people were, they were capable and advanced enough to work with this iron-like material. He picked up one of their weapons. The short-shafted spears, topped with a sweeping blade, were both ornate, like the lethal spears of the Kudaness, and precisely weighted like a fine Lyran sword. He hefted the weapon and worked through a few intricate attack moves with it. The weight felt good, efficient and deadly. All of these things worked together to build a storm of dread in his chest.

"They were killed with ascard," Ian commented.

Yiloch nodded. "An adept. I wonder what became of him?" His gaze swept the remains of the inn.

"Or her," Ian added pointedly.

Yiloch ignored him. Indigo was behind them now and he couldn't dwell on her until Lyra was secure again. He wasn't going to let Ian's well placed comments distract him from his purpose. "The important thing is that we know they can be killed. These are the first bodies we've seen from the Grey Army. I wish we could talk to whoever killed them."

He attached the spear to his saddle and mounted, but he waited, noticing that Ian's focus had turned inward, his brow furrowed with intense concentration. After a few minutes, a small shudder passed through the creator's lean frame and he met Yiloch's eyes.

"The signature on the ascard that killed these men is Myac's."

A chill raced up Yiloch's spine, though he managed to maintain the appearance of calm. Myac must have come after Indigo. Why else would he have been here? He'd followed her trail this far. "Is he still alive?"

Ian shrugged. "I can't tell. I can feel his signature in that building as well, but I can't tell from that if he's alive or dead, or where he went from here if he is still alive. All I know is he isn't physically here anymore."

Yiloch took a deep breath, trying to chase away the malignant worry creeping through him. "We didn't cross paths with him on the way here. If he was still after Indigo, we should have run into him."

"Maybe," Cadmar said, "if he wanted us to."

Yiloch scowled at him, hoping he would realize how unhelpful he was being.

The big warrior simply shrugged.

"If it took someone of Myac's power to kill them, I don't suppose that says much for our chances."

Turning the scowl on Ian, he said, "None of this

helps. Do either of you plan to give up on Lyra?"

"No." Ian's look indicated that the answer should have been obvious. He looked reassuringly offended by the question.

"I do not plan to give up on Lyra's people," Cadmar answered.

That was good enough. "Then we keep going. I'm worried about Indigo as well, but she and Myac can't be our primary concerns right now."

Tantrum danced sideways, done with breathing in the smoke and ready to be away. With a quick correction, he settled the stallion and turned back to his companions. They both looked weary, but they watched him attentively, waiting for his orders. Whatever he asked, they would still do, even Ian whose lingering resentment over his mistreatment of Indigo colored their every conversation.

Yiloch scanned the surrounding forest then, his gaze coming to rest on the tree line to the northeast of the village. "This attack is fresh. With only three of us, we can take the game trails at speed and make our way to Yiroth. We can travel much faster than the Grey Army can and our route will be more direct. We should be able to beat them to the city by a few days even if they don't take time to rest."

"Lead the way," Cadmar urged.

Ian glanced southward with a look of longing, wondering after Indigo again. With a heavy exhale, he turned back to Yiloch and nodded.

Yiloch nudged Tantrum with his heels and directed him around the debris of a collapsed house. Once clear of the obstruction, he upped the pace, moving into the woods at a fast trot. The other two fell into a line behind him and he began to weave a path through the trees, searching out the game trails. This part of the forest had little undergrowth, allowing for easy movement. Tantrum responded fluidly to his direction, winding around and through the trees like a great serpent. The stallion broke over into a canter and Yiloch smiled, letting memory take him back to the hunts of his youth, a time before his mother died and everything changed, a time when life had been simpler.

He and Adran had camped and hunted together in these woods often in their youth. On occasion, Adran's sister Eris or Captain Kardyn—both of whom had lost their lives helping Yiloch overthrow his father—would join them. Even more rarely, they would allow his younger brother Delsan, to join them. Delsan had little interest in learning combat skills. On hunts, he would never take a shot with his bow, no matter how good the shot was. The younger prince was never a killer. In retrospect, maybe that wasn't such a bad thing, but their father had put him to death for it.

So many people had died in the war between him and his father. The pain of those losses was still fresh. How many more would die before this new enemy?

Myac hated as he had never hated before in his life. Not even Yiloch, his mother's murderer, inspired this level of loathing in him. Hatred boiled through him, searing his mind with its intensity, scorching and ineffectual. No matter how much he hungered to make these men suffer, he couldn't take back control of his power.

From the moment he woke after falling debris knocked him unconscious in the burning inn at Ahn-Segys, he knew something was horribly wrong. The soldiers of the foreign army were riding all around him and he lay slung uncomfortably in front of someone's saddle, his hands and feet bound. None of that mattered though. What mattered, what sent icy blades of terror stabbing through him, was that he could do nothing about it. Whatever the foreign adept had done to him, Myac could still feel his connection to his inner aspect, but he could no longer control it.

When they realized he was awake, they unbound his feet and offered him a horse. With no viable alternatives, he mounted the animal as best he could with his hands still bound. They continued, one of the warriors leading his mount. Another warrior riding near them led four more horses. He realized the extra horses must belong to the men he had killed. The thought brought no satisfaction. He was broken. The burden of defeat weighed so heavily on him he was surprised it didn't slow his horse down.

The link that bound him was perfect. The adept who controlled it allowed him enough control to analyze the fine workmanship of that binding, perhaps as a way of mocking him. There was an elaborate ascard working not only coiled around his inner aspect, but also penetrating it, drawing from it like a blood-sucking parasite. If he could find a way to mimic that creation, it could be a very useful tool.

Was there a backlash on the controlling adept if someone bound to them in such a way died?

There was no way to answer that. For now, he could do nothing. They had effectively raped him of the power that defined him. Unless he could find a way out of this predicament, being able to analyze the working was of no value to him. He would find a way to kill the adept who'd bound him or die trying, even if he had to use his teeth to do it.

None of the soldiers made an effort to communicate with him for the first few days. They gave him food and tended his needs in an impersonal way, neither cruel nor kind in their treatment, simply indifferent. He didn't even see the adept who bound him or the warlord he had encountered in AhnSegys until the third day.

The army had stopped in an open field and was arranging itself in ranks. They appeared to be preparing for a confrontation. Lord Inaki's holding was nearby. Perhaps they meant to eliminate the potential threat before moving on again. Myac didn't know what losses the lord might have suffered in the campaign to overthrow Emperor Rylan, but he'd had a considerable force prior to that and Lady Shyalis would bring her soldiers to his aid in an instant. With the barrier abilities Myac had witnessed during his own battle with some of these warriors, he wasn't sure how much damage even a substantial force could do to this army. It was always worth hoping.

He could speculate about the foreign army, but he had no way to know what was really going on. Their language was completely strange to him. Listening to their conversations had taught him only that they appended something, perhaps a family name or honorific of some kind, to their common name when addressing one another. Thus far, he had come up with no way to use that information to his advantage.

Myac could feel the adept approaching long before he saw him. The malignant presence attached to his inner aspect grew stronger when he came close. Warriors parted and bowed their heads to the man who walked through ahead of the adept. Upon closer observation, Myac noted an elaborate pendant hanging at the throat of the lead man, and the small plates of his armor were individually painted with the same design as the pendant in painstaking detail. The young man and the adept who flanked him on either side wore the same armor as the rest of the warriors, only the small plates woven into theirs were darker in color. There were also a few among those men surrounding them who wore the darker shade. An indication of rank, perhaps.

The leader stopped a few feet in front of Myac and exchanged words with the adept then turned to him. The young soldier flanking him made a sharp gesture toward Myac, holding his hand out flat and pushing down with it. Were they telling him to bow down?

Myac lifted his head and glared at the warlord.

All of a sudden, he felt his own power draining from him as a leech might drain his blood, then power, bearing his own ascard signature, began to press him down. He tried to fight both the draining and the pressure, but he could do nothing. Humiliation and rage burned through him, heating his face as he sank to one knee beneath the pressure. The warlord approached him and gazed down, the dark eyes on either side of his broad nose full of an almost paternal patience. It was the regard of someone who knew they would win.

Myac spat at the warlord's feet. A bludgeon, formed of his own stolen power, struck him across the face, sending him sprawling on his side. Blood burst through his mouth along with something hard. A tooth. Furious that he couldn't do so much as stop the blood with his power, he spat the tooth at the warlord. The younger man surged forward then, his leg swinging to land a fierce kick in Myac's gut. He curled around the burst of agony.

"Na-jnai!" The warlord snapped.

The young man, Na-jnai, dropped to his knees, bowing his head almost to the ground and uttered something in their strange language, his tone thick with remorse. He addressed the warlord as Ksa-jnai, appending something else that sounded like a title to the name. Through the haze of pain, Myac clung to the fact that the two shared the same honorific, if that's what it was. The information might prove useful somehow. At the very least, the thought gave him something to focus on. Ksa-jnai nodded and said something to the adept. Again, Myac felt his own power being used on him, this time to force him to rise against his will, ending in a kneel with his head pushed low enough that he had to put his bound hands out in front of him to keep his balance.

The warlord addressed Na-jnai again, his tone scolding, while the adept healed Myac's injuries. The tooth was gone, but the torn gums and cheek mended quickly. Apparently the adept's abuse was acceptable, while the kick Na-jnai had given was not. He yearned to understand the difference. There were so many possible answers and, without understanding their language or being able to read their emotions with ascard, he couldn't know the right one.

Fighting an urge to curl on the ground and give up, he turned inward and made himself inspect the working that controlled his power again. What little he could access of his inner aspect was barely enough for him to recognize that the invasive working was there. Beyond that, he couldn't even begin to build up enough strength to try to counter it. His weak probing met with a laugh and Myac glanced up to see the adept's gloating smile. The warlord looked over then and saw the smile as well. His lips pressed together in a firm line.

To Myac's considerable surprise, the warlord sharply reprimanded the adept, and Myac finally caught the man's name, Ini-jnai. All three shared the same honorific. What was the connection? They didn't look like family, though it was hard to make a real assessment of their unfamiliar features.

The adept accepted his reprimand with a nod to his warlord, then he turned to Myac and bowed his head, lowering his eyes in a manner that he could only call apologetic. He said a few things under his breath and the warlord nodded approval, then turned a disturbingly fond smile on Myac. Confusion and frustration raged through him like a tornado. There was no doubting that he was a prisoner. The peculiar treatment made no sense, unless…

Fresh fury boiled through Myac. He wasn't being treated like a prisoner. He was being treated like a wild horse. Ksa-jnai had an enemy adept in his army and he needed to break him in properly. Firm treatment had to be mixed with kindness when bringing any creature to heel.

Still, there was a certain respect in the warlord's manner, perhaps because of the power he had seen Myac wield or his defiance despite the odds. That grudging consideration confused him, giving him a rock to cling to in a sea full of predators. Surrounded by the hostile army and rendered powerless as he was, it was hard not to want to turn to the warlord for protection. That too, was probably a calculated outcome on Ksa-jnai's part, but knowing that the foreign warlord was manipulating him didn't seem to change the effects of that manipulation.

They could heal, or at least Ini-jnai could. It was important to keep that in mind because it significantly pushed out the limits on how much they could hurt him if he didn't behave the way they wanted him to. He met the warlord's eyes. There was respect in those dark depths. Staring down at Myac, he made the same gesture the young warrior made earlier, indicating that he should bow his head, but the gesture was gentle, more of a request than a demand. When he made no move to submit, Ksa-jnai tilted his head ever so slightly to one side and continued to watch him, patient.

I must hate you. Myac memorized every feature of the warlord's face and drew in a deep breath. *I must hate all of your army, but you the most.*

There was no press of power this time. He bowed his head on his own. The weight of that submission was crushing. The warlord spoke a few words then walked away, Ini-jnai and Na-jnai following. Someone brought a horse up next to Myac and another warrior took his arm, helping him to his feet with a grip that was only as firm as it needed to be. As he mounted, he ran his tongue over the right side of his lower jaw, feeling the gap left by the missing tooth. It wouldn't be so hard to remember to hate Ksa-jnai.

The entire army mounted and finished organizing in ranks. The soldier leading Myac's mount moved up through those ranks until they were only two rows of warriors behind the warlord when the army surged into motion. A shudder coursed through him. This wasn't where he would prefer to be if the army was heading into a battle. Ideally, he would like to be somewhere on a tower or fortified wall, watching from above. At worst, down in the thick of things was tolerable, if he had a plethora of barriers and his immense ascard power to throw around. If Ini-jnai died in the fighting, that would be worth it, but he doubted Inaki and Shya-lis combined had the military might to face this army down, especially with the magnitude of the combined power Ini-jnai wielded.

Did any adept in the army have control of his own power? It was pointless trying to pick out the other adepts without being able to use ascard. Even Ini-jnai wielded one of the bladed spears and his armor was no different from that of the other ranking soldiers. When he had tried to face the adept down in AhnSegys, he had felt that combined power and it was substantial, the power of hundreds of adepts woven together with remarkable mastery. Given those numbers, he should have seen at least a few adepts by now, which suggested that they all wore the same armor and carried the same weapons as the warriors.

The kind of working that bound the adepts together was something he'd encountered before. Combining power was difficult because a group of adepts had to feed their own power willingly into one leader who then had to weave it together and control it. It was hard enough to find adepts who would relinquish control of their power, finding someone willing to control that blending with the risk of someone pulling out at a critical moment was nearly impossible. This method of binding, however, eliminated that risk. The adepts on the feeding end had no control at all. If all of them were bound as he was, Ini-jnai could draw from them as much or as little as he needed whenever he wanted to.

Did these foreign adepts give themselves willingly to such servitude?

A wave of motion moved through the army as they drew their short-hafted weapons. Myac tensed, wishing he had at least enough power left in him to burn through the rope that bound his wrists. It would be far easier to ride without his hands bound and control of his horse in someone else's hands. It would also be easier to get his hands on a weapon and go after Ini-jnai in the heat of battle. Hence the reason his hands remained bound, and he didn't have enough ascard at his disposal to do anything about it. He was essentially blind without his power, unable to reach ahead and search out the opposing force, unable to feel what the other adepts in the army were doing.

There was a sudden drain on his power, not enough to weaken him significantly, but enough that he noticed. Focusing on the power wrapped insidiously around his own, Myac found that he could feel some of what was going on through Ini-jnai. The lead adept was drawing on the adepts to sustain a powerful barrier over every man and horse in the entire army. The concussion of ascard assaulting areas of that barrier from without reverberated through the other adept, jarring Myac slightly. The incoming attacks were inadequate against the combined power the warlord's primary adept wielded.

With his power being leeched from him and his focus following Ini-jnai's workings, he was caught off guard by a group of mounted Lyran soldiers surging into the midst of the army. The attacks of the Lyran soldiers bounced uselessly off their targets, but a few of Ksa-jnai's warriors were imbalanced by the force behind those attacks. One Lyran soldier spotted Myac, a flicker of surprise lighting his eyes, then bright red blood choked up through his lips in sharp contrast to his pale skin as a swept blade punched through his chest.

The warrior leading Myac's mount turned his own horse at an angle in front of him and several other warriors formed up protectively around him. They weren't willing to lose such an asset. Under different circumstances, the realization might have been flattering. Here it only ensured that no one was going to get close enough to help him escape.

Leaning to look around the warriors blocking him in, he saw that Ksa-jnai was no longer in front of them. Following the binding that linked him to

Ini-jnai allowed him to locate the adept and Ksa-jnai whose side he rarely strayed far from. The warlord was at the head of a charge that swept around one side and surged toward a second group of Lyran soldiers charging into the heart of the army. The Lyran tactics were haphazard and reckless. It was a suicidal charge, a ruse, and judging by the rage on Ksa-jnai's face, he knew it.

Leveling the short-hafted spear with its long swept blade, the grey-skinned warlord charged at the opposing soldiers. In the last instant, the nearest soldier spun to face him, the man's long, pale hair flowing out beneath his helmet as he spurred his mount toward Ksa-jnai. His sword came forward in a fierce thrust, powered by the lunge of his horse. The sword struck the warlords chest and rebounded to the side, twisting from the soldier's grasp. He caught hold of the front of his saddle with one hand to keep from falling. Ksa-jnai's bladed spear swept up, sunlight sparkling on the polished steel, then it swung down and around, slashing through the Lyran man's neck effortlessly. So effortlessly, in fact, that Myac was certain Ksa-jnai had used ascard to add force to the strike.

Moments later the battle was finished. The opposing force had been small and fierce. Too small for this holding. A decoy for an escape. If he judged right, Lord Inaki, and likely Lady Shyalis as well, would be well on their way out of the area by now. They must have gotten warning about the coming army. It was a desperate and costly move, but it might pay off.

Ksa-jnai sneered at the bodies of the Lyran warriors, then his gaze lifted and locked on Myac. There was smoldering anger there, lighting a fire in those dark eyes. For a tense moment, Myac wondered if the warlord intended to take that molten store of emotion out on him, then Ini-jnai leaned in close to Ksa-jnai and said something. The warlord held Myac's eyes for a moment longer, then he nodded and turned away, barking out orders. The army fell back into their ranks.

he trip back to the Murak village on the northern border went quickly. A brief respite from the more intense heat allowed for longer and faster hours of travel. Suac Chozai and the Murak warriors traveled with single-minded intensity, focusing on the coming conflict now that the suacs had committed to action. In the silence of her own head, Indigo wondered if all that had happened had perhaps driven her mad. Was she really attempting to influence the outcome of war? Who did she think she was?

She was one woman, one adept, now turned traitor to her country for the love of a man who hated her. Despite that, she was going to try to help him save his empire just as she had helped him win it in the first place. If she could see Yiloch again and talk to him more about how she had come to betray him, perhaps show him how she meant to help Lyra, would the uncertainty swelling in her chest disappear?

As soon as they were back in the Murak village, Suac Chozai retreated to his hut with a group of men, one of whom he had pointed out to her before they left for Farid. The man was the Murak chief, though she had yet to see him do anything that suggested significant authority. Although impressive in appearance, the chief appeared to defer to Suac Chozai in most things.

Abandoned by the suac with no one else to talk to, she turned to wandering through the village, watching the people and listening to their conversations in an effort to pick up some of the language while trying to ignore their suspicious looks. At least they had stopped glaring at her outright. Something in the way the suac treated her had gained her a grudging respect from the people of the tribe.

After a time, she wandered back to the suac's hut and waited outside, fighting the urge to eavesdrop with ascard. She yearned to know what they were talking about, but they were certainly speaking Kudaness and knowing how they felt about ascard use made her feel self-conscious when she used it anyhow, even when they had no way of knowing she was doing it. She waited, picking at her fingernails until other men finally left the hut. Then she hurried in, heart thrumming double-time in her chest.

She stopped inside the entrance and stood silent a moment, considering what to say and recognizing that he might not appreciate her barging in as she had without invite.

The eyes of the suac turned to her from where he sat cross-legged in the center of the hut. His head dipped in the slightest nod of acknowledgement, showing that her unannounced entrance at least hadn't offended him.

She took a few steps closer. "Is it possible to direct a walk with the gods in order to see something that's happening now?"

He tilted his head to one side, brow furrowing in thought, the expression rearranging the shape of the tattoos there. When he spoke this time, he mixed in a few words in the Murak dialect, letting her translate through context. "Direct, no. You must make your desires known to the gods. If they feel your need is great enough, they will guide you to what you seek."

She chewed at her lip. Was it wise to continue using the drug? What might it be doing to her? She glanced at Chozai's copper eyes and yearned for a mirror, but there were no such frivolities here. She would have to take her chances or abandon the idea.

After a moment, she nodded. "I would like to try."

"You know where the sucar is." He swept a hand toward the cupboard in the corner.

The thrumming in her chest became a violent pounding. Both times she used the sucar, once she recovered from its effects, her connection to her inner aspect had felt stronger than before. That didn't lesser her fear of the vile substance. "Will you…"

His level look silenced her. "I have many things to do if my people are to go to war. You do not need me there to walk with the gods."

She took a deep breath to ease the tremor of fear in her chest. When that failed, she clenched her teeth and made her feet move to the corner. The skin waited, pushed to the back of the cupboard, ominous in its shadowed place. She grabbed it, strode over to a rug with forced courage in her steps, and sat. Pulling off the stopper, she glanced at Chozai. He nodded and she lifted it to her lips, taking a quick swallow. A dark hand moved into her periphery. She handed him the skin and succumbed to the swaying rhythm of the drug.

•

The blackness hung with her, wrapping around her and clinging to her. The tremor of fear became a panicked bird, its wings beating against the inside of her chest, demanding release. There was a spinning feeling in her head and she thought she might throw up, then vision returned, pushing through dizziness and pain.

She left her body behind, abandoning it to its suffering, and soared above the desert, the fear in her chest giving way to excitement as the landscape sped by beneath her. The northernmost Murak village vanished behind her and the first Lyran town appeared, the dead rotting in the silence the Grey Army left behind. She was high enough up that she could almost believe those myriad lumps on the ground were something other than bodies. As she moved swiftly north, the changing landscape blurred some below her. There was enough time to notice that every town along the main roadway was silent like the first, but not to absorb the grisly details of each massacre.

The one passing beneath her now had burned and some buildings still smoldered. She knew the Grey Army had suffered their first losses here, though how she knew that, she wasn't sure, given that the bodies all looked the same from her vantage.

Still heading north, she caught up with the Grey Army. Thousands strong and all mounted on sturdy, compact horses. Every man carried a bladed spear and was protected by a barrier of ascard. She knew that only because she had encountered them before and had investigated the barrier then. She couldn't sense the power now, perhaps because she wasn't there in the flesh, but she didn't doubt it was still there.

The Grey Army was traveling slower now, creeping

north toward the capital city of Lyra. Dropping in closer, she spotted the man that led them in the midst of his army. Stocky and thickly muscled with dark eyes and wild dark hair, he exuded the power and confidence of a great leader. A leader unfamiliar with defeat. His nose was wide and flat and his skin, like that of all his men, had a slight Greyish tone. He glanced up as he rode along, as if he somehow knew she was watching them and she backed away, rising up higher.

Where were Yiloch, Ian and Cadmar? They should be on the trail of the Grey Army. Might she have missed them in the trees? The Grey Army was traveling at a deliberate pace now, conserving strength. It was possible that Yiloch and the others had overtaken them by now if they kept an aggressive pace, in which case they would be trying to make their way around the army without being seen. If not, they should be somewhere close behind.

She turned and began to retrace her path, sinking down to scan along the roadway for them. Someone was calling to her now. She tried to ignore the summons—she hadn't found what she was looking for yet—but it pulled at her, demanding her attention. It was dragging her back toward Kudan. She tried to fight it, resisting the pull. She had to find Yiloch, had to know he and the others were still alive. What if they had caught up with the army? What if the army had spotted them and they were already dead?

•

She woke with a choking gasp, as though sucking in the first breath after almost drowning, then turned on her side and vomited. Purged of the vile substance, she rested there for a few minutes, shaking. Turning inward, she took inventory of the state of her ascard connection. A thrill of excitement and fear charged through her and an ironic smile twisted her lips.

This time, she had paid careful attention to the strength of her connection before swallowing the rank, viscous fluid. Now, as she focused her ability in on the connection to her inner aspect, she was certain it was stronger. It wasn't a significant increase, but enough of one for her to notice.

What else might the drug be doing to her?

Excitement faded and she turned her attention away from her connection, remembering her experience with a flash of annoyance at the abrupt end. The high priest still sat where he'd been when she started, cross-legged on a rug nearby, now watching her thoughtfully. The elaborate tattoos took on an illusion of movement in the fading light of evening, writhing about his arms and torso, climbing his neck to his face, and causing her upset stomach to turn alarmingly. Using a touch of ascard to ease the nausea, she sat up and faced him.

"You said I should take this walk alone." The words came out more snappish than she intended and he narrowed his eyes at her. She swallowed her irritation and forced a more respectful tone. "Why did you pull me out?"

"One should never overstay their welcome among the gods."

"I hadn't found what I was looking for yet," she objected, aware that she sounded much like a spoiled child.

"Sucar is poison," he replied, patient, but firm. "It is given only to those deemed strong enough to be chosen by the gods. Among those few, many still die their first time. If your system isn't allowed to purge what it can't yet handle, it could still kill you. You should not stay away too long or you might never come back."

She stared at him, letting his words sink in, forcing her to acknowledge the unpleasant truth. A chill swept through her, bringing goose flesh to her arms. "That's what happened to the dead man in Suac Therah's hut."

Chozai nodded.

She thought back on the day he had first given her the sucar that the priests of the Ithik Ani consumed to initiate a walk with their gods. Anger flickered to life, starting as little more than a spark and flaring until it blazed through her, poisonous in its own right. "You could have killed me that first time."

Suac Chozai held her gaze, unmoved by the accusation. "It was the only way I could know if you spoke the truth."

"But you didn't expect me to survive it." This wasn't accusation. It was fact. She could see that much in his eyes.

"You would live if the gods wanted you to. If not," he shrugged, "it would have simplified things." Reaching out, he placed a finger against her jaw and turned her face so that her cheek was to him. "This was your third walk with the gods. You should have an identity so they will know you the next time you come to them."

She drew back from his touch. Undeterred, he repeated the gesture, this time moving his finger to trace a pattern along her cheekbone. With a growing sense of alarm and something else, something a lot like pride, she realized he was suggesting a tattoo. All of the Kudaness had the symbol of their tribe and their role within it tattooed on their face. The suacs, the high priests, also had tattoos over most of their body along with the uncut, long black hair done into small braids weighted with beads.

"I'm Caithin. I'm not even of your people," she objected, moving back away from his hand again. She wasn't ready to let him distract her from her anger with him yet. "How could you treat my life so superfluously?"

He lowered his arm and smiled so that his sharpened teeth showed. "If the gods had not shown you favor, your life would mean nothing to me even now. However, it seems that, even though your flesh is Caithin and you are an adept, the gods have chosen to embrace you. You are of the Kudan in spirit. I would not have known this if we had not walked with the gods together."

She met his dark copper eyes, his steady solemn regard telling her that he believed his words. Caithin would regard her as a traitor. She was an exile with no home. If she went back now, they would certainly arrest her and perhaps even put her to death. The man she loved had turned her away and not without good reason. Regardless of her intentions, she had betrayed his trust, inadvertently caused the death of one of his closest companions, and left him stranded in Kudan while an army invaded his empire. He would probably never accept her back into his heart after all of that. Maybe it was time to let her past go and create a new life. She had never envisioned herself living in the desert, but at least here, the tribe's high priest was inviting her to embrace a new identity as one of them. With his acceptance, others would accept her in time.

"Perhaps you're right. I am no one now."

Suac Chozai nodded and rose, long, muscular limbs unfolding smoothly. "Wait here, Indigo un Ani."

She watched him leave, something frightening and wonderful blooming in her chest. Indigo un Ani, he had called her. The Ithik Ani were the Kudaness priests. Suac was the title granted to the highest of that order, but un Ani was an honorific appended to the names of lesser priests. To the best of her knowledge, there were no priestesses and almost certainly no foreigners among their ranks. The identity he offered her was one of great respect and honor.

A woman entered the hut and collected the rug on which she had thrown up the sucar. A few minutes later, Chozai returned flanked by a muscular man carrying an assortment of tools for tattooing. A young woman also entered, her purpose unclear until she settled on Indigo's left and dumped a selection of beads on the rug next to her. The man with the tools sat on her right. Chozai stood behind him and reached down, tucking her hair behind her ear. He traced a pattern with one finger and discussed it with the man in Kudaness. She caught a tiny fraction of what they said. She was picking up some more common words, though it would be a long while before she didn't have to rely on the Lyran trade dialect for communication.

How long had it been since she had spoken her own tongue? That question brought a flood of memories to mind that she did not want to consider now. There hadn't been a need to speak Caithin since she boarded Captain Murchadh's boat the night she fled Demin after freeing Yiloch and Ferin, killing Jayce, and attempting to do the same to Myac with less success.

She swallowed around a knot in her throat. "When will the tribes be gathered?"

"Soon. Do not speak while they work," Chozai snapped as he sat cross-legged in front of her.

She forced herself to be still, trying not to let her thoughts become caught up with the permanence of the choice she was making. The quick, sharp stabs of pain as the tattooist began his work were unpleasant in a way, but they also brought a heightened sense of clarity after the dizzying effects of the sucar. She met Suac Chozai's gaze and held it, refusing the temptation to use ascard to mitigate the pain. He would notice the lack of reaction and respect her less for it. On her left, the woman began to work some of her thick, dark hair into a delicate braid.

Chozai watched in silence for a time, perhaps ensuring that the work was done to his satisfaction. Eventually, he responded to her question.

"The southernmost tribes, Denilik and Chusin, will head north. As they cross the lands of the tribes to their north, those tribes will join them. This process will continue until all have arrived here, at the northernmost Murak village. This is the most efficient way."

She started to nod her agreement then caught herself. It was best not to move while someone was pounding ink into her cheek with a sharp implement.

Chozai continued. "When all the tribes have gathered, the Dursik un Kar will move into Lyra. This is as you wished it, Indigo un Ani, is it not?"

His teasing smirk told her he was baiting her to see if she would forget and move. She held still and marveled that this powerful man, religious leader to a people who considered use of ascard to be sacrilege, had already become so at ease with her. When she first arrived here, he'd been hostile, not only due to her race, but also because he hadn't foreseen her coming as he had that of her companions. It was a tense encounter, very different from the relative comfort that was developing between them now, after such a short time together. Since the first time she walked with the gods with him, he accepted her, even brought her under his protection, because he believed the gods accepted her.

She waited, wincing as the tattooist began to work over her cheekbone. When he paused to wipe away the blood, she took advantage of the moment.

"It is as I wished," she confirmed, hoping her words might prompt him to say more.

Chozai nodded, his gaze turning inward. "Yes. But why do you wish it? The Blood Prince has rejected you." She struggled not to frown at his use of Yiloch's old derogatory title, not daring to speak in his defense now that the tattooist was working again. "Why do you risk yourself for him even now after he has turned you away? Perhaps it has something to do with this thing you call love. This thing you told me I know nothing of."

She flushed, embarrassed to be reminded of the hateful words she had once spat at him. Chozai smirked and shook his head, dismissing her shame.

"Your words were not wrong, not in regards to the type of love you spoke of then. I love my people. I loved my parents. I love being alive. I love the gods that guide, protect, and challenge us. None of these things is the same as the love you have for Emperor Yiloch. Or the love he has for you."

She placed her fingertips on the tattooist's arm, stopping his work with a light touch. "You told me that he hates me now, did you not, or were you only being spiteful when you said that?"

"Part of him did hate you. Part of him will never stop loving you. It is because of the strength of that love that your betrayal ignited an equally passionate hatred. He does not hate you now."

She lowered her hand, allowing the tattooist to continue. There were many things she wanted to ask, not the least of which was how he could possibly know how Yiloch felt toward her now. His power of prophecy had been proven more than once, but it was unlikely that he would spend his time among the gods trying to divine the Lyran emperor's feelings for her. There was too much emotion wrapped up in the subject though, so she opted for settling into the silence forced by the tattooist's work.

Chozai continued to watch in silence, only offering the occasional word of advice to the two who were building her Kudaness identity. His critical observation, noting every flinch or twitch of a finger in response to the pain, didn't bother her as it once would have. After all she had been through and done to get to this point, the judgment of others wasn't something she was willing to waste energy on. She had killed men in war to save Yiloch. She had killed her ex fiancé in an act of hatred and fear. She could try to convince herself that was self-defense, but it didn't matter in the end. No justifications would make him any less dead. As far as her king and country knew, she had freed the man who ordered the assassinations of King Jerrin and his family. She knew Yiloch wasn't guilty of the crimes, but they didn't, and she could do little to prove that from here. Now she had put into action her plan to see the Kudaness army come to Lyra's aide against the Grey Army that was marching on the capital. With all of that already resting on her shoulders, Chozai's scrutiny didn't have the power to unsettle her.

The woman finished three beaded braids in her hair and left the hut. A short time later, the tattooist finished his work and left the hut as well. Chozai considered her for a long moment, taking her chin and turning her face first to the left so he could look at the tattoo, then to the right so he could see the braids. After a few minutes of this contemplation, his expression unreadable, he nodded.

"You are now a priest of the Ithik Ani."

Her cheek throbbed, the lines of the tattoo stinging, needling her with an acute awareness of the choice she had made. "Don't you mean priestess?"

He shook his head. "There are no Kudaness priestesses."

She stared at him, confused.

"It is good," he continued, ignoring her expression. "Now everyone will know who you are." His tone suggested a depth of knowing that went well beyond that of simply knowing someone's name.

"Yes, everyone except me." She recognized her words as a shameless grab for guidance even as she spoke them.

Chozai chuckled and smiled at her with reserved fondness, the expression looked out of place on his strong, tattoo-covered features. "With that I cannot help you. You must figure that out for yourself."

The heat of embarrassment rose in her cheeks and she lowered her gaze. Oh, to have the nearly black complexion of the Kudaness, at least then her embarrassment wouldn't be obvious at all.

"Yes. I realize that."

"I know you do," he replied. "Keep the tattoo protected from the sun until it heals," he instructed.

She nodded understanding as he turned and left the hut. Running her fingers absently over the soft textures of the woven carpet on which she sat, she contemplated healing the tattoo with ascard. Such a simple act, using the very skill she had trained for so long to develop, would lose her considerable ground with Suac Chozai. Something that was such an integral part of her would always be blasphemy to the Kudaness. No matter what her new identity declared her to be, she would never truly be one of them. Still, she had gained far too much ground with the suac to destroy it in a moment of indulgence.

Donning a hooded wrap, she left the hut and walked to the edge of the village, her soft shoes sinking a touch in the rocky sand. Continuing out away from the huts, she stopped next to a large bush, gently touching the tip of a thorn with one fingertip. All the plants here had thorns. Many of the creatures were prickly too, the Kudaness people included.

Watching the ground for snakes and scorpions, she continued walking until she could no longer hear the sounds of the village. Then she stopped and closed her eyes, feeling the heat of the sun blazing down, the lingering pain of the fresh tattoo, and the contours of rocks mixed into the sand under her feet. She stood there for several minutes feeling the desert and listening to the sounds of birds and other creatures that lived there. When she opened her eyes, a wild dog stood no more than ten feet away, watching her. The animal was still in the way only a wild animal could be. She yearned for that stillness, staring into the wild dog's eyes with a longing to understand its nature. The animal held her gaze for a long, breathless moment, neither hostile nor friendly. Then it turned and trotted away from her.

Realizing she had been holding her breath, she let it go and inhaled the warm evening air. The sun was touching the horizon. It was time to go back to the village. No one wandered the desert after dark given a choice. There were far too many dangers lurking in the sand, scorpions and other such poisonous creatures, that might be missed in the dark. The voices of wild dogs sang her along her way and she smiled to herself. They were predators of the desert, but so was she now. In that sense, they were kin.

CHAPTER FIVE

The sitting room was empty. Lush gold chairs accented with maroon detail waited in quiet repose. Caplin walked to the far corner of the room and slumped into one with a distinct lack of grace. Somehow, he managed not to spill his wine in the process. One elbow came to rest on the arm of the chair and he pressed the wine glass against his forehead, closing his eyes.

Her face waited in the darkness. Not Andrea's, not the face of his fiancé that should linger in that special place within his mind. If he tried to picture his fiancé, he could pull up her image for a moment, but her green eyes always turned a deep blue, her reddish hair morphing to a luxurious golden brown. Indigo's lips filled his thoughts, begging for a kiss, offering a smile that could drive away the deepest sorrow with its sweet sincerity.

Why hadn't he listened? He might have heeded the ache in her voice, the desperation. She might be here now, not run away to Lyra, not wanted as a traitor to her own people… like her father before her.

Indigo, what have you done? Where have you gone?

His memories of her were so vivid, so intense, that he could smell her and feel her smooth skin under his fingertips. With a soft exhale, he slid further down in the chair, resting his head against the plush back. The

room rocked, given motion by the intense weariness
that dragged at him. There was somewhere he was supposed to be soon, but he couldn't dredge up enough
interest to remember where that was. Opening his eyes,
he gazed into the dark red liquid, swirling it in the glass.
The glass was created. Imported from Lyra where using
ascard for such things wasn't a crime.

Only it wasn't a crime here. Not for everyone. They
had creators of their own in the palace. There weren't
many creators, but they were there. He knew that now.
So many of the things he thought to be true had been
revealed as false since he became prince of Caithin.
They had their own secret group of creators and adepts,
but all of the created glasses in the palace were still imported from Lyra. The creators of Caithin didn't use
their power for benign purposes, like the creating of
unbreakable glass. They were weapons for the king.

He swirled the wine again, his eyes refocusing on
the glass that contained it. It's clear, flawless curves
embraced the fluid. As perfectly beautiful as the pureblooded Lyran people themselves. Was that what drew
her to Yiloch, that unbearable perfection? The man
moved like water flowing, flawless and beautiful. Eyes of
pale silver-blue, like daggers of ice, a sweeping cascade
of silver hair, the man almost made him wish he were
interested in his own gender.

Caplin swallowed the rest of his wine in a bitter gulp
and threw the glass. It struck the marble mantle and
bounced away, not even having the decency to shatter.
The glass protected by the power woven into it. How
much did such a creation cost?

The glass rolled in a smooth arc back toward him,
coming to rest at the toe of his boot. It left a trail of red

drips behind, like small droplets of blood. Rage flooded him then and he stood, kicking the glass with all the power he could muster. It flew across the room and struck the doorjamb as the door opened, still not breaking. His father frowned at him. His father the king.

Dizzied by his abrupt rise and a few too many glasses of wine, Caplin wavered and dropped back into the chair, staring sullen into the empty fireplace.

"I'm pleased you got that out of your system," Gavin remarked, his gravelly voice rumbling out in its customary growl like the purr of a huge cat.

Caplin dropped his forehead into his hand and closed his eyes.

"You are aware that we have a council meeting in less than an hour."

Caplin waved a dismissive hand toward the door. "Whatever."

The door slammed. He opened his eyes to see his father scowling at him as he strode into the room, stopping on the other side of a center table. He averted his gaze, finding it less uncomfortable to stare down at his father's feet. There was a long silence while Caplin waited for the scolding to rain down on him, but when Gavin finally spoke, his tone was gentle.

"You have to let Indigo go, Caplin. There is no way she could ever be yours. Not now."

"I don't... I..." Caplin sputtered and fell silent, staring open mouthed at his father.

"Don't lie to me. I'm your father. I know your feelings for her have changed over the years. Her past would have made her a poor match for you before, but now she is well beyond redemption. You need to turn your attention back to the woman who is here now.

Andrea loves you. She is warm and willing to be yours."

Leaning forward, Caplin rested his elbows on his knees and stared at the toes of his boots, fighting the ache within. "I can't let her go," he whispered.

"You can and you will. Even if she came back, she chose to betray her country. No matter what her reasons, she can never be a part of this family."

Wringing his hands, he muttered, "What if she was right? What if Emperor Yiloch wasn't behind the assassinations?"

"She should have spoken to someone in charge instead of acting on her own."

"She tried." His voice cracked and he swallowed, struggling for control. "She came to me, but I refused to hear her. I wanted him to be guilty because I thought that would end her love for him. I let my jealousy drive her away."

Gavin nodded. "Perhaps you did, but she should have tried another way. She could have requested an audience with me or spoken to Lord Serivar."

"Considering how fast we put the first three adepts to death, she probably didn't think she had time."

Gavin stepped around and sat on the table. His simple attire, the same sedate colors and inexpensive fabrics he had always worn, made it easy to forget that he was now the king. Caplin met his deep brown eyes. Eyes full of patient understanding.

"They all signed confessions. Without any proof to the contrary, we can only believe that our course was the right one."

Caplin searched his father's face for a moment, seeing the tight line of his lips, the faint circles under his eyes, the worry etching lines in his brow. "You doubt too. You haven't declared outright war on Lyra, haven't attacked them while they're vulnerable."

Gavin exhaled now, lowering his gaze. He rubbed one thumb with the fingers of the other hand as though it pained him. "I suppose you're right. I don't know Indigo as well as you, but I know her well enough to have a hard time accepting that she would do something so drastic unless she truly believed she was in the right."

They sat in silence for several minutes more, the king rubbing his thumb, Caplin massaging his temples. Somewhere in their conversation, a headache had snuck up on him.

Lyra had never been more vulnerable. With the upheaval from Yiloch's takeover on top of the distress that Rylan's madness had placed the empire in prior to that, the once invincible country was disorganized and crippled, a shadow of its former self. This was the perfect time to retaliate for the assassination of Jerrin and his family. The actions of one woman stayed their hand.

"If she's here, if she comes to me, I won't place her under arrest," Caplin stated.

Gavin regarded him with the thoughtful look that meant he was considering how best to tell his son that he was being a fool. His lips pressed into a tight line within the frame of his neatly trimmed beard and moustache. "You realize that you would not necessarily be doing her a favor in that circumstance. If you arrested her, you could at least ensure her good treatment and see to it that she got a chance to explain herself."

Caplin ground his teeth, staring into the empty fireplace. How could the man always be right? It wasn't natural.

Abruptly, Gavin placed his hands on his knees and pushed himself up. "Sober yourself up for the meeting. I'm planning to send Lord Theron to Yiroth to gather information and to speak with Lord Terral and Lord Captain Adran about the situation."

Caplin sat up. "Indigo's Uncle?"

Gavin nodded. "He's the most reliable and effective emissary we have and he'll bring Indigo back alive if he can find her."

"If she even is still alive," Caplin muttered.

Gavin scowled.

Ignoring the look, Caplin rose. "Don't worry, Father, I think I'm sober now."

The gruff man's expression softened again and he squeezed Caplin's shoulder. "Good, I have need of your support."

●

"Yiroth has requested a temporary stay of hostilities. They haven't heard back from the group they sent in search of Emperor Yiloch and they now have a foreign army marching on the capital city leaving a path of destruction—"

"An army?" Lord Davrick interrupted, winning himself a cold glower from the king. "From where? Kudan?"

Gavin wetted his lips with his tongue and looked down at the table. A gesture Caplin was familiar with. It meant, 'I'm too annoyed with you to look at you right now,' and it was always pleasant to see that look directed at someone else.

"The army comes from beyond the Rhuakhine. It matches up with information we received from Lord Edan before he too vanished without a trace. We have no word on his current whereabouts or those of Lady Indigo Milan. Without Emperor Yiloch to face the accusations against him or Lady Indigo to explain her actions, it makes sense to me that we should give them some time to deal with this new threat. I—"

"We should crush them. Make them pay for their crimes while they are at their weakest," Davrick interrupted again with an arrogant toss of his dusty blond hair.

"I think I like these meetings better when you send a representative to sit in your stead, Lord Davrick."

Davrick's face went red and Caplin rested his chin on his hand, hiding a smirk behind his fingers.

Gavin nodded approval of the resulting silence and continued. "Under the circumstances, they have shown the presence of mind not to request aide from Caithin. Given that they seem to be cooperating, I think it makes sense to give them time to deal with their problems and try to track down some of our growing list of missing people." Gavin paused for a few seconds, apparently long enough to invite another interruption.

"Perhaps we should offer them aide," Serivar said.

Caplin suspected his stunned expression was much the same as that on his father's face. "I seem to recall you being adamantly against aiding Emperor Yiloch in taking the throne from his father. Why so eager to help now?" Caplin asked, an edge of annoyance sharpening his tone.

Serivar glanced from Caplin to his father.

Gavin lifted his brows. "It seems like a reasonable question, Lord Serivar."

The Academy Headmaster sat back in his seat with a pained expression as all eyes turned to him.

Think quickly. Caplin offered him an uncharitable sneer.

Serivar's brown eyes flickered up in controlled recognition of the look. He took a moment to clean something out from under one fingernail then set his hands out, palms down on the table and met the king's eyes. "Lyra could still be a powerful ally under proper leadership. This foreign army might not be so congenial. It seems that the wiser move would be to support the power we're familiar with rather than risk a hostile force taking over." There was a soft grunt of consideration from Gavin and even Caplin had to agree that there was a certain sense to the argument. "Such a gesture, if executed properly, would also put us in a position of considerable influence in any future negotiations with Lyra."

"There is a certain logic to what you suggest," Gavin stated, "but we must not appear to take the crimes they have committed against us lightly. I will think on this and discuss it with the council in two days. Right now, I'm going to advise that our next action be to send an envoy to Yiroth to meet with Lord Terral and Lord Captain Adran in an effort to assess the situation."

There were murmurs of assent around the table at that. There was little to argue with in such an action. Anything they considered doing now required more information about the foreign army and the status of the search for Yiloch and the others in Lyra.

"I recommend Lord Theron."

Caplin had been watching Serivar intently since the headmaster suggested aiding Lyra. Now he saw the flicker of something, panic perhaps, or maybe irritation, flash across his features. The emotion was carefully smoothed away an instant later, but his curiosity was piqued. There was something going on with the headmaster.

"Given the situation with Lady Indigo I think someone more impartial to her would be a better choice," Serivar suggested now, his tone reasonable if one ignored the faint tremor in his voice.

"I must disagree, Lord Serivar," Gavin countered. "Lord Theron is now, and always has been, a most successful and loyal representative to the Caithin throne. I have no doubt that he can handle this delicate situation better than anyone."

The king's expression was stony as he regarded his old friend. The long friendship between the headmaster and Gavin was less amiable since they argued over Indigo after she set Yiloch and Ferin free. Serivar's less than complimentary comments about her during that argument won him no favor with Gavin. Gavin had never been open about his affection for Indigo, not even with his own son. His confession in that particular argument that he thought of her as a daughter had been news to Caplin as much as it was to the headmaster.

Caplin watched with interest as Serivar struggled against the downward curve of his lips, trying in vain to maintain an expression of neutrality. Many other members of the council shifted in their seats, none of them blind to the tension in the room.

Remembering his father's request for support, Caplin cleared his throat and said, "Lord Theron's record of service is flawless. Even when his brother was declared a traitor for his sabotage of the slave trade, Lord Theron continued to manage diplomatic missions for the kingdom without issue. His loyalty didn't falter then. I see no reason we should expect anything less from him now."

There were grunts and nods of agreement around the table. Gavin caught Caplin's eye and he gave the slightest of nods to show his appreciation.

"When will he return from his current mission?"

Caplin had been too busy watching Serivar and his father to catch who spoke, but Gavin responded quickly, not allowing room for more arguments.

"Lord Theron returned yesterday. He is not averse to heading out on this mission immediately. I have suggested that he go in the company of two warships, a gesture to remind Lyra of whom they are dealing with in this. I do not think he will have any difficulties, but a small display of strength is not out of line in this situation I think."

There were nods around most of the table, though Serivar still looked somewhat petulant. The headmaster appeared to understand that he wasn't going to win this. Theron's reputation was impeccable. He would be hard pressed to find any fault that would convince them not to send the man. Something in the headmaster's behavior bothered Caplin, but he couldn't figure out exactly what it was. It was like a bad itch he couldn't quite reach. Whatever it took, he intended to find a way to scratch it.

Wild dogs sang Indigo to sleep every night in the desert, but it was cries of war that startled her awake this morning. Pulling on a Kudaness wrap, she managed to be on her feet and heading out of the hut a few strides behind Suac Chozai. Outside, in the near blackness of early dawn, she could see nothing but a sea of dark-skinned warriors spreading in all directions. So many tribes, many of whom spent much of their time in conflict with one another, were coming together to honor the rite of the Dursik un Kar, a gathering of the many tribes' warriors into one army to face a common enemy. Pride filled her, warming her in the chill of the desert morning. Her actions had set this Dursik un Kar in motion. It might have been a crazy thing to try, but it had worked.

The new arrivals regarded her with surprise and disgust when she walked out among them, at least until they spotted the still healing tattoo, a delicate rendition of the symbol of the un Ani, on her cheek. Then the disgust in their dark eyes was pushed aside by surprise and they inclined their heads in a show of respect for her rank, reluctant as the gesture might be in most cases. No one questioned the wishes of the gods it seemed, and she couldn't help marveling at the conviction of their beliefs. They kept to their tribal groups, but their shared faith bound them together more strongly than ties of blood. If they believed the gods willed something so, then they would accept that, no matter how foul a taste it left on their tongues.

It took a powerful leveraging of self-control for her not to jump when a hand rested firmly on her shoulder. A quick touch of ascard told her it was Suac Chozai. The suac adjusted her direction of travel with the pressure of his hand.

"This is our army, but it is your spirit journey," he murmured, speaking in the Murak Kudaness dialect. He had been drilling her on it relentlessly since their return to the village, speaking less in the Lyran trade dialect and forcing her to learn through context. "You will join the suacs."

She allowed the high priest to guide her to the center of the village near the watering hole. The suacs of the other eleven tribes waited there, an ornate display with their tattoos and the beads in their long braided black hair, copper eyes alert to everyone and everything around them. All turned toward Indigo and Chozai, none of those metallic eyes failing to take note of her fresh tattoo. Most stared at the symbol with a calculated lack of expression. A few even nodded to her, including Suac Kipith of Denilik whose expression was the most welcoming. Suac Therah of Farid offered a feral grin and she had to struggle to keep from shuddering in response. She nodded back to those who acknowledged her and reciprocated the indifference of the others.

Chozai collected a cup of water from the well. This he held out in the center. Every suac drew their blade and she tensed at the hiss of steel sliding free of leather sheaths. Then they drew the blades across their palms in turn, each man allowing a few drops of blood fall into the offered cup. When the cup stopped in front of her, it was all she could do not to step back from it. Suac Therah offered her the hilt of his blade and she could see the gleam of amusement in his eyes.

Determined not to lose whatever ground she had gained with these men, she took the blade and drew it across her palm as she had seen the others do. She couldn't stop a small intake of breath in response to the sudden pain and a few of the suacs grinned, though their expressions were more teasing than mean as she might have expected. Holding her hand out, she let a few drops of her own blood fall to join the mix in the red tinted water, then offered the hilt of the dagger back to Therah. Giddy pride swelled in her chest in response to his reluctant nod of approval when he accepted the weapon back. Chozai gave her a quick warning glance and she accepted the cloth he offered to stop the bleeding rather than giving in to instinct to heal it.

Chozai made his offering last and swirled the cup. His eyes met hers expectantly. Not sure how to respond, she gave a nod, hoping that was sufficient. The faintest hint of a smile tugged at the corners of his lips. Turning away, he dumped the bloody water back into the well and she winced slightly at the thought of the blood mixing in with the village's water supply.

"The Dursik un Kar is initiated," Chozai announced. "We fight the Grey Army as one tribe."

There were solemn nods around the circle.

"We will rest tonight and head out with the morning sun," Suac Kipith said.

Indigo tensed. "Can we not leave today?"

Twelve pairs of dark copper eyes turned toward her and she regretted her words, wishing she could disappear from their cold scrutiny.

"The trek across the desert is a hard one, Indigo un Ani, and we have traveled at great speed," one Suac explained. "We must rest."

Remembering Chozai's lessons, she identified his tattoo as that of the Shirid tribe. Their tribe was the furthest south on the western edge of Kudan. They had indeed traveled far, but she feared that they would come to Yiroth too late if they delayed much longer. She opened her mouth to argue, and stopped, catching the small shake of Chozai's head. Working to calm the worry that made her nerves dance, she inclined her head to the Shirid suac.

"Of course. You have indeed traveled far."

Chozai took a few moments to call in several women who he set about the task of helping the other tribes' suacs settle in around the village. As the group dispersed, he stepped in close to her.

"Go to the hut and rest. The journey ahead will be a hard one. Walk if it will help you keep your path clear."

From his tone, she understood that the walk he was suggesting didn't involve her feet. Perhaps he was right. If she used the sucar again, maybe she would be able to find Yiloch, or perhaps check on events in Caithin. The added bonus of strengthening her connection had its own appeal as well. What could it hurt for her power to grow, if that truly was what was happening when she used the drug? Lyra would need her as strong as she could be.

She nodded and left him, returning to his hut. A young woman followed her, somehow privy to her purpose, and stood by in silence while Indigo collected the sucar and arranged herself on a rug. Drawing out the stopper, she grimaced at the stench of it and her stomach clenched in dreadful anticipation. Steeling herself, she took a swallow of the thick fluid. The woman stepped forward and took the skin. She stoppered it and put it back in the cabinet before leaving the hut.

Swaying, Indigo focused her thoughts on Yiloch. She wanted to know what was happening in Caithin, there were people she cared about there, but she had to know that he was still alive first.

Blackness embraced her and the falling sensation was brief this time, the cramping in her stomach an annoyance she was learning to cope with. When the falling stopped, she still drifted in a sea of blackness. Swaying with the strange motion the drug incited, she waited. Nothing changed.

Yiloch. She projected her need into the darkness, feeling a tickle of apprehension at the base of her spine. *I have to know what's become of Yiloch.*

What if something was wrong? What if she never left the darkness this time?

There was a dizzying sense of motion then. When it stopped, she stood in the center of a circle of tall mirrors. There were more mirrors than she had ever seen in one place, every one perfectly flat and smooth as though created with ascard. Images of her own swaying form reflected a thousand times over. For a minute she could only stand in awe of the display, then her eyes refocused on the primary reflection in the mirror in front of her.

The tattoo on her reflected cheek had nearly healed. One line started a little under her eye, dropping down and then sweeping back up in a graceful arch that traced along her cheekbone then curved back down, ending in a spiral near her hairline. There were two dots just above the end spiral. Below her cheekbone at the center of the gradual arch, a short detached line swept down toward her lower jaw, with a second shorter line angling back from the center of that line towards the corner of her jaw. In front of the downward line were two more small dots.

All said, it was a graceful pattern, far more attractive than some of the tribal symbols and far less masculine than the warrior tattoo. A faint smile curved the reflection's lips, a hint of amusement with the way the honored symbol moved with her expressions. Then the smile dissolved. There was something different about the reflection in the next mirror over.

Turning, she regarded her reflection in that mirror and gasped. The eyes that looked back at her were dark copper, the exact image of a suacs eyes. Unnerved, she turned to the next mirror. Here, the tattoo was gone and her eyes were blue again. In the next, she wore an elegant gown of Lyran make. In another, the tattoo was back and her eyes were mostly blue, flecked with copper. In the next...

She stepped back from the mirror, the reflections around the circle moving with her. The image that stared back at her was much like the first, but her hands were red with blood. Blood dripped from her fingertips, landing in stark red splotches on the pale skirt of the dress she wore. The eyes staring back at her were dark, almost black, the face expressionless. The ink of the tattoo bled from her cheek, running down in black rivulets and dripping from her jaw to mix with the blood on the skirt.

With a cry, she staggered back and stumbled, sitting down hard in the midst of the mirrors. The image before her remained standing and replaced the images in all of the other mirrors. Sweat broke out on her forehead. Her gaze darted around, searching for a way out, or, at the very least, something else to see, something that might offer a glimmer of hope amidst the fear.

"No." She screamed at the image, pulling her knees in to her chest and wrapping her arms around them. She hid her face in the circle of her arms and whispered the word over and over again. "No, no, no, no—"

"Indigo un Ani."

The voice was firm and strong hands shook her shoulders. Opening her eyes, she saw Suac Chozai's copper eyes staring down at her, his brow furrowed in concern. Twisting away from him, she heaved up the remaining sucar on another rug. A woman came and collected the soiled rug, retreating quickly to leave them alone in the tent. Lying back, Indigo panted and wiped at the sweat on her brow. After a few seconds, she became aware of the tears that trailed down her cheeks and wiped those away as well.

Without looking at Chozai, she asked, "Do you always know what your walks with the gods mean?"

He gave her a level look. "Meaning is not always clear at first."

"I—"

"No." She flinched at his harsh tone and looked over to see him shaking his head, warning her to silence with a stern glower. "When we walk alone, we do not share what we see. That is between the walker and the gods."

Staying still, she focused on the vivid images from the mirrors. The images of blood on her hands and ink running down her face remained burned into her mind. Why? What did it mean? Were the images meant to represent some future possibilities? If so, what decisions would lead her to that final image? Or did its taking over all the mirrors mean that she'd already made those decisions?

She surged to her feet and started for the door of the hut muttering, "I need to wash my hands."

Chozai watched her leave in silence.

Outside the hut, she walked to where the wash water was kept in a separate pool. They refreshed that water only when necessary to avoid waste. Grabbing a rough cloth, she squatted down and scrubbed her hands until the skin was raw. The image of blood on them couldn't be washed away. Sighing, she dropped the cloth and stood. The thousands of voices drowned out the sounds of the desert. Warriors stretched as far as she could see. Escaping the village to find a quiet place wouldn't be easy. She selected a direction at random and began to walk.

The sun blazed down brutally now, its unforgiving heat supporting the decision not to begin the trek to Lyra today. She had left her wrap in the hut, so she surrounded herself with ascard, a cocoon of pure, strong, and refreshing power. Dark skinned warriors, women, and children stared as she passed, unaware of the sin she committed before their eyes. When she was beyond the bounds of the village itself, only warriors watched her walk. They moved out of her path quickly, bowing their heads so fast that she wondered at her own expression. Did her distress and intensity show through that strongly? Whatever it was, it was more than simply the tattoo. She hadn't gotten this much of a reaction before.

Eventually, she stopped and stood in the midst of a sea of dark skinned warriors, most of who now sat in groups in the sand, gazing up at her with curiosity when she didn't move. There was a lull in their conversations. After a short time, they resumed talking, but in lower voices. She swept over them with her gaze.

How many of you will die in this fight?

Whose blood would she have on her hands when this was done? Even if things went well, some of them would die. More would be injured. She rubbed at her hands. Could she live with more bloodstains upon her soul if it meant Yiloch was safe? It wasn't only him anymore, though. It wasn't even the others she cared about who were with him. The Grey Army posed a threat to more than Lyra if they defeated that empire. How much blood would have to be spilled to stop them? How many lives stood to be saved?

Once again, she looked over the warriors around her, seeing their faces this time, not just their forms. They were strong and beautiful in their own magnificent way, every one of them.

"I'm sorry," she murmured in Caithin, knowing they wouldn't understand her. It was probably better that they didn't.

Despite the power Ini-jnai had at his disposal, it was becoming apparent to Myac that the foreigners didn't diversify widely in their uses of ascard. Primarily they used it for binding and for protection with a few other applications branching predictably from there, such as using barriers to push things away. In order to create a barrier as strong as those Ini-jnai created, a portion of every ability he drew upon had to be dedicated to that skill, including his own. Only Ini-jnai and Ksa-jnai appeared to have branched away from that primary skill set in some ways, but even they had not done so significantly from what he had observed.

Given how seamless Ini-jnai's control of the combined power of their adepts was, Myac suspected it was a common practice among their people to have one lead adept running a large number of others. With so few adepts in control of their own power, it made some sense that there might be less individual experimentation and, as a result, less diversity of skills. There was so much they could learn from him if they could only understand the language. That alone gave him a reason to appreciate the communication barrier, despite the other challenges it presented.

Efforts to pick up on their language were minimally

productive. The structure was different from anything he knew and the sounds strange to his ears and tongue. Rather than waste time on that, he pondered ways to escape, running scenario after scenario through his head. It would be so much easier if he could simply bolt. The opportunity to try to flee had presented itself a few times already. Unfortunately, bound to Ini-jnai as he was, he would be leaving his power behind as long as he left the adept alive and they would always be able to track him through that connection. He could run with the intention of finding help, but then he risked not getting the chance to destroy the adept and regain his power. Death was far preferable to life with some other adept's binding keeping him from controlling his ability. Therefore, whatever he did, it had to involve Ini-jnai's death.

When he wasn't running through futile scenarios in his head, he let his consciousness ride along on the link to Ini-jnai, learning what he could of the adept and the army that way, or wiled away hours cursing Indigo in his head. In many ways, she had helped bring him to this dismal situation. It did no good to think of her though. Every time her image coalesced in his mind, desire rose to greet it, desire for her power and beauty, desire for her suffering. The desire was like a fever that refused to break. It clouded his reason, making it hard to think rationally, and he hated her for that.

Most nights he found it almost impossible to sleep, his hands bound before him, his mind restless and defiant for all the good it did him. Through the binding on his inner aspect, he could feel when Ini-jnai slept. The controlling adept had no trouble at all drifting off into peaceful slumber, while Myac's lack of sleep wore away at him. During the day, his sleep-deprived mind wandered more and more, distracting easily. If he hoped to take advantage of an opportunity to escape, he needed to be sharp, but tonight was no different from any other. Sleep eluded him.

The army as a whole rested well. Lord Inaki's distraction had been their only organized resistance since they had taken Myac captive and that had been less effective than his own confrontation with them. To Inaki's credit, the suicidal attack had allowed him and Lady Shyalis to make good their escape with the majority of their forces. Perhaps Lord Terral and the others realized the Lyran army was still too scattered and weakened by Yiloch's campaign to face this army on open ground. Secure behind the walls of Yiroth, they might hold out for a while, but the people along the route would continue to suffer. On the other hand, maybe Lord Captain Adran and Commander Hax simply refused to make a move without their precious emperor to guide them. Either way, it looked as if this army would reach the capital virtually unchallenged.

Myac sucked in a breath of surprise as the ropes fell away from his wrists. He stared for several long minutes at the frayed objects lying on the ground. Ascard. An adept, or more likely several adepts, outside the camp had managed to move power in undetected and free his hands. What did they hope to achieve? Was this some act of heroism to rescue a fellow Lyran or did they hope he would lash out against his captors and create a distraction. It didn't really matter what they intended, there was only one way he was leaving this camp and that was with Ini-jnai's blood on his hands.

Without getting up, he glanced around to see if any of the sentries were watching. They rarely paid him much attention and now was no exception. When he felt confident that no one was looking his way, he moved to push himself up with his freed arms. It was all he could do not to cry out as muscles in his shoulders and back flared with agonizing protest. For many days, those muscles were restricted to a limited range of movement and this was the price of that restriction. Rolling on to his back, he moved the muscles a little at a time, his breathing punctuated by the occasional soft grunt as he tried to work through the pain.

Some miserable time later, he checked the sentries again and rose to a cautious crouch. He could feel where Ini-jnai was in the camp and began to pick his way through the sleeping bodies. A few horses shifted as he passed, not upset by his movement as much as they were simply curious. A tiny glint of steel in the moonlight caught his attention when a warrior he was close to shifted in his sleep. A knife lay on the ground alongside the man. Myac waited for a minute, crouched in the shadow of a stocky mare until the man's breathing was even again. When the man settled back into deeper sleep, he eased the blade away and moved on.

Ini-jnai was close now. In a Lyran army, the warlord and his officers would have some kind of tents erected for discussion of strategy and sleeping. Ksa-jnai lay on the ground with the rest of his men, his ranking warriors arranged around him. The adept, Ini-jnai, and the young favored warrior, Na-jnai, were also in that circle.

Myac paused outside the circle, struggling to keep his focus. Hatred pounded through him like a drug in his veins, the nearness of freedom more intoxicating than any alcohol. Emotional and physical weariness from the days of captivity clouded his thoughts, counteracting the heightened alert of his nerves. He rubbed at the wrist of the hand holding the knife, feeling abrasions on the skin and a deep ache in the muscles from the ropes.

It didn't matter if someone woke while he was still there, so long as they did so after Ini-jnai was dead. With his power back in his control, he could escape the army and take many of them down in the process, of that he was confident. At the absolute worst, he would die trying, which was better than this raping of his power, better than feeling that power lingering just out of reach while someone else did with it as they pleased.

His lip rose in a silent snarl and he crept forward. Closer. Softly closer. Pause. Hold breath and watch for movement. Inch closer again. The adept was sleeping, the grey flesh of his throat giving off a dull gleam of reflecting moonlight. The first strike had to be fatal. If the adept got any chance to fight back, it was over. The mere thought of such an outcome sent a shudder through him. It had to end now.

Closer.

A short distance away, beyond the sleeping form of Ksa-jnai, Na-jnai stirred. Myac froze and waited. He stayed there for a few minutes, each second passing with agonizing slowness. There was no more movement. Wishing the blood would stop pounding so loud in his ears, Myac closed the remaining distance. The thrill of victory waited, coiled in his chest in anticipation of the lethal strike. He sneered down at the adept. Sound asleep, his protections inert, he was as vulnerable as any man. His power slept with him. The power of all of the adepts slept with him. Tying off such a massive working in order to keep it active even in rest was too much for even him. If Ini-jnai died, would the other adepts be ready to control their own power. Would they come after him?

It was too late to worry about that now.

Sinking to one knee, he brought the blade down level with Ini-jnai's throat and started to sweep it in a path that would cut deep into his neck. At that same instant, there was a movement to his right and the soft whistle of something cutting through the air. There was barely enough time for his heart to jump into his throat before the thrown knife plunged into his upper arm. The force of the throw sent steel driving deep into the muscle. The injured arm jerked out of position and the blade swept up instead of across, cutting a line from under the adept's ear up to the point of his chin.

Before Ini-jnai's eyes were fully open, Myac was flying backward through the air, the power behind the push so strong that he felt the bones of his lower legs shatter, jagged edges tearing through flesh, when he struck ground. He cried out, a hoarse scream that didn't even sound human in his ears. He lay where he landed paralyzed by an agony so intense he was scarcely aware of the army surging to life around him. Whoever had freed his hands wasn't going to be coming to his aid now.

Pain. Everything in his world was now pain. His entire life narrowed down to the mind-numbing anguish of his shattered legs. Even the blade embedded in his arm was an itch by comparison. He couldn't imagine anything hurting more, but Ini-jnai hadn't gotten a chance to express his anger yet.

Someone stood over him, speaking in low, sinister tone. The words made no sense, but the intent was crystal clear. Horror filled Myac the instant before a deep gash opened on one hand, splitting the flesh from his wrist to the tip of his index finger, laying it open to the bone. Pain like fire burst from the wound, violent enough to distract from his legs, burning away all remaining coherent thought as blood gushed out hot over his hand. His free hand clamped around the wrist of the wounded hand, desperate to stop the gushing of blood, then a matching wound split it open.

He felt another wound split his cheek along the line of the cheekbone as someone reached down and wrenched the blade from his arm. The sound of his own voice howling out in agony filled his ears and beneath it all, some part of him was aware that it was his own power being used to torture him. Even in the midst of that immeasurable pain, humiliation and rage surged through him. Simultaneously, wounds opened across his chest and higher up in both wrists. His lungs seized with the shock of the myriad deep wounds and the blood he had already lost.

Black spots swam in his vision, the warriors staring down at him faded. He was faintly aware of another gash opening across his ribs. Blackness wrapped around him and he welcomed its embrace when it sucked him down into unconsciousness.

●

"Ini-jnai." The First Maker ignored him and rage flared in Ksa-jnai. No one ignored him. "Ini-jnai," he roared.

His First Maker turned, dark eyes crazed with anger, blood running in a thin rivulet down into the collar of his shirt from the shallow cut that stretched from under his ear to his chin. Close. The foreign maker had nearly sent his Bloodnau into the Afterworld. Remarkable. What courage and determination it must have taken for him to risk such a move in an army full of enemies. He could have run, but he wanted his power back enough to risk his own life to get it.

Ksa-jnai gazed down on the still foreigner. The pale man's breath was coming in shallow gasps. Awareness had left him. Not a surprise given the extent of his injuries. He would die soon if his blood continued to drain out into the grass with such speed. A waste of extraordinary power. This man, though not born to the Khajikan, was bold and strong enough to be one of them.

He became aware of Ini-jnai trembling next to him, overcome with a fury born of pain and fear. The First Maker wasn't ready yet to face the Afterworld and they both knew it. He had nearly taken an early trip.

"I expect you to save his life," Ksa-jnai stated. Silence met his words. Glancing at his Bloodnau, he saw that the maker's face had gone a pale, ashen color, his jaw hanging slack with disbelief. It would be very difficult to pull the foreign maker back from the edge of death at this point. Let the strain of that effort be a lesson to Ini-jnai to control his temper. "Only when that is done may you heal this." He ran a rough finger across the cut under Ini-jnai's ear.

The adept flinched and lowered his gaze, though not fast enough to hide the flicker of fresh rage that flashed in his eyes. "I'm not sure I can, First Legend."

"This one is stronger than you, my Bloodnau, but you are the First Maker. His power makes yours greater. It makes this army greater. I expect you not to waste such a thing."

The First Maker nodded and sank to his knees next to the mangled creature in the grass.

"Make certain he bears the scars of this day as a reminder," Ksa-jnai added. When he felt the vast store of power Ini-jnai commanded focusing down into the dying maker, he turned his attention to the surrounding warriors. "Whose blade is this?" He held aloft the weapon he had pulled from the foreign maker's arm.

Na-jnai stepped forward and knelt, bowing his head. Ksa-jnai nodded. He had suspected as much. Holding the weapon by the pommel, he offered it to the First Warrior.

"The blood is yours," he stated.

Na-jnai looked up, gaze alighting on the bloodied blade. "Thank you, Ksa-jnai, First Legend." He spoke with breathless reverence, accepting the hilt.

He placed the weapon to his lips in a soft kiss, blood painting those lips black in the moonlight. Closing his eyes, he licked the precious liquid from his lips.

Ksa-jnai considered the youth for a long moment, appreciating the deep respect he showed for the honor he'd been given. The First Warrior rivaled Ksa-jnai in strength, both in physical and now in blood strength. He was devoted to their cause and respectful of their traditions. Though he lacked any maker's skill, he would be a worthy successor. It could be dangerous to name one so young. The impatience and impulsiveness of youth were always a risk though Na-jnai was less im-pulsive and hot-tempered by far than Ini-jnai who was many years his senior. This felt right, and Ksa-jnai always followed his instincts.

"You have done well, Na-jnai." When he spoke, the First Warrior's eyes snapped open, their dark depths reflecting the moonlight. Lifting his voice, Ksa-jnai proclaimed, "I name you Bloodjen, next ruler of the Khajikan."

Na-jnai's smile was transcendent. "My blood to honor you," he said in response, bowing down until his head touched the ground at Ksa-jnai's feet.

Ksa-jnai nodded. The choice was well made. Glancing over his shoulder, he caught Ini-jnai's eyes before the First Maker looked away.

"Finish your work," he said in a low tone edged with threat.

One day, his Bloodnau would fail him. He knew that with the same certainty he knew Na-jnai was the right choice as his Bloodjen. Right now, he had no replacement for the First Maker. Eventually, maybe…

His dark gaze shifted to the foreign maker. The wounds were closing one at a time as his Bloodnau worked to fulfill his orders. In his mind, he saw the man again, standing in the doorway of the burning inn, wielding such awesome power to take down his warriors. This man needed to live. His blood holding was already great. Though he did not know it yet, he had horses, wives, and children among the people of Khajikan by Rights of the Conqueror. If only they could breach the barrier of language, he might become a willing power in Ksa-jnai's army.

With a gesture, Ksa-jnai released his new Bloodjen and returned to his resting spot to wait and see if his new maker would survive.

strong desire to talk to someone who shared at least some of his devotion to Yiloch drove Adran out of the palace in search of Hax. With his sister and Commander Dalce dead, there weren't many people left to go to. He and Paulin had never been close, Ian was off with Cadmar and Indigo in search of Yiloch and Ferin, and he had no idea where to begin to look for Leryc. The young new captain had left their bed early that morning to lead a patrol in the city.

He managed a small smirk of amusement that he now considered it *their* bed.

Who else, other than Hax, came close to understanding the extent of his frustration and worry around the current situation? There was the Lady Auryl of course, but what she loved was the idea of Yiloch, not the man. She hadn't been around him long enough to understand why his captains loved him.

He and Hax had spent a lot more time together of late. A relationship once based on necessity and grudging respect had changed to one of mutual dependency as they sought solace from the anxieties they shared. Adran still found her rather caustic, though he agreed with her cynical outlook more and more as time passed without word of Yiloch. This morning he had nearly let the weight of constant worry keep him in bed. It was hard not to hide away in his rooms and let the deep melancholy take over, but he needed to be involved in the affairs of the empire if he was going to ensure things didn't fall apart in Yiloch's absence. Hax's somewhat abrasive temperament helped him focus.

This time of day, the commander was usually making rounds on the inner wall. Patrols had been doubled and the inner gates were opened only with the permission of ranking officers, which meant Hax, himself, Paulin, Leryc, or the emperor regent Lord Terral. The prophecy of war brought to them by Suac Chozai had become a thing of concern when many other parts of his prophecy came to pass, primarily, the betrayals that led to Yiloch's disappearance. Now, numerous reports of that prophesied army from across the Rhuakine and the carnage it left in its wake had reached the palace. Based on those reports and the weakened state of Lyra's military, it made sense to prepare for quick lockdown of the city and plan to face the army from behind the protection of the city's walls.

They had a war marching their way and he could do nothing but worry about Yiloch. Even his newfound love for Leryc did nothing to tame the long-time love he had carried for his friend and leader. He lived so much of his life for Yiloch. What was he supposed to do if the man never returned?

Battering his way through the crippling ache within, Adran trudged about a third of the way around the top of the inner wall before he heard Hax's raised voice and spotted her down by the main barracks reprimanding a group of soldiers for something. He couldn't make out her words, but her sharp gestures and tone betrayed considerable anger. Facing Hax angry was an intimidating prospect, but not as daunting as that of wallowing in his melancholy alone. Without hesitation, he hurried down the first set of stairs he came to and made a direct line for the main barracks.

When he reached her, Hax was sending the soldiers away, their worried looks hinting at some threat of further discipline. Her expression darkened even more when she glanced over one shoulder and spotted him coming. Her long braid of pale blond hair whipped over her shoulder as she spun to face him.

"Come to pine away over your lost love some more?" she snapped.

He was getting used to letting her sharp words slide off him like so much water thrown in his face. He'd even gotten past the wincing in response. Knowing that beneath her cold exterior she yearned for Yiloch's return almost as much as he did made it easier. "I was wondering if you might be interested in sparring again later."

Her expression brightened at the prospect of giving him a sound thrashing. They had faced off over practice swords with some frequency of late. Hax outclassed him in skill, or perhaps she was simply more willing than he was to cripple a comrade, but the challenge was an effective distraction for him and Leryc enjoyed fussing over his bruises and sore muscles.

"Of course. How about…?"

The hint of a smile disintegrated and her face darkened like a sudden storm, her gaze shifting to something behind him. Adran turned and saw the gate to the inner wall gradually swinging open. Before he could say anything, Hax was stomping past him, her black look knocking aside everyone in her path. Adran hurried after. Watching Hax chew someone to pieces might at least be entertaining.

"The inner gates are supposed to stay closed to all visitors without proper clearance. I don't see anyone here authorized to give that clearance."

Even though he wasn't the intended recipient of her anger, the snarl that followed up her shout made Adran wince. He felt a touch of sympathy for the gate guards as they turned to face her. One of the guards, a young soldier barely old enough to have completed his initial training, bowed deep to the commander. The youth's pale face flushed, supporting the perception of inexperience. The other, an age worn woman who was probably mentoring the youth, narrowed her eyes and lifted her chin to face the charging commander head on.

"Commander Hax, I felt it safe to assume that those orders could be overridden by Emperor Yiloch," the woman replied with a satisfied smirk.

Adran's heart skipped a beat and Hax glanced back to meet his eyes, hers brimming over with the same shock and hope he felt. They both sprinted over to where they could peer through the opening gates. The opening was barely wide enough to admit one rider when the dappled grey stallion charged through. Yiloch's silver hair blew out behind him, his unmistakable, flawless features shadowed with hardship, weariness and worry. Close behind him came Ian and Cadmar, slipping single file through the narrow opening. Indigo and Ferin were ominously absent.

Neither the dark warrior nor the slender Lyran creator slowed to acknowledge them. They followed Yiloch past at a gallop heading to the stables. They all pulled up hard and were on the ground passing off their horses to palace grooms when Hax and Adran ran up behind them. The horses' ribs heaved and sweat ran off them in rivulets. They had been traveling hard. Adran yearned to embrace his longtime friend, but he forced himself to hold back, fighting the sting of relieved tears as Yiloch's piercing silver-blue eyes swept over him with a flicker of acknowledgement before riveting on Hax.

"I want all archers and ranged adepts running a rotating patrol of the inner and outer walls at full force. Both gates need to be closed to general traffic and send our fastest riders out to call in reserves."

Hax bowed her head, her obedience unquestioning. Curiosity could wait. "It shall be done, my Lord."

"Now," he snapped, his curtness with her giving true measure to the extent of his worry over the coming threat. Judging by his behavior, Adran knew the army must be at least as deadly as earlier reports suggested. "When you have those things taken care of, meet us in the council room. Bring Captain Paulin and Captain Leryc if you can get them quickly. Adran. Ian. Come with me. Cadmar is yours again," he added with a wave to Hax. The dismissal was abrupt, but the solemn look and respectful nod he gave the dark warrior conveyed a sense of gratitude.

As he turned toward the palace, Yiloch met Adran's eyes for a second and the regret in that glance made his chest tighten. They were in serious trouble.

Both Hax and Cadmar nodded understanding, their gestures going unnoticed. Hax touched Cadmar's arm and they strode away with a sense of urgent purpose. Now wasn't the time to be sensitive.

Adran trotted after Yiloch, falling into stride on his right, across from Ian. The guards on the palace doors bowed deep as they opened them for the three men. In the instant before their faces lowered, Adran saw shock and perhaps a bit of alarm in their typically restrained expressions. Yiloch's clothes were tattered and bloody in places. His refined features had picked up lines of worry and fatigue. In many ways, he looked worse than he had after he escaped the seven months of imprisonment at the hands of his father.

"It's good to have you back, my Lord," Adran offered as they passed through into the palace.

Yiloch gave a quick nod. "It's good to be back. I only hope it isn't too late. Where's Lord Terral? I assume he's been put in charge and kept under proper supervision I hope."

"Last I heard he was breaking fast with the Lady Auryl on the ocean terrace," Adran answered, delighted, despite the sense of impending danger the emperor brought with him, to be serving his beloved friend again.

Yiloch altered his course and Adran noted the shadows under those beautiful eyes. Whatever had befallen him in his absence, it hadn't been pleasant.

"Might I ask where Ferin and Lady Indigo are?" Adran dared, watching Yiloch's expression as they walked.

The emperor's jaw tightened and the hint of moisture glistened in his eyes before he blinked it away. Sudden dread struck Adran. Ian glanced at him and he saw the same pain in his cousin's pale eyes.

"Lord Ferin is dead," Ian stated, confirming part of his fear. "Lady Indigo stayed with Suac Chozai."

Adran stumbled and Yiloch's hand snapped out reflexively, catching his arm to steady him. Gathering his composure and falling back into stride, Adran nodded absent thanks to Yiloch. The moment slowed them for mere seconds, though it had a much more powerful impact on his body, leaving him feeling as though he'd been punched in the gut... twice.

He swallowed hard to keep sorrow over Ferin in check. There would be time later to mourn. "She stayed with Suac Chozai? Why?"

"Where is she supposed to go?" Ian replied, his gaze stabbing daggers into Yiloch's back.

Yiloch's head snapped around toward the young creator and Adran suspected there was a reprimand in his expression from the haste with which Ian averted his gaze, now staring at the floor. He longed to dig deeper into the matter, partly out of curiosity, partly to distract himself from the loss of Ferin, but it appeared to be a volatile subject. Now was not the time to go rubbing salt in wounds.

"What are we up against?"

"An army. Not surprisingly from across the Rhua-kine," Yiloch added with a fierce scowl. "They've destroyed everything between the central Denilik lands and here. They have substantial ascard protections like nothing I've seen used here. Until recently, they suffered no losses, but someone managed to kill a few in AhnSegys. According to Ian, the dead warriors bore the signature of Myac's power. The army could be less than a day behind us depending on how fast they're moving now."

Myac.

The adept he'd failed to kill when he took the throne was the only one who'd been able to harm this new enemy. That must be a considerable blow to his ego on top of having to admit that Suac Chozai was right. A cold calm settled over Adran. War was coming to Yiroth and the enemy wasn't one they knew how to fight. He had to believe they would find a weakness. Otherwise, there was little point in even trying to fight.

As expected, Lord Terral and Lady Auryl were still chatting on the terrace. It was a pleasant day, sunny and not too warm with a clear view of the water below. The three stepped out onto the terrace and Terral's charming smile transformed to a look of openmouthed shock when he saw Yiloch. The little color drained from his face and he froze midsentence. In sharp contrast, Lady Auryl's eyes brightened and she smiled, rising from her chair to execute a graceful curtsey before her emperor and fiancé.

"My lord," she greeted. Her brow furrowed with concern when her pale violet eyes skimmed over him, noting his ragged state, but she kept her voice steady as she lowered her gaze and said, "It is so good to see you."

Terral hesitated, staring at her for a few seconds as though in need of guidance before he followed her example, bowing to Yiloch. "Emperor Yiloch, what a relief it is to have you back."

"I'm sure it is." Yiloch's words dropped like blades of ice on Terral and Adran could feel the restrained anger chilling the air. Did he have new information about Terral or was it the startled reaction by itself that earned the man such a frosty reception? Regardless, Adran was glad he wasn't the recipient of the emperor's unpleasant smirk. There was something in that expression that reminded him of when Yiloch returned from his father's prison and slew the man who'd betrayed him in front of them, a glint of fury so intense it danced on the edge of madness. "Why so shocked, Cousin? One might think, judging from your expression that you expected me not to return."

"Of course I hoped you would return, my lord. I only feared that you might not, given the ill fate of the other adepts in Caithin," Terral responded, managing to sound calm despite the bright fear in his eyes when he met Yiloch's cold gaze. There was little doubt that Yiloch saw that fear as well. Terral's gaze flickered away and he licked his lips before speaking again. "There was a man, an envoy from Demin, who came here looking for the Lady Indigo Milan? Did you encounter any such man?"

"We saw no one," Yiloch replied curtly. "He may have fallen to the Grey Army. Come, we have much work to do. Please excuse us, my lady," Yiloch said, the ice melting from his tone when he spoke to Lady Auryl.

To Adran's surprise, he actually waited for her nod of acknowledgement before he turned back into the palace. There might be hope for some relationship there after all. He hoped so, for her sake.

Terral scampered to catch up, falling in to step next to Yiloch when Ian made room for him. The creator gave Terral a chilly scowl of warning and Adran marveled at how he had changed. Once he had feared Yiloch, now he bristled by the emperor's side like a devoted guard dog ready to kill for its master, but he wasn't afraid to speak his mind in front of that master either. It was a change that pleased him to a degree, but he also feared for the young creator. Eris had died because she was willing to sacrifice everything for Yiloch. How long would Ian last at the emperor's side? Would the next battle be his last?

They were heading toward the council room on the far side of the throne room. Despite his travel worn attire and the weariness that drew dark circles around his eyes, Yiloch was every bit the proud, magnificent leader Adran had followed and loved most of his life. His strides were bold and his head high, determination in the tightening of his jaw as he led the three men through the halls.

"Lord Terral." Yiloch spoke as they walked, not looking at his cousin, who visibly tensed in response to that deceptively casual tone. "You are close to being the only family I have left and certainly the only family in a good position to betray me. Suac Chozai's prophecies, though somewhat misleading in ways, have been remarkably accurate so far. Might I suggest that, if you have betrayed me or plan to, you take some time to consider how much protection the ties of blood afforded my father."

Yiloch never once looked at Terral as he spoke, but Adran did. The emperor's cousin hung his head, chewing at his lower lip for a moment before opening his mouth as if to speak. He hesitated then, perhaps unsure of his words and several uncomfortable seconds passed. When they slowed in front of the council room, he said only, "I understand, my lord."

Adran didn't believe that was what he originally intended to say and the desire to hear the words he'd swallowed back made his skin itch. It certainly wasn't a denial.

"That's good, Cousin," Yiloch replied, glancing at Terral as he allowed an attendant to open the door. "We have powerful enemies. I would hate to waste effort guarding my back against my own kin when we could be working together against much greater threats."

They followed him into the room then, three dogs on the heels of their master and happy to be there for the most part. It was hard to imagine Terral betraying anyone. He simply didn't seem the type. He reminded Adran in many ways of Yiloch's late, mild-mannered brother. The blood he shared with Yiloch showed in his striking appearance, but beyond that, it was hard to tell that they came from the same line. In the past, Terral did exactly as much as he had to do to maintain his standard of living and nothing more. The effort of executing some complex betrayal was so out of character. Although, if someone else was pulling his strings who he feared more than the emperor, it could happen. Cowards could be the most dangerous of allies.

Hax, already in the room, faced them as they entered, offering a respectful nod to Yiloch. "The first shift of full force patrols is arranged, my lord. All gates are being closed."

Yiloch nodded. "Your haste is appreciated, Commander Hax. Please sit." His expression was somber as he took his own suggestion and sat at one of the chairs around the square council table. When all of the others had followed suit he turned his attention on Hax again. "Where are Captain Paulin and Captain Leryc?"

"Paulin is out doing field work with some recruits and Leryc was running a patrol in the city."

"They should be called in immediately."

"Already done, my lord," she replied. "I sent two soldiers out to find them and call them back."

The ghost of an appreciative smile touched his lips before his gaze moved to his hands and he frowned. Adran ached with the beauty of him. For all that he adored Leryc, his love for Yiloch was built upon a lifetime of experiences together and the new emperor was always the most strikingly handsome in moments of trial.

"Unfortunately, I still don't know much about our enemy. The Kudaness call them the Grey Army. Given the few bodies I have seen and descriptions I've heard, it's an appropriate name. From what I understand, they have a large number of adepts and seem immensely skilled at the creation of protective barriers. The first and, as far as I know, only casualties the Grey Army has suffered were in AhnSegys and appear to have involved a face off with a very powerful adept. Un…" Yiloch trailed off, his eyes going to Terral who had stiffened a fraction in his chair. "You think this might be the envoy from Demin?"

Terral shrugged, trying to dismiss his own reaction, but he wasn't so skilled in the political art of deception.

Yiloch's eyes narrowed. "You failed to mention that he was an adept. An important point under the circumstances, don't you think?"

Terral nodded, lowering his gaze. "Yes, my lord. You have my apologies."

Yiloch's eyes remained narrowed and Adran wondered if he would tell Terral that Myac was the adept. Could the envoy to the palace have been Myac in his disguise? He wished now that he had been more insistent on staying in the room that day.

"Keep your apologies and give me your loyalty, cousin," Yiloch snapped. "As I was saying, that adept is either dead or moved on—"

"Might they have taken the adept captive?" Terral interrupted.

"It's possible, though they hadn't shown much tendency toward taking captives up to that point. Regardless, we will have to discover their weaknesses on our own. Ian?"

The young creator was in complete attendance, his entire being radiating attention to the council. Not so long ago, he would have been sitting with his gaze downcast, locked on his hands as he wrung them nervously in his lap. The disappearance of that timidity was Yiloch's doing. Adran hadn't necessarily agreed with his method of dragging the boy into the heart of things then, but now, as Ian met Yiloch's gaze with confidence and a flicker of challenge, Adran had to appreciate the success.

"Yes, my lord."

"You said there was a powerful barrier around the army?" Ian nodded. "Do we have anyone among the ranks of our adepts with the skill to bring down a barrier that strong?"

Ian started to shake his head, and then paused, his expression turning thoughtful. "I don't believe any one adept could, but perhaps, if we can mimic what Lady Indigo did when she and I took down the barrier around the traitor at the rendezvous camp, several adepts working together might be able to bring it down."

When Ian mentioned Indigo, a shadow fell over Yiloch's features for a few seconds, guilt and sorrow rising in his eyes.

She's here even when she is not. Adran gritted his teeth against a twinge of jealousy.

"Good. Go now and start work on that. We should also have some strong defensive groups ready in case that effort fails."

Ian stood and gave a quick bow. "My lord," he acknowledged before leaving the room with purpose in his long strides.

Yiloch regarded the rest of them. "Hax, get our troops ready for combat. If the adepts can bring down the Grey Army's protections, I want everyone ready to attack. Have Leryc assist you when he returns and send Paulin out to work on evacuation plans in case things don't go our way. Terral, go with Hax and see that your troops are also prepared. When you're done with that, find a quiet spot to sit and consider your next move."

Hax and Terral followed Ian's example, Terral with a hint of relief in his drawn face as he hurried from the room.

When the door clicked shut, Yiloch rose, slow movement attesting to a deep exhaustion. Adran followed him from the room. With no orders to act upon and no dismissal, it seemed the obvious choice. Yiloch walked to his personal chambers, leaving the door open behind him, confirming that he expected Adran to follow. He closed the door behind them and turned in time to watch Yiloch sink down onto the chaise with a bone-weary elegance. He rested his head back and closed his eyes, long silver hair cascading over the edge.

"Give me just a moment," he said. His voice was little more than a drained whisper.

After a few seconds, his breathing became steady and shallow. Adran smiled fondly at his sleeping friend, then he sat in another chair and put his feet up, settling in to give Yiloch his *moment.*

Yiloch woke with a start. The speed with which he had fallen asleep the second his body contacted the comfortable surface of the chaise, heedless of the threat to his empire, vexed him and brought to painful clarity the level of complete mental and physical exhaustion he had reached. The confidence and power he was accustomed to feeling were lost behind a weary, heartbroken haze, tauntingly out of reach. Like a sniff of good wine from a broken bottle, the aroma so perfect you would almost lick the floor for a taste.

His body demanded a stretch while he struggled to banish the fog that filled his mind.

"Feel better?"

Finishing his stretch, he turned, setting his feet on the floor, and regarded the other man. His sense of decorum told him to gloss over the truth, to put on a strong face, but this was Adran. Adran often knew how he felt before he did.

"Worse," he muttered. "A little comfort was all it took to bring the strain of this entire ordeal crashing down on me. I must be getting old," he added, looking at hands that appeared as smooth and strong as ever. "I thought I said I only needed a moment."

Adran's smile was gentle, sympathetic, and not even

a little apologetic. "You needed a long moment. Dare I say, a much longer one than you took?"

Yiloch, fighting a powerful desire to lie back down, forced himself to sit up straighter. "Perhaps, but there isn't time."

Adran snorted and Yiloch scowled at him.

"You've set everything in motion," Adran argued, meeting his eyes unflinchingly. "There isn't anything else for you to do right now. Without some more rest, you will be no use to anyone."

He rubbed his temples and sat back. Adran was right, there was nothing more he could do, outside of fretting over the coming conflict, an activity he was unaccustomed to. There was so much he didn't know about their enemy and what he did know only made him nervous. He yearned for the certainty he felt when he campaigned against his father. If only Indigo were here.

He let out a heavy exhale. "I'm not sure I know how to defeat this enemy. What if Chozai was right? What if Lyra is doomed to fall to these foreign warriors?"

"I think we should plan for the worst, but go forward as though we believe we can win. What good does it do us to believe otherwise?"

He grunted noncommittally. Perhaps it was the fatigue and loss that left him feeling defeated before the battle had even begun. With a little more sleep, things might not seem so bleak.

"What happened with Indigo?"

"I treated her unkindly and she wisely chose not to return with us," he replied, kicking up his feet onto the table and grimacing at the memory. "I was a fool."

"She did imprison you," Adran offered.

The man was trying to defend his actions for him, but Yiloch didn't want the support in this case. He didn't deserve it. "She was tricked into it."

"If she truly loves you, she should never have believed you guilty," Adran countered, his tone unforgiving.

Yiloch gave him a stern look. "Have you ever considered that maybe she is the sensible one. In her shoes, what would it take for you to believe that a man who beheaded his own father in front of you to take the throne would order the assassination of a foreign king who helped enslave so many of his people? Pitting that and the word of people she's known all her life against a rather irrational love, I should not have expected anything else." His biting cynicism seemed to strike Adran like a blow and the other man glanced away, perhaps trying to hide the hurt in his eyes. He continued in a gentler tone. "Given some of the things she's seen me do and Myac's involvement in the situation, I can forgive her for falling victim to doubt."

Adran nodded. When he said nothing, Yiloch leaned back into the chaise and closed his eyes again. He was nearly asleep when Adran's voice broke the silence.

"I have always loved you," he murmured. "I would never doubt you."

"You have always known me." Yiloch replied. To lighten the mood, he cracked one eyelid to peer at the other man and added, "And who can blame you. Have you looked at me?"

Adran grabbed the pillow next to him and hurled it at Yiloch who deflected it with a chuckle. Adran rolled his eyes, though he laughed as he shook his head at him. The levity felt good for a moment, but the feeling didn't last. There was too much to worry about. This was what he had chosen though. He wanted to rule, wanted the responsibility his father had carried, and he didn't regret that it was now his. He only wished he knew more about this enemy.

"Are you worried about Indigo?"

He glanced at Adran and started to say that he was, but when he thought about the question for a moment, he realized with a mild surprise that he wasn't all that worried about her.

"No." Adran raised his eyebrows in an expression of disbelief. "I'm worried about many things, mostly the coming army and the damage it has done—the damage it may still do—to my country and my people. Indigo has proven herself capable many times over. Whatever compelled her to go into the desert with Suac Chozai, I can't believe she went without a plan. If he expects to take advantage of her in some way, I pity him."

Adran chuckled and smiled, his gaze becoming distant.

"See," Yiloch remarked with satisfaction, "even you're fond of her."

Adran gave him a look of mock severity, then he grinned, but the grin faded too fast. "I do wish she were here."

Yiloch didn't have to ask why. She would be more likely than anyone to have the strength and skill necessary to bring down the barriers around the Grey Army. He was convinced now that even Myac would have been no match for her the night he took the throne if she hadn't come into the confrontation exhausted by long days of healing and then masking their presence on the way in. Even with those things, it had taken the adept some time to build up enough power to break her hold on him. Enough time that Emperor Rylan was dead before Myac could interfere.

If only he hadn't acted out in his rage and sorrow like a spoiled prince and driven her away.

Myac.

The miserable bastard had gone on to Demin after fleeing the palace. There was little doubt that he played a part in manipulating Indigo into this mess. The man that had followed her into the prison when she had freed him and Ferin, the man he learned later was Myac in disguise, had been Caithin by all appearances. He'd only noted the individual for his brief involvement in the betrayal, but the circumstances had etched his image in Yiloch's mind.

A Caithin adept. Yiloch let out a soft, animalistic snarl and Adran's eyes widened in surprise.

"What is it?"

"Did you see the Caithin adept that came here to talk to Terral?"

Adran nodded. "I was wanting to talk to you about that—"

"Describe him?"

Adran's brow furrowed at the interruption, but he didn't hesitate to answer. "He was a young man, Caithin, average looking…"

"Slightly dingy brown hair almost down to his shoulders, dark eyes, relatively fit, average height?" Average in all the ways necessary to avoid drawing too much attention to himself.

Adran nodded, the furrows in his brow deepening.

Yiloch jumped to his feet. It had to be the same man. That adept was Myac and he suspected Terral knew as much. Striding to the door, he reached out with ascard, trying to locate Terral in the palace. His skill with that kind of detection wasn't overly developed, but it ought to be good enough in this limited range.

"What's wrong?" Adran asked, jogging after him.

"My family has already betrayed me," Yiloch hissed. *There!*

Terral was in the palace library. Adran asked no more questions, he followed Yiloch at a swift pace through the palace. They startled several servants and more than one royal guard who all hurried out of the way. One of the double doors to the multi-level library stood ajar. Yiloch threw them both the rest of the way open and stormed in. Terral stood along one book lined wall smiling and talking to Lady Auryl. When he turned toward the sound of the opening doors, his face paled, the smile dissolving, and the book he held dropped from his hands, forgotten.

Yiloch used a touch of ascard to speed his movement across the remaining distance between them and grabbed Terral's shirtfront, slamming him back into the shelves. Several books fell from their perches. Lady Auryl backed away, her mouth opened in a silent "o" of surprise. She caught one heel on her own skirts and nearly fell, catching herself on a shelf and knocking another two books to the floor.

Terral gasped, trying to catch his breath through the pain from the impact.

"You've been working with Myac," Yiloch accused, fighting the fury that made him want to beat the man in front of him senseless.

Terral's eyes jumped to Adran and then to Auryl as if hoping one or the other might come to his defense.

Lady Auryl only looked confused and frightened, her eyes darting from Yiloch to Terral and back again. Adran, who had gone to her side, glared at Terral, more than willing to believe the accusation.

"Why?" Yiloch demanded, punctuating the inquiry by lifting him with the help of ascard enhanced strength and shoving him harder into the shelves.

Terral grimaced and defeat broke across his handsome features. In the end, Terral simply wasn't a fighter.

"Myac is… powerful," he managed between gasps of pain. "He's also… my son."

It was as if someone had kicked Yiloch in the gut. Unable to draw a breath, he dropped Terral, who slumped to the floor, cowering against the shelves amidst a pile of fallen books. Yiloch turned away from him and dropped, listless, into a nearby chair. He scowled at nothing for several long seconds, then he faced Terral, finding his breath again.

"Myac's your son?"

Terral nodded and started to stand, but he winced part way up and slumped back to the floor. "He's my only child."

Yiloch shook his head, closing his eyes for a few seconds. This was far more complicated than he had imagined it would be. Myac himself was family then. It wasn't a revelation that pleased him in the least.

"What is he trying to accomplish?"

"He wants to put me on the throne and make himself the rightful heir to the empire," Terral responded, his voice still tight with pain.

The man looked truly wretched crumpled there and Yiloch felt a bitter stab of satisfaction. "All of this is merely a grab for power?"

Terral's eyes narrowed and the misery transformed, giving way to a sudden and unexpected sneer of rage. "No," he snarled. "The power is only an extra incentive. Something to sweeten the revenge."

Yiloch shook his head, mystified by Terral's words and the sudden change in his demeanor. "Revenge for what?"

"You killed his mother" Terral was shaking now, though whether from pain or passion was hard to tell. "You cut her down like an animal."

Myac's face flashed in mind from the moment he stood trapped by Indigo's power, near panic as he watched Yiloch cut down the emperor. The image transformed, the eye and hair color changing, becoming the panicked features of a youth standing in the doorway of a burning house. A boy who had watched Yiloch kill his mother. Images of his own mother's death flashed through his mind then, the crossbow bolt punching through her slender throat, bright blood on pale skin and the fading of the light in her eyes as she left him. He could recall the feel of her warm blood covering his hands, soaking into the fabric of his pants when he pulled her to him and struggled to stop it.

His stomach turned and an involuntary moan escaped his lips.

Fate was a cruel mistress. He may as well have murdered his own mother. Myac, in a terrible way, was another version of him, seeking vengeance for the exact same loss that had led Yiloch to that village, to that moment, in the throes of a blind rage stoked to a killing frenzy by Emperor Rylan.

Yiloch jumped to his feet, knocking over the chair. His gut was a nest of knots and hollow regrets. He turned, kicking the toppled chair. It flew into a freestanding shelf, one ornate wooden leg snapping as the shelf rocked and more books fell to the floor. He slid his hands behind his neck and bowed his head before the weight of a new, overwhelming misery. They balled into fists there and he grimaced, yearning to lash out at anything or anyone to release the turmoil within, but that passionate fury was what led him to this miserable place.

Lashing out won't help, a voice said in his mind, sounding disturbingly like both Indigo and his long dead mother.

An icy calm suffused him then and he lowered his hands, seizing control. He turned, his gaze locking on Terral. The other man had gotten to his feet and stood there hunched with pain. Now he stepped back, bumping into the shelf before Yiloch's cold stare. Another book fell, clipping his shoulder on the way down.

"I can't change the past," Yiloch stated.

"Neither can I." Terral lowered his gaze, rubbing at the bruised shoulder. "I never wanted any of this."

"I know."

Terral glanced up at him, his brow pinched with confusion.

Yiloch responded with a bitter smile. "You never had any ambition, Cousin. You and my brother were much alike in that way. I guess Myac must take after his mother." She had been beautiful and determined. A woman trying to save herself and protect her son before he cut her down. "He will never stop looking for revenge. He has to die."

Terral deflated, sliding down against the shelf so that he was once more sitting on the floor amidst the fallen books, his long hair fell forward to hide his face when he hung his head. Yiloch went to sit in another chair. Lady Auryl watched them both, quiet tears tracking down her soft cheeks. Whether or not she understood all of what had passed between them, she would have to be all but dead not to feel the ache of loss that filled the room. Adran stood with an arm around her shoulders, deliberately looking at neither of them.

"Maybe if I talked to him," Terral started, gazing up at Yiloch, his voice little more than a whisper. Yiloch gave him a sharp look and he sighed again. "No. He'll never listen to me. Do you think you can defeat him?"

He regarded Terral. The man's tone was flat, expressing no emotion either way. Perhaps part of him wanted Myac gone. He was an illegitimate son, not that most nobles didn't have one or two illegitimate children. This was the first time Yiloch had ever seen the man look truly miserable. His son's ambition and hunger for vengeance had driven him a very long way out of his comfort zone. Did he even care that Yiloch had killed the woman who fathered his only child? He certainly didn't appear to share Myac's thirst for revenge. There had been that brief flicker of anger, but even that had been fleeting.

Yiloch looked away from his cousin, feeling a swell of disgust with his lack of devotion to his only son and the woman who mothered him. "If he is alive and we get through the coming battle we are bound to find out sooner or later," he said finally.

All four of them turned when Ian cleared his throat. The young creator stood in the doorway of the library, looking only at Yiloch first then he started to look around, his brow knitting in a puzzled look.

"My lord, I apologize for interrupting this..." he

trailed off and his gaze meandered over the fallen books around a rather humble Lord Terral. "Shall I call someone to come clean this up?"

A spike of frustration lanced through Yiloch. He closed his eyes and took a few deep breaths to bring it under control. The last thing he needed was to let his frustration drive him to start attacking his most valuable people without cause.

"I…" he trailed off, fighting the edge of anger that still tried to creep through in his voice. "I suspect you came here with some other purpose," he said, managing an even tone this time.

"Ah… yes." Ian met his eyes and Yiloch realized the poor creator was probably running on even less rest than he was. He mustered a smile, hoping the sympathy in the expression would help. Ian answered with a rather tremulous almost-smile and continued. "Lord Theron Milan is at the inner gates. He is here as an emissary from King Gavin to request an audience with Lord Terral and Lord Captain Adran." He nodded to each man in turn, then a sudden bemused grin cracked his features. "Convenient that you're all in one place. He doesn't appear to know that you have returned, my lord," he added, his gaze drifting back to Yiloch.

Theron Milan. Indigo's uncle and a highly regarded representative of the Caithin kingdom. Yiloch had never met the man, but he had heard his name mentioned respectfully with some frequency during his stay in Demin. More than one member of the King's High Council had boasted of Theron's skill in handling sensitive diplomatic missions. This one fit that description remarkably well. Despite his exhaustion, he was eager to speak to the man, though he suspected it had a lot more to do with his family ties than his political prowess.

"I imagine he's about to get more of an audience than he bargained for," Yiloch replied. "Ian, find someone to escort him to the throne room then go get some rest."

Ian's expression hardened, a sudden clarity in his gaze. "*I* will attend you, my lord, in the throne room along with Lord Terral and Lord Captain Adran. The Caithin will not get a second chance at you so long as I draw breath."

The fierce conviction in his tone surprised and pleased Yiloch. There would be no arguing with the creator and he found he wasn't inclined to do so. He nodded. "So you shall, though I recommend that we both change first." His gaze slid past Terral and came to rest on Lady Auryl. "Lady Auryl, I apologize for startling you."

"I am fine, my lord." Her voice trembled, but she lifted her chin and pulled her shoulders back, regal as ever. "I will retire to my rooms and let you attend to your business."

They all wished her good evening and Yiloch waited until she had left the room, then he turned to Adran. "Captain Adran, please escort Lord Terral to his rooms. Ian, go with him and see to it that he cannot leave said rooms for the time being. When that is done, clean up and join me in the throne room."

There were questions in the widening of Ian's eyes, but his firm nod said he would leave them to a more appropriate time. For now, he would do as ordered.

Terral swallowed with the expression of someone who had tasted spoiled wine, but the wary glance he gave Ian was enough to assure Yiloch that he would offer no fight. Terral would have to wait until they were done with Lord Theron and he wasn't about to have the traitor wandering freely about the palace any more than he was going to allow him contact with the Caithin emissary.

When they were all gone, Yiloch sat a moment more, considering the mess he had made. The collection in the palace library was exceptional, boasting books from several different countries, many rare and highly prized tomes among them. He scanned the floor, hoping nothing valuable had been damaged in the encounter.

After a few minutes, he became aware of another presence in the room, tensing when the individual drew on ascard. She had entered from a small servant's door tucked into a wall of books. Her pale lips curved up, increasing the wrinkles around her eyes, and she curtsied to him, then looked up and caught a book as it rose from the floor and glided into her hand. The book opened and pages flipped past under her scrutinizing gaze. When the book closed, she looked up at him and smiled again.

"Still here, my lord? I can take care of this." As she spoke, the book traveled through the air, landing back on its shelf and another rose to her hand.

"It appears that you can," he replied with an amused smile. How many times had he caught his younger brother, Delsan, sitting in a cubby watching palace librarians moving books around with ascard? For the first time, he felt a true pang of remorse for the loss of his brother and guilt rushed in on its heels. Maybe he was even more like his father than he cared to admit. It was something to consider and perhaps try to improve upon going forward.

"A good evening to you," he murmured, as he rose to leave the room.

"And to you, my lord," she called softly after him.

The man the usher announced as Lord Theron was a handsome individual… for a Caithin gentleman. Well-groomed dark hair brushed his shoulders, the length a little longer than was typically popular in Caithin society. Dark eyes peered out of a face that had nobility and refinement etched into every curve or well-defined angle. The fitted doublet he wore was fashioned in a rich chocolate color so dark it looked almost black, with Caithin red and gold embroidered sparingly down the sleeves, the red and gold hawk above a crown, the crest of the king, stitched over the left breast. He moved with considerable grace, almost worthy of a pureblooded Lyran and, to his credit, his stride and expression didn't falter when he saw Yiloch sitting on the throne. With only one tiny hint of a twitch in one finger, he continued to the foot of the dais and bowed deep.

"Lord Theron Milan," Yiloch acknowledged.

Given that Caithin had committed a crime against Lyra by taking him hostage, it would have been reasonable to at least make Theron wait a while in that bow before acknowledging him, but desire burned in Yiloch. A desire to learn more of Indigo through this man who had helped raise her and he made little effort to quell it. Besides, there was far too much at stake for him to indulge in petty punishments, even for as serious an offense as that of which Caithin was guilty.

"Your Highness, I must confess that I am somewhat surprised to find you here."

"So am I," Yiloch replied with wry humor. "I only made it back here a few hours ago."

Theron met his eyes, his expression tightening, not in anger, but in a quick grimace of emotional pain. An ache resonated through Yiloch in response. The grimace and the faint flicker of hope that sparked in the emissary's eyes spoke volumes that he suspected the man would never put into words without prompting.

Taking a chance, he said, "I regret to inform you that Lady Indigo is not here, but she was well when last I saw her." *Heartbroken and adrift without a place to call home, but well enough.*

Theron ducked his head, trying not to let his emotions flavor the audience, but not before Yiloch caught the faint smile and the shine of relieved tears in those dark eyes.

"Thank you, my lord," he said after a brief silence, his voice, tight with emotion, barely crossing the distance between them.

"I did not make her do this," Yiloch stated, relenting to an odd inclination to defend himself.

A startled noise came from Adran and, to his surprise, Theron laughed.

"No disrespect, my lord," Theron said, gathering his composure. "You may be an emperor, but it would take more than a mere emperor to force that woman's hand."

Yiloch surrendered to a fond, nostalgic smile. This was complete madness. Given recent events, the room ought to be frozen over with hostility at best. Theron, however, didn't seem to harbor as much animosity toward him as he would have expected and he found himself wanting to trust the man. They had a common bond in their love of Indigo and perhaps that connection was something they could build upon.

"Lord Theron, I realize our countries are on uneasy terms, to put it rather mildly. The things we meet now to discuss could well lead to war between us. However, I will soon have another army pounding on my gates and I could use a glass of wine to ease my tension. Would you be willing to retire to a more comfortable room and have a drink while we speak?"

Theron's gaze swept over him, taking his measure. After only a few seconds hesitation, he nodded. "I would, my lord."

"Send food and wine to the crystal sitting room," Yiloch ordered, catching the eyes of an elderly attendant who waited at the corner of one edge of the dais. The man bowed and vanished through a doorway. The usher also vanished, going ahead to ensure the room was properly prepared.

When they entered the crystal sitting room, candles burned and a warm fire crackled merrily in the hearth. The reflections of the fire and candles danced about on the created crystal windows that lined one wall, much like those in his private chambers. This room, with its pale ivory and bleached wood furniture had been one of his mother's favorite rooms. Delicate, created crystal wind chimes hung outside a window that looked out on a small flower garden she had cultivated herself. Beyond the garden was a magnificent view of the gilded straight second only to that from his chambers. He had avoided the room since taking control of Yiroth, but tonight, with an army marching on the city and the alliance with Caithin on the verge of complete collapse, it felt like the right time to use it. Now, while Lyra was still his.

"Please, make yourself comfortable," Yiloch gestured to the room, sweeping Adran and Ian into his glance to ensure they understood that the offer encompassed them as well.

Wine and a tray of bread, fine meats and cheeses arrived as they were sitting. When the attendants left, Yiloch met Theron's discerning look. The man rested back in the chair he had selected, crossed his legs, and took a sip of the wine, offering a nod in appreciation of the fine vintage. Then he rested the glass on a small side table and leveled a steady gaze at Yiloch.

"Emperor Yiloch, my primary goals in coming here were to learn what I could of the efforts to find you, which I think was sufficiently covered upon my entering the throne room, and to investigate the rumors of this army invading Lyra. I also hoped for some word of Lord Edan and..." he trailed off, catching Yiloch's quick scowl. "I get the feeling you have something to say about him, but, before we discuss that, I want to articulate that I am willing to give you every opportunity I can to explain things. Lady Indigo had some reason for risking so much to set you free. I wish she was here to explain it to me herself, but, in a way, I am also glad that she is not. At least this way, I'm not obligated to place her under arrest.

"Tell me, Emperor Yiloch," he uncrossed his legs and leaned forward in the chair, "why would she give up everything she held dear to set you and Lord Ferin free?"

Now Yiloch eased back in his chair and took a sip of his drink. He stalled a minute longer, gazing into the dark red depths through the perfect window of the created wine glass. With an effort, he managed to hide the twisting guilt that rose up with thoughts of Indigo and kept his expression casual. "I will tell you what I know. Creator Ian traveled with her for a time when they were trying to find me and may be able to fill in some blanks."

There was the slightest flicker of unease in Theron's eyes as he glanced at Ian now, recognizing who and what he was, but he nodded and sat back again, prepared to listen.

"The first I knew of King Jerrin's death was after I arrived in the prison Lady Indigo and Lord Serivar placed me in. I never ordered any assassination." Theron met the pronouncement with an expression of forced impartiality. He'd most certainly heard about and perhaps had even seen the confessions of the three Lyran adepts. Confessions that had to have been forced upon them in some manner that involved either ascard manipulation, torture or some combination of both. He swallowed a flash of fresh anger and continued. "When they took me prisoner, I believed Indigo knew what she was doing."

Theron raised an eyebrow at the informal address and Yiloch answered with a slight narrowing of his eyes, daring the man to take exception. Theron's chest lifted and fell with a deep breath, but he held his tongue.

"As far as I could tell at that time, I had been betrayed by Caithin and she was the executor of that betrayal. Later she destroyed the prison, stranding Ferin and I in southern Kudan."

"At least you ended up on the proper continent," Theron offered.

Yiloch answered with a bitter smile. "The same continent, perhaps, but worlds away. I'll spare you the details of the long walk, but along the way, we came upon the trail of a large army heading toward Lyra and found nothing but dead in the first several Kudaness villages we came to while following that trail. More importantly, there were only Kudaness dead. Not one of the invaders died in those attacks. In later villages, they had warning that the army was coming and abandoned their homes to seek safety elsewhere. In the Silik lands, Ferin was killed by a band of Kudaness warriors, so his freedom ended up being merely a brief stay of execution."

Theron inclined his head in a show of respect. "I am sorry to hear that."

"Are you?" Yiloch asked, bitterness slipping through in his tone.

"Emperor Yiloch, it is my place to assess political situations and come up with reasonable solutions. I do not blame Lord Ferin for anything at this point and I am sorry for his loss. I try to avoid passing judgment without adequate information, which I do not feel I have in this situation. The death of the royal family is not something I have been involved in, beyond a personal sense of loss, until now. As I am now involved, I must gather all the information I can and I require your help to do that, so please, continue."

Yiloch checked his temper. He couldn't let his pain and loss damage their tenuous rapport. "Fair enough. I crossed paths with Indigo, Cadmar, and Ian when they came looking for me in southern Murak, where I proceeded to treat Indigo rather harshly because of her role in my capture and, unfortunately, managed to chase her off. I held her accountable, unfairly it seems, for my imprisonment and for the circumstances that led to Ferin's death. I'm afraid I was rather unkind to her. That is the extent of my involvement in the death of your former king and those who arrested me for his assassination."

Theron's face clouded over, his fingers tightened on the wine glass.

Yiloch waited. Theron's next words would give considerable insight into whether they had any chance of understanding one another.

"This army…" Theron trailed off, a flicker of distress in his eyes. He clenched his teeth hard enough to make the jaw muscles bulge then his composure cracked. "Where is Indigo now?"

That was exactly the reaction Yiloch had hoped for. Theron couldn't abandon his concern for Indigo, not even for the sake of his position as a much-lauded emissary. There was hope for peace in that. "Indigo chose to remain in Kudan with Suac Chozai of Murak."

Theron stiffened. "The Devine have mercy. You left her with the Kudaness? They hate Caithin and they hate adepts. She's as good as dead."

Yiloch met his eyes. "She *chose* to stay in Kudan and they *chose* to let her. This is Indigo we're talking about, not some halfwit who can't manage the duties of a scullery maid. She is quite capable of making her own choices and standing by them, as you so eloquently stated earlier."

Theron's jaw worked, but he was unable to argue the point. He leaned forward, resting forearms on his thighs, looking every bit the worried father in that moment. "It should come as no surprise to you that, as her ward, I am rather disturbed by how well you seem to know her."

Yiloch met his gaze, seeing the demand for explanation in his eyes. Let him wonder for now. Not knowing might unbalance him some, but not as much as the truth would. They weren't here to discuss Indigo, after all.

Adran shifted in his chair and Ian sat forward a touch, both uneasy with the current tension.

"It comes as no surprise, Lord Theron. In fact, it pleases me to know you're concerned for her wellbeing, but that isn't why you're here, not really." Theron's eyes pinched with a flash of irritation, but he said nothing. "You see, from there I continued north with Ian and Cadmar. We managed to pass the army using a more direct route than the main roads their numbers restrict them to, but they could arrive any day now. They have impressive skills in the use of barriers, but beyond that, I know little about them other than that they are ruthless and effective killers. They eliminated the entire population of several villages in Kudan and many Lyran towns along the route north from Kudan. They only suffered losses in one instance that I know of and I have reason to believe that may have involved the man you call Lord Edan."

Theron nodded, rubbing his chin in thought. "So the army is real. I don't envy you your position in that. King Gavin is not overly enthusiastic about the idea of giving aide at this point, though the subject has come up. I might influence that decision one way or another if you can give me adequate reason to. Which takes us back to the assassinations, if you didn't order them, who did and why did your adepts confess to them?"

Yiloch took a long drink of his wine. None of this was going to be easy to explain. It was hard enough to make it all clear in his own head, especially now that he knew Myac was family. That was one thing Theron didn't need to know. In fact, he meant for very few people to ever know about that particular blood tie.

"I have a very powerful enemy, Lord Theron. His name is Myac and he is a creator adept who served under my father. His power is remarkable, almost unmatched. After I claimed the throne, he apparently went to Demin and has been masquerading about, orchestrating my downfall under a created disguise as one Lord Edan."

"Lady Indigo believes he is behind the assassinations. She also thought he may have helped compel the three Lyran adepts to sign those confessions and perhaps believe their own guilt," Ian interjected into the brief pause.

"But he could not have managed all of that on his own," Yiloch added. "No matter how powerful he is, he's still only one man."

Theron sat straighter, a challenge rising in his eyes. "We restrict all training and use of ascard in Caithin to healing. Who would have had the necessary skills to help him?"

Meeting those dark eyes, Yiloch considered how much to say. If this man was as important to the throne as his reputation implied, then he had to know about the King's Order. But there was so much he might not know that would make all of this even harder for him to swallow. Still, without Indigo here to support him, he had to do the best he could to try to make the man believe and that meant exposing his knowledge of some things he shouldn't know much about.

"I know that is a lie, Lord Theron," he dared. "I'm fairly certain that you do as well."

Theron resisted. "How would you know if that was a lie?" His tone was calm and reasonable.

Yiloch couldn't help admiring his composure. "I have received created missives from King Jerrin in the past."

Theron shrugged it off. "A very benign and useful skill. Not one that would be of much use in a deception of this magnitude."

"And Indigo told me about the adepts and creators of the King's Order."

Theron's lips pressed into a tight line. Thoughts raced behind those eyes. "What would Indigo know about the king's affairs? She's only a healer."

At this point, there was little reason not to divulge more. It wasn't fair to Indigo to expose her, but the fate of his country and their alliance with Caithin required this man's support. "Indigo is much more than a healer. She is the strongest adept I have ever encountered. Without her help in my campaign, I might not have taken the throne from my father. Lord Serivar has been training her for the King's Order since before she came to Lyra the first time. Hasn't he told anyone that yet?"

His face clouding over with anger and an encouraging flicker of uncertainty, Theron shifted forward in the chair as though ready to rise and stared at Yiloch. "Indigo is only a healer," he said again, though his tone lacked conviction this time.

"Lady Indigo is an amazing adept, Lord Theron," Ian said, the flash of enthusiasm in his eyes making him look as young as he was and, whether intentional or not, it added convincing sincerity to his words. "If she were here now, we would be certain to defeat the Grey Army," he added, throwing a quick, accusatory glance at Yiloch.

Theron put his elbow on the arm of the chair and lifted his hand, resting his forehead against the fingertips. He looked suddenly very tired. "I won't say that I believe you, but, if everything you say is true, you must realize what that implies."

"Yes, I do. Indigo told me she suspected Lord Serivar of some sinister intentions back when she was here with the Caithin healers. She was worried because she found out he hadn't told the king about her."

Theron's eyes narrowed to angry slits and he snapped, "Why would she tell *you* this and not me?"

Yiloch shrugged. "Perhaps she simply wanted to talk it out with someone outside the situation before she made such an accusation to someone who could do something about it."

"Perhaps you could stop avoiding and explain to me what your relationship is with her. Maybe that would shed some light on this situation."

The emissary's voice was tight with hurt and anger. Yiloch was reluctant to upset him further, but it was a little too late to turn back now. "Indigo is a remarkable woman, Lord Theron. I couldn't help taking an interest in her and I spent perhaps a little too much time around her whenever the situation allowed."

"He loves her," Ian piped up and Adran's head dropped into his hands as he muttered a soft curse under his breath. Yiloch gave Ian a warning look, though it was much too late for warnings. Ignoring the look, the creator added, "She loves him too, or at least she did before he chased her off in Kudan."

Theron looked dazed, as though someone had struck him a solid blow to the skull.

"It's growing late." Adran cast a pointed glance at the windows. "Perhaps we should adjourn for the evening and get some rest. I'll see that proper accommodations are arranged for Lord Theron if that is acceptable."

Theron glanced at Adran, looking as though he equally loved and hated the idea. Yiloch could sympathize. There was so much more to say, but he needed sleep and this wasn't going exactly as he had hoped it would. The only consolation to that was that he suspected Theron felt equally out of control of the conversation. If only Indigo were there. He needed her testimony for Theron. He needed her power against the army. More importantly, he needed her, just her, if for no other reason than to lose himself in those vibrant blue eyes.

"Is that agreeable, Lord Theron?" Yiloch asked, anxious to leave all of them so he could struggle with the swell of misery and heartache away from prying eyes.

To his relief, Theron nodded.

"Good. We will continue in the morning when we have all rested and our heads are clear."

Adran rose and asked Theron to follow him. A few minutes after they left, Yiloch felt a light touch on his arm, not a physical touch, but a touch of power. Glancing up, he saw Ian leaning against the doorjamb, watching him. The youthful exuberance was gone from the creator's eyes. He looked exhausted… and determined.

"You should consider the impact of your words before you say them," Yiloch snapped.

Ian's expression hardened. "You need to sleep. Now."

"When did you become so bossy? I should never have encouraged you."

Standing, he walked out through the narrow space Ian's lean frame left open in the doorway, noting that the youth made no effort to give him more room. His father would have punished such behavior and perhaps he should as well, but he had grown to like the creator. The last thing he wanted right now was to get into a power struggle with the talented youth. Ian was loyal, formidable, and smart. That seemed like a good combination, one he needed to have on his side.

"My lord," Yiloch hesitated in the hallway, glancing back over his shoulder. "You can take credit for a lot of who I am now, but Indigo gets credit for this part."

"Belligerent," Yiloch muttered, but he couldn't stop a weary and much too wistful smile. "Get some sleep."

CHAPTER ELEVEN

Indigo's breath created a ghost of white in the air before her. The landscape, lumpy with the moon-lit shapes of resting warriors, was growing quiet as sleep called most of them into its embrace. The Kudaness travelled fast on foot, faster than she would have thought possible, and they slept hard as a result. Even the horse she rode, grown lean and hard with so many long days of travel, was weary from the speed of their journey and rested soundly.

Sleep proffered no warm embrace for her. There were battles coming. A strange and powerful army marched toward Yiroth. Toward people she cared about. People she loved. She needed to be as strong as she could be to help them and there was one way she knew now to strengthen her already formidable ascard connection. Whether the sucar truly increased the strength of her connection or simply enhanced her control of it made little difference. Either would be useful in trying to bring down the barriers that protected the Grey Army's warriors. Those barriers had to come down if Yiloch's army was going to have any chance of defeating them.

Her breath came fast, each exhale creating a brief white wisp in the darkness. Moving with quick light steps, she snuck to where Suac Chozai slept. He carried a small skin of sucar in his pack. One never knew when a walk with the gods might be necessary. Every suac in the Dursik un Kar carried some, but she didn't dare *borrow* from anyone other than Chozai. Using ascard to hold those resting nearby in sleep, she knelt by Suac Chozai's head and slipped a hand into the pack he was using as a pillow. She jumped when he shifted, her heart pounding, but the influence of her power kept him from waking as she resumed her search.

When her hand closed on the small skin, she let out a shaky exhale and drew it out. A light breeze tickled along her skin, making her shiver as she hurried back to where her own packs lay next to her horse. When she was hunched down beside the animal, she drew back her power, letting those she'd influenced return to a normal sleep. For a few minutes, she listened to the sounds of the night, the breathing of the horse beside her, the calls of owls. The nervous flutter in her chest reminded her of times she'd snuck out with Caplin as a child when her uncle took her into the city with him.

Dear Caplin.

What was he doing now? Did he worry about her or had her apparent treason and his jealousy turned him cold to her?

Dashing away the thoughts with a shake of her head, she pulled the stopper from the skin, grimacing at the pungent aroma wafting out. She would never get used to that stench. Drawing in a breath to steel her nerves, she lifted it to her lips.

A hand grabbed her wrist. She let out a soft cry and twisted to face Chozai. His copper eyes took on an eerie glow in the moonlight and his furious scowl threw hard shadows over the planes of his tattooed face. She yanked her wrist away, scowling back at him in the darkness.

Defensive anger quickly gave way to the heat of guilt rising in her cheeks and she was thankful that the moon hung behind her in the sky, hiding her face in shadow.

"There is no need for you to walk with the gods now," he growled in a low voice, switching indiscriminately between Lyran and Kudaness in his anger. "You have accomplished your task. The Kudaness are on the move."

"We haven't defeated the Grey Army yet," she hissed, also keeping her voice low and stretching her ability to keep those who slept near them from waking.

He gestured to the sucar. "How is this going to help?"

"It…" She hesitated. Should she tell him the truth? Given their beliefs around ascard use, was there any way to make him understand or would the truth only make him angrier? She needed to take the chance. "My ascard connection grows a little stronger every time I walk with the gods," she confessed, yearning for him to understand and accept. He had to see that this made sense in light of the current situation.

Suac Chozai was silent, but his rage magnified, blasting against her extended ability with enough force that she stepped back into her horse. The tired animal shifted the foot he was resting on and she placed a hand on his shoulder, more to calm herself than to soothe him. The Murak suac turned slightly away from her, his sharp movements further attesting to his anger, but his silence suggested uncertainty. After a long pause, his glowing eyes bored into her again.

"Do not," he growled, his gaze jumping to the skin for a second. "The gods will demand payment for the gifts they give you. The more you accept, the greater that price will be."

For a few seconds she considered arguing that she didn't believe in his gods. She held the sucar tight to her chest, longing to drink from it in spite of his warning. To defy him now would be to throw all of his trust back in his face. It would destroy the relationship they had developed.

Still, she hesitated.

He breathed deep, the intensity of his rage fading as he exhaled. "You are wrong. Sucar destroys the connection to ascard. It always has."

She stared at him, trying to absorb what he was saying in context with her own experience. She reached out to all the Suac's in the army. In them, she found only the faintest trace of an ascard connection. Extending further, she found the lesser priests and discovered something different. The all had varying degrees of ascard connection, most strong enough to be pressed into training as a healer in Caithin, but it was changing, becoming something different with a different feel to it. Startled, she reached back into Suac Chozai and found that altered connection there. It was incredibly strong in him, that changed ascard connection. It wasn't gone at all, only altered so that the individual was no longer aware of it and could no longer consciously control it. That must be how they managed the prophecies, though she still didn't understand how one could see future possibilities, with or without a conscious ascard connection.

Why wasn't her connection changing in the same way? Could it be the healing she did after every session to minimize the damage from the poison?

Something else occurred to her then and she lifted her lip in a silent snarl, fury burning through her as though her blood had turned to acid. "You tried to take my power from me."

He lifted his head, defiant of her anger. "The sacrifice of that power is a part of becoming un Ani."

"When were you going to tell me that? Were you going to give me a choice or wait until it was already gone?"

He met her eyes, his jaw set with the righteousness of his conviction. It was so tempting to tell him the truth right then, to tell him that his connection wasn't gone, only altered. How would he accept that? How would it sit with him to know his belief that he had eradicated that power in devotion to his gods was false? How did she feel knowing his acceptance of her was only a trick to gain her trust and eradicate her sinful power?

The fury burned out, sinking in her chest like a stone in water. He was a product of his culture. It didn't make the things he'd done right, but the fact that he hadn't killed her outright for the mere offense of being a Caithin adept was a profound defiance of his beliefs. He was trying to fix her. To give her a chance to become something better, in his estimation, than she was when she came to him.

She placed the stopper back in the water skin and handed it to him. He yanked it from her grasp and she watched him stride away, a shadow storming through the sleeping warriors. Restless and miserable, she wrapped herself in a blanket of warmth drawn from ascard in the ground and lay down. Sleep was slow to come.

•

The insipid light of predawn found her back in the saddle with dark circles under her eyes. Sleep had come in brief fitful spells. She moved along amidst a vast sea of dark-skinned warriors. They ate as they walked, breaking their fast on the move. When they finished eating, the pace would increase to an easy lope that the gelding could match with his reasonably comfortable trot.

She chewed listlessly at some dried meat. It was bland, reminiscent of that Yiloch had offered her in his father's prison. Two people brought together in the strangest of places by the strangest of circumstances. His recent rejection of her stripped the memory of its odd sweetness. She had to force herself to continue chewing.

How could she have sunk so low as to try stealing some of the sucar? It wasn't like her to be so deceitful. Then again, what right did Chozai have to try taking her powers away without telling her? She was a grown woman. She had the right to decide for herself who and what she wanted to be. He should have explained the risks and let her make her own choices.

She sat straighter in her saddle, proud of all she had accomplished of her own volition. Seconds later, her shoulders sank and she hung her head again.

No matter how much she had to be proud of, no matter what he kept from her, in this she was wrong. She should have at least asked to use the sucar rather than sneaking it away in the night like a petty thief. Then, at least, they could have had a calm discussion about her reasons for wanting to use it. That she had felt it necessary to steal the sucar suggested that her need wasn't so justified. It wasn't love that drove her to take it. It was hunger. It was greed. It was the promise of more power. It didn't matter how she meant to use that power.

The realization made her body ache with weariness. Such things had never driven her before. The thirst for knowledge and the desire to escape a dreadful life with an abusive husband had driven her. What had changed?

A dark hand reached into her line of sight, patting her horse's shoulder. She looked at the black tattoos wrapping the wrist, reaching with tapering tendrils over the hand and up the fingers and blew out a weary exhale.

"Suac Chozai," she acknowledged in a small voice.

"Indigo un Ani un Yiloch," he greeted in return.

There was a painful twisting in her chest and she wondered whether the title binding her to their priesthood or that binding her to Yiloch caused it. Probably both and she suspected the inclusion of *un Yiloch* had been an intentional torment meant as punishment for her actions. As much as she wanted to snap at him for it, she couldn't muster the energy to do so.

"I told you, Emperor Yiloch turned me away," she reminded him, resigned enough that there was little emotion in the statement. The words floated up from the hollow in her chest and dropped from her lips.

Chozai made a soft noise in his throat that managed to communicate both disagreement and disinterest somehow. "Your eyes already show the mark of the sucar. If the gods want you to have a stronger ability to manipulate ascard, perhaps that is good for the trial ahead. Do not expect it to come without a high price."

Her hand went to her face as if she might feel the change in her eyes. She forced the hand back to her reins, a shudder rushing through her as she recalled the images from the mirrors in her last walk with the gods.

"What kind of price?"

"You know sucar is a poison. It will change you and it may kill you if you take too much." His impatient tone suggested that she already knew this and shouldn't have to be told again. "The gods may be helping you or they may be tempting you with this power, testing your integrity."

"Why would the gods lure me to my death now? You said they had accepted me." *I thought you had accepted me*, she added silently, the ache of his deception twisting like a dagger in her chest. Was this how Yiloch felt when she betrayed him? Given the comparative depths of the relationships, her betrayal had probably been much harder to take.

She hung her head, hoping he wouldn't notice the shine of unshed tears.

"Perhaps you have served your purpose," Chozai snapped.

Another shudder moved though her. The suggestion of such fickleness in their gods horrified her, as did his easy acceptance of it. She reached out to him with ascard, inspecting the confusing array of emotions that came from him. Disappointment and affection were strong among them.

Guilt flushed her cheeks again and she drew her power back into herself.

"I know what is in your heart. You tell yourself you want to be stronger so you can protect those you love. Power is addictive and it will kill you at least as quickly as the sucar will if you allow it to control you."

She swallowed and nodded. "I understand."

They continued in silence until most of the warriors had finished their scant meals. The pace would be increasing soon. If she wanted to say more, this was the time.

"I'm sorry, Suac Chozai Galal un Murak un Ani. I was not myself last night and—"

He made a sharp gesture with his hand, cutting her off. Then he took hold of the horse's reins and stopped them. The rest of the Kudaness continued to pass around them like a river parting around a rock. His copper eyes burned with anger.

"I cannot forgive *you* if you were not yourself. Perhaps you will explain to me who you were?"

There was a hard edge to his tone, a coldness that chilled her far more than his anger the night before, but she understood his point and inclined her head in a small bow of deference.

"*I* was wrong, Suac Chozai Galal un Murak un Ani. I ask your forgiveness for my actions."

He gave a quick nod. "You are young and the responsibility you take upon your shoulders is great. This has not been the first time nor will it be the last time you stumble upon this road. I forgive you, Indigo Milan un Ani un Yiloch."

She bit her tongue, fighting the urge to yell at him for his insistence that she was Yiloch's somehow. She had his forgiveness, but his manner remained distant. It would gain her no ground to argue with him over that now. She had to pick her battles.

"You earned that tattoo just as any Kudaness man would have. Do not shame it."

"Did I earn it?"

He gave her a hard look. "You would not wear it otherwise." Turning, he started to walk again, tugging the horse along with him. "Sometimes our circumstances drive us to do things we might not have considered otherwise. Even things we will regret. We must accept those actions that shame us just as we would those that bring us pride. You know this. As does Emperor Yiloch."

Not giving her time to question the last comment, Chozai jogged away and the army increased their speed. She urged the gelding up to a trot to keep pace with them. How she wished what he intimated with his words was true. Would Yiloch welcome her back now that he had time to consider what had passed between them? Would she let him do so after their last encounter? The man might as well have cut her heart out and carried it away with him.

Her hand went to her chest where her old ring now hung on the chain Yiloch had worn for so long, the band cold and hard against her skin.

•

It was coming on evening when the army halted again without warning, coming to a surprisingly smooth stop considering their numbers. She moved her horse out and around, trotting to the front to see what had stalled them.

A group of seven warriors and five of the suacs had gathered in a precise circle at the far side of the rough track. She directed her mount over to them. One warrior stepped into the middle of the group and raised his spear. Between two of the men, she could see a figure lying prone on the ground. The warrior started to bring the spear down fast toward the fallen figure. Lashing out with power, she knocked the spear from the warrior's hands and pulled the horse to a hard stop at the perimeter. She jumped from the saddle and strode into the circle. An uproar arose among those close enough to see what had happened. The disarmed warrior scowled at her, hate in his eyes.

Ignoring them all, she knelt beside the prone figure. He was Lyran, his light blond hair worn long and his skin pale as snow, though his facial structure was a touch too rounded and rugged for someone of pure blood. At first, she thought he was dead. His chest didn't appear to move and she didn't feel a pulse when she pressed her fingers to his throat. Using ascard, she delved in deeper, finding a very faint pulse and the shallowest breathing.

"What were you thinking?" She glared up at the men around her. "This man is alive."

The warriors all scowled at her and looked away, as if she were unworthy of their acknowledgement. She started to repeat the demand in Kudaness, but stopped when Suac Chozai stepped forward. There was a look of warning and disapproval on his face.

"The man is nearly dead. It is a mercy to end his suffering," he explained.

"There are better ways," she hissed and turned back to the man.

The injuries were several days old. A deep gash laid open his left thigh, the proud flesh hot and reeking with infection. A broad puncture in his chest also stank of infection. She could see the swept bladed spears of the Grey Army in her mind as she examined the wounds. She laid a hand on his chest to feel the heat there and started when his hazel eyes fluttered open.

How are you still alive?

She set a gentle hand against his cheek, hoping to comfort him. His face was blazing hot, his pupils large and unfocused. She doubted he even knew they were there.

Closing her eyes, she focused ascard into him. The infections were severe, his fever high enough to injure his brain. His heart strained, near to failing. There was a chance she could save him, but it would take everything she had, and even if it worked, he would require continuing care for some time.

What was one life worth?

Tears streamed down her cheeks when she opened her eyes and glanced up at Chozai. His expression was unyielding. He gestured to the warrior who had retrieved his spear.

"He will end this man's pain."

"I will do it," she countered, speaking in Kudaness so the warrior would also understand her.

The warrior, Farid tribe from his tattoo, stepped back and bowed his head, respecting her choice now that she agreed with their decision. Chozai looked displeased, but he also stepped back, giving a sharp nod.

She took a deep, shuddering breath and closed her eyes again. The man's heartbeat was so weak. A little longer, an hour or two, maybe half a day, and it might give up on its own. Then again, it might not. He might continue to suffer for a long time before his body gave up or, worse yet, predators found him, predators that would feast on him alive or dead. How had he ended up here, several miles from the nearest village? Was this where the army had cut him down? Had he drug himself from the village south of them perhaps? What need kept him alive that she was now going to override? What right did she have to force him to give up?

She fought back a sob, her throat tightening with the effort. Focusing her power, she wrapped it around his heart and, with a firm squeeze, stopped it beating.

There was no resistance. A final breath gasped between his lips. Then his body stiffened and relaxed. He was gone. Death was too easy to give.

She rose and walked out of the circle, looking at none of them. Whatever they thought of her powers and how she used them, she didn't care to see the judgment in their eyes right then. Stepping up to her horse, she mounted and continued down the rough track that would take them to Yiroth. Tears ran down her cheeks unchecked and she didn't look back to see what the army was doing. With surprisingly little sound, the Kudaness followed after her.

CHAPTER TWELVE

What are they stopping for?" Lady Auryl's voiced trembled when she spoke.

Yiloch glanced over his shoulder to see Terral resting a comforting hand on her arm. He jerked it back to his side when he noticed Yiloch looking and stepped away from her. Perhaps he feared igniting his jealousy.

If only I felt something more than pity when I look at her.

Still, Terral's discomfort brought him a small satisfaction. By going along with Myac's plans, he'd helped bring much misery upon them. His cousin knew well enough that the ties of blood were no deterrent. Yiloch had killed his father, he would kill Myac, and he would even kill Terral if he decided it was necessary. He did feel guilt over the death of Myac's mother, but he'd felt that long before knowing who she was and guilt had no place in the running of an empire. The night he killed his father and took the throne, Myac hadn't only tried to kill Indigo when he escaped her power, but he had taken time to make her suffer first. The man would never settle for some compromise that let Yiloch go unpunished. Leryc had told him horrifying tales of how Myac dispatched those who displeased Emperor Rylan.

Hatred and thirst for vengeance had given him a penchant for cruelty.

From this vantage, in the highest room in the southeast palace tower, they could see a portion of the Tygis River. They couldn't see all the way to the crossing where reports said the Grey Army was setting up camp. He had come up here with Adran a few hours ago to consider their options before meeting with Lord Theron again. Terral he dragged along because he felt a need to keep a close eye on the man, especially with the Caithin emissary in the palace. Ian arrived a few moments ago with the news of the Grey Army, having tracked Yiloch there with ascard, and Auryl had followed him up. The room, a small observation chamber that boasted a couple of chairs and a small table, was getting rather crowded.

"He may be giving his army time to rest before attacking. Or perhaps he hopes to lure us out," Yiloch said.

He grimaced as he stared out toward the crossing. Perhaps he should have led his forces against them earlier to try to save the river towns instead of simply sending riders out to encourage evacuation. By now, given the Grey Army's efficiency, anyone who had stayed in those towns was long dead. Within the city walls, they should be able to hold out until Cadmar and the other riders Hax had sent out returned with reinforcements, though it was questionable what help those reinforcements would be against this particular foe. He itched to do something though. Sitting back to wait while the army slaughtered his people was enough to drive him mad.

"He?"

Yiloch glanced at Auryl again, reminding himself not to be impatient with her. She was out of her element. "The Grey Army's warlord," he answered before turning back to the window.

It was hard to believe that she couldn't feel him. The warlord's presence was like a foul smell on the wind. Along with him, there was another adept out there whose considerable power was a tremble in the earth, resonating through the walls of the palace.

"Maybe he hopes to intimidate us," Ian muttered, a tremble in his voice.

Yiloch placed a hand on the younger man's shoulder, noting that the creator stood a little straighter in response to the contact. If the ascard presence of the warlord and his adept had this much effect on him, he could only imagine what it was doing to Ian who was far more sensitive to such things.

"If he hopes to scare us into surrender, he doesn't know Emperor Yiloch very well," Adran stated.

Yiloch smiled and, for the first time in his life, he envied Adran his lack of ascard connection. If he felt the enemy power at all, it was probably more like a minor itch at the back of his skull, annoying, but not suffocating. Not terrifying.

"It didn't feel like this when we saw the army before," Ian said.

"No, I'm certain this is deliberate. They're playing with us. Trying to break our confidence before they attack."

"They're doing a good job."

Yiloch glanced at Ian, concerned by the faint tremor he felt pass through the young creator. He needed Ian now, perhaps more than he ever had. If only Indigo were here to block this. There was no doubt in his mind that she could. What couldn't she do?

He let out a heavy exhale. "Don't let him win without a fight, Ian."

Ian bowed his head, a light flush rising in his face. Perhaps he was ashamed by the show of vulnerability. "I am fighting," he murmured, his voice low enough that only Yiloch could hear him.

"I know your strength, Ian." Yiloch gripped his shoulder a little tighter. "This power is a storm. It is strong now, but it will blow itself out and the whole army will die with it." He hoped Ian couldn't hear the doubt behind his words.

Another figure appeared in the stairs, an attendant who stepped aside and introduced Lord Theron as he strode into the room, the strength of his presence making it feel several times more crowded.

His dark eyes met Yiloch's. "The army is here?"

Yiloch nodded and stepped to one side to make room for Theron at the window. Adran and Ian also moved back to accommodate. He pointed out toward the crossroads. "They are setting camp in those trees there, just beyond the river. I take it you have no notable ascard ability."

Theron peered toward the river, shaking his head. "No, why?"

"They've been projecting power out over the palace and city, trying to intimidate my adepts and creators."

Theron's lips pressed into a tight line as he gazed out the window, squinting his eyes as though he might be able to see through the trees if he tried hard enough.

"Why did they come?" Auryl asked in the moment of silence.

Yiloch shook his head. Lady Auryl was soon going to break the fragile control he had over his temper with her pointless inquiries. He had to remind himself that she was not like Hax or Eris. War and its politics were never part of her education. She was bred and raised to society life, trained in the frivolous skills of fashion sense and charm. A flower meant to please the senses and distract from such weighted affairs, not assist with them.

She wasn't Indigo.

"Resources perhaps," he offered. "We know nothing of them or their culture. We can't know what drives them."

"It's sad really." She sighed, moving closer to the window in the narrow space Adran and Ian had left. "Such a shame that their circumstances should drive them to such action."

Yiloch sneered, hatred pulsing through him, amplifying his sense of helplessness. "They're no strangers to this brutality," he growled, muscles tightening through his arms as he gripped the sill of the window. He couldn't afford to show his frustration in front of the emissary. "They're much too good at it."

Auryl stepped back from him, driven away by the angry edge in his tone and the sudden tension in his posture. From his other side, Theron regarded her thoughtfully. Yiloch yearned to know what the other man was thinking, but he wasn't apt to say much in this situation.

"Perhaps I should go." She lowered her gaze to her clasped hands.

"I think that's wise. There are things we need to discuss that you needn't worry about."

He knew his cold manner hurt her, but he was close enough to turning his fury toward the Grey Army on her that it made sense to send her away. He heard the door open and click shut again as she left.

"That was unkind," Adran said under his breath, stepping close as he spoke so Theron wouldn't hear. His tone was informative rather than accusing, as if he thought, or maybe hoped, that Yiloch was unaware of the harshness of his treatment of her.

Ignoring the comment, he gestured Ian forward and said, "Can you reach them? Perhaps read something of the skills of their adepts."

Ian shook his head. "Indigo could. Their barriers are too strong for me alone. I can only feel what they want me to feel."

Yiloch ground his teeth and glowered at the trees that hid the crossroads as though willpower alone would reveal the army hidden there. How long would they wait, resting while they used ascard to try to unnerve the creators and adepts within the city? Without a way to bring down their protections, going out after them would be suicide. He wasn't willing to throw his people away like that.

And yet, if he allowed them to rest undisturbed, they would be fresh and strong when they came against the city. He knew from what he'd seen and what others had told him that they were a powerful force. There was also the deep uncertainty within, created by Suac Chozai's prophecy that his empire would "fall in a storm of fire and blood" to this new threat. So far, the Murak suac had been right in most of his prophecy. Why should he expect this to be any different?

Was it hopeless?

Because of these things, because of a fear of what he knew and a fear of what he didn't know, he was reluctant to move against the Grey Army without some certainty that his forces could so much as touch the enemy warriors. The city walls should hold against them for some time, though even that wasn't certain. Knowing that fear held him back filled him with shame, which only fed his restlessness and rage. Auryl was better off staying away from him. Adran knew how to deal with his tempers and Terral made a nice target should his rage get the better of him. Ian? The powerful young creator's distress was comforting to him. It justified his fear somehow, making if feel less like plain cowardice. That and their shared love for Indigo made him welcome at Yiloch's side.

"No matter how strong their power, they can't keep this up indefinitely. Soon they will make a move. At least then, the waiting will be over. We'll find a way to make them pay for the lives they have taken," Yiloch stated, wishing he believed it.

Ian's jaw tensed and his eyes narrowed, remembering the lives the army had taken and the massacres they had seen. There was a burning hatred in the creator's eyes that Yiloch had never seen before and, in that moment, it pleased him.

"Yes, and then they'll be sorry they ever came," Ian said through gritted teeth.

Yiloch smiled, finding that Ian's bold statement bolstered his own confidence. "That they will," he agreed. "Ian, gather the adepts and creators. Do what you can to help them deal with the effects of this power and work on some ideas for bringing those barriers down. Don't hesitate to ask for anything you need to make that happen."

Ian bowed and strode from the room, fresh determination in his eyes. The young creator would do everything he could. Whether it would be enough remained to be seen, but Yiloch couldn't shake the sinking feeling that it would not.

He turned to Theron. "You should return to Caithin now. You could end up trapped here when they make their attack."

Theron responded with a wry smile. "I've already sent word back to Demin that I need more time here. I hope you don't mind. I am curious to see who these people are. Besides, my niece is out there somewhere. Without her, it is going to be hard to convince anyone of the things you've told me, myself included."

Yiloch shrugged. "Suit yourself, Lord Theron, I cannot guarantee your safety in these circumstances."

Theron nodded. "I knew that before I made the decision to stay."

Raising his eyes, Yiloch looked beyond the tree line. She was out there somewhere, on the other side of that army. He could only hope she was safe. It was out of his hands for now. Now all he could do was try to get through this, preferably with his empire intact.

•

The palace was beautiful. Myac wasn't sure he had really appreciated that before. Certainly never with this kind of desperate longing in his heart.

Sunlight danced over the created crystal ceiling of the throne room, creating a blaze of fiery brilliance that was almost hard to look at, like a land-bound second sun. The white walls that surrounded the city and palace were stark and brilliant, blending with the backdrop of the distant waves beyond like the massive foamy crest of frozen whitecaps.

Standing quiet at the edge of the trees, the reins of his mount hanging loose in one hand, he ached for that city. His hands remained unbound since the night that he tried to kill Ini-jnai. It wasn't a kindness. It was a way of saying they believed he had learned his lesson. The worst part was that he had. The healing of his injuries from that night was imperfect. Every movement caused stinging pain in one of the cuts or his perpetually aching legs. As if that wasn't enough of a reminder, his sleep was tormented with nightmares reliving every second of fear and pain. The mere thought of trying it again made him nauseous. He had been trained. So much power, rendered so useless.

His hand tightened to a fist on the reins, fingernails digging into his palm. Then rage at his weakness faded, overwhelmed by exhaustion, and he relaxed his hand. He stroked the horse's face, moved by the animal's enduring patience.

There is much people could learn from such a creature.

He waivered on his feet then, weakened by constant pain and lack of sleep. If only he had Indigo's ability to understand new skills so quickly, he might have discovered some way out of this imprisonment by now. He had to work hard for every skill he had developed and, while his connection was perhaps as strong, that talent for picking up new things gave her the potential to be far more powerful.

Myac leaned on the horse's shoulder and focused on his breathing. The emotional assault Ini-jnai and Ksa-jnai were projecting out over the city was a muted, tormenting buzz in the back of his mind. The fact that his ascard was part of the blend of power behind that working buffered him from the full effect. He couldn't imagine how unnerving it must be to those within the city, to Yiloch.

A rare smile touched his lips. He'd been hungry for the man's death for so long now. Hatred coursed through him, warming him like a good wine, adding a cruel edge to his smile. It felt good. Recent events had driven him to doubt his course, to doubt his strength. Now, knowing Yiloch suffered, his purpose refreshed, sharpening to a dagger point in his mind. He wanted to hurt the emperor, to make him suffer, but he had to be patient. Somehow, he had to escape this. It wouldn't do to let someone else take the insufferable man's life. Ini-jnai had to die before that happened.

He stroked the horse's coat, smooth under his fingertips.

The opportunity would come. He only had to wait for the right moment, and while he waited, he could rest. There had to be a way to destroy the controlling adept. He needed to be ready when the time came to bring Yiloch's world crashing down around him.

Remembered pain sent a shudder through him and he gritted his teeth against it. The horse nudged his arm and he turned towards the stocky animal. The white star on its forehead drew his eyes and he began to scratch there, then he moved around to scratch behind its ear. The horse's lips quivered and he smiled in response to the simple pleasure.

Ksa-jnai's voice drew his attention then, wiping away his smile. The warlord was approaching, approval in his eyes. They prized their horses, so Myac suspected his growing rapport with the animal was the source of that approval. Behind the warlord, Ini-jnai and Na-jnai strode, neither sharing their leader's approving expression. Glancing away so they wouldn't see the flush of fear in his face, he knelt down. The fierce resolve of a few minutes ago vanished in a haze of panic as the sharp tang of fear filled his mouth. He clenched his jaw, trying to ignore his own voice screaming *coward* in his head.

They stopped in front of him and Ksa-jnai said something. When he looked up, Ini-jnai stepped forward and held out his hand. His fingers uncurled and Myac's heart stuttered in his chest. The key stones for the Serroc prisons sat in the adept's palm. He had forgotten about them. His hand twitched in response to the swell of longing within him. If only...

Ini-jnai's mouth curved in a wicked smile then and Myac realized with a sudden dread that the other man would feel that longing through the binding. His eyes focused on the chipped, dirty fingernails as Ini-jnai's fingers closed around the stones and he drew his hand back to his side. Hatred burned through Myac so hot that the other adept flinched when it flashed along the binding, his eyes widening in surprise. Then Ini-jnai's lip twisted in a snarl and he stepped forward. Myac's palms began to sweat, icy prickles of fear creeping up his spine as crisp memories of the man's torture flashed through his mind.

Sensing the tension or perhaps the rising power from Ini-jnai, the warlord grabbed the adept's arm and snapped something at him. The adept stepped back quickly, lowering his gaze. Such complete obedience. Trembling, Myac bowed his head to Ksa-jnai, understanding that the warlord had saved him from more torture. A few more words were exchanged and Ini-jnai and Na-jnai retreated, their feet disappearing from the circle of his vision. After a few more minutes of silence, Ksa-jnai crouched down in front of him.

Strong, calloused fingers slid under his chin and lifted. Inwardly, Myac recoiled from the touch, but he clenched his teeth and forced himself not to fight it. When his eyes rose to meet those strange, dark eyes, the warlord released the pressure and took his hand away. He considered Myac for a minute or more, then he nodded, rose again, and patted the horses neck before walking away.

Frustration and an intense urge to scream or weep, or both, rushed through Myac. Beyond the departing warlord, Ini-jnai stared at him, his eyes full of undisguised loathing and something more, something that he could only identify when he touched along the binding. Jealousy. The other adept was jealous of the warlord's attention, attention Myac despised at least as much as Ini-jnai hungered for it. Despair filled him so full that he doubted he had the strength to stand under the weight of it. Twisting around, he sat on the ground next to the feet of his horse and stared out at the city of Yiroth. The city that should be his.

He still remembered the first time he'd seen it. He had been travelling from his father's manor. Rejected. Hiding burn scars, sorrow, and rage beneath a cloak with a deep hood. He'd come seeking revenge, somehow believing that his righteous anger at the senseless slaughter of his mother and the rest of their village would be enough to carry him to the emperor and his cursed son. Enough to bring him the vengeance he deserved.

The beauty of the place had felt like a mockery. A deliberate attack on the beauty he'd lost to horrible scars. His hair burned away, his face disfigured, one eye blinded by a spray of hot ash. The palace itself, with the soaring created crystal ceiling above the throne room sparkling in sunlight, was an image of perfection, gloating at him.

It was during a period of relative peace within the empire in spite of the recent murder of the empress. Peace at least for those who hadn't been targeted by a cruel emperor and his son for harboring the empress's murderer. It didn't matter if the accusation was true or not. He and his mother had known nothing of such things. Neither of them deserved the punishment they were given.

He should have made his father suffer for turning him away, but he had fled instead, fled the horror with which Lord Terral had regarded his disfigured son. Now he had only a burning hatred for those who had led him to this end. It was all that kept him going.

Inside the outer gates, he had stalled in a crowded marketplace, overwhelmed by all the people and animals and smells and sounds. Someone had bumped into him. A gust of wind, twisted by its passage between buildings, caught his hood and flipped it back. A woman, no beauty herself, saw his scared features and screamed. Someone shouted, "What the hell is that thing?". Myac turned and fled from the city. He ran to a grassy knoll just off the road where he dropped to his knees and wept like a child beneath the aged branches of a lonely tree. Wept like a coward.

It was there that Serivar found him. He was traveling with a quiet man who Myac later learned possessed great talent at sensing ascard ability. Serivar was traveling in Lyra to learn about how the Lyran people used ascard. He was kind to Myac. He offered him food and a place to stay in Caithin. Offered him education and a way to transform his burned features into something that people wouldn't shy away from.

Serivar, not yet headmaster of the Caithin Healer's Academy or a member of the King's High Council, was looking for a toy. A foreign adept he could experiment with in secret to learn more about ascard power. Myac's extraordinary ascard connection was too much for him to resist. At the time, Myac didn't see the hidden agenda behind the kindness. He saw only someone who wasn't screaming in fear or mocking or turning him away. He saw hope and safety. He saw a future that would someday bring him the vengeance he needed.

This moment, this reliving of his first sight of Yiroth, wasn't that future.

CHAPTER THIRTEEN

There was only one day left. One day before the wedding he wasn't at all ready for. Caplin woke early, slipping quietly out through the palace kitchens to grab a bite. In the stable, he shifted restlessly from one foot to the other, watching the Lyran groom as he saddled the black mare, Velvet, the mare Indigo had ridden so many times. The mare wasn't his regular mount, but she satisfied a tiny fraction of the yearning that had drawn him from his rooms much earlier than he usually rose.

The servant who was saddling her, Terun, had moved along with most of the family horses when their household relocated into the palace. He handled the big animals with a deft patience that they responded to well. He was also a handsome man in the way of any man from a purer Lyran bloodline and every movement held a certain grace that defied his low station. The royal grounds seemed to embrace him as though he belonged there and he looked better in that environment than Caplin had ever seen him look, stronger and healthier.

"Is something wrong, my lord?"

An elegant voice as well. Caplin met his eyes, only then realizing that he was scowling at the man. He shook his head, schooling his expression to something more neutral.

"No. I…" He trailed off, searching those light green eyes. So much serenity in those pale depths. How could that be? He'd been sold off into slavery by his own people. "You… Your manner… You strike me as a nobleman, Terun. Were you? Before…"

Terun's expression turned wary.

"I apologize. It's not appropriate of me to ask such a thing," Caplin said, taking the reins and stepping up beside the horse.

"Yes."

Caplin hesitated then turned to face the man. He was almost surprised to realize that they were about the same height. Odd that he had always thought of Terun as much shorter. "How…? Doesn't it…?" He fumbled and fell silent. Where had his usual charisma vanished to?

"Yes, it makes me angry at times, but I gave my freedom in exchange for protection for my family. That they are safe comforts me and my fate could be much worse. Your family treats us all fairly and I have always enjoyed working with horses." He stroked the mare's nose and she pushed it into his hand, eliciting the faintest smile from him.

Caplin rested a hand on the cantle. He should mount and leave now, before he said something else foolish. He stayed where he was. "Now that Emperor Rylan is gone, do you wish you could go back?"

Terun's eyes blazed to life, his jaw tensing. "You never struck me as a cruel man, Prince Caplin. When you were younger, such a question might be excused, but I think you are old enough to know better. False hope is not something you lay at the feet of a man who has made peace with his fate."

Caplin winced. He considered apologizing, but he had known it was cruel when he asked it. Apology would be for his own benefit only. Terun made him think of Yiloch and for that, he had wanted to cause the man pain.

"You're right Terun. Perhaps I envy that you have found that peace."

A bitter smile flickered across his lips. "Royalty and peace are uncommon bedmates, my lord."

Caplin grimaced. "So I've noticed."

Swinging up into the saddle, he trotted Velvet from the stable. Outside, four guards fell in behind him. He would have preferred to go without the escort, but he would never hear the end of it from his mother and Andrea if they found out. Accepting the shackles his newfound royal status came with was easier than fighting them. Passing through early morning streets brought a different kind of torment that built up on top of the angst within him. The way people moved out of the way and bowed their heads when they saw him, the way they watched him with eyes full of expectation and envy. There had always been some of that, as the king's nephew, but not to this degree. He was their future king now and they longed for him to be great in so many different ways. He could never live up to all of their many disparate expectations.

Irritation became an itch over his entire body and he urged the mare up to a canter, weaving quickly through the streets. The guards sped up to keep pace and the clatter of hooves on the cobbles warned anyone who might step into their path. They left the city behind, but the pressure of obligation and responsibility remained, wrapped around him in a suffocating embrace. He urged the mare faster until she stretched long, her ears pressed back against her neck in response to his volatile mood.

He didn't pull her back down until they reached the turn into the clearing by the river. The place he and Indigo had spent so much time in their youth, dipping their toes in the river and sharing silly daydreams. The horses were all sweating and breathing hard. Velvet's sides heaved under his legs and he patted her neck absently as he turned her into the clearing. Dismounting, he led the mare to the river and let her drink, placing a hand against her side to feel the powerful beat of her heart. The rhythm was comforting. He closed his eyes, letting the fast, hard rhythm fill him, thrumming through his mind, chasing everything else away.

How long he stood that way, he wasn't sure. Eventually, the black mare's lips, cold and wet with river water, nipped at the arm of his shirt. Caplin opened his eyes and held a hand out, letting her lip at his palm in search of treats.

They had received a missive the prior evening from Lord Theron. There really was an army marching on Yiroth, due to arrive within a few days if the reports were accurate. Indigo was somewhere in Kudan and Lord Edan's whereabouts were unknown. Emperor Yiloch was in Yiroth, returned to the capital less than a day before Theron arrived. That came as a shock, almost as much of a shock as Indigo in Kudan. The emperor claimed she was there by choice, though Caplin couldn't help doubting that. Why would anyone, aside from the Kudaness themselves, actually want to linger in Kudan?

Theron advised that they take no action against Emperor Yiloch until after the coming army had been dealt with and an attempt could be made to find Indigo.

That suggested that she might indeed have information they needed to confirm the emperor's guilt or innocence. Theron ended the missive stating that he intended to stay in Yiroth until he could learn more. Curiously, he offered no opinion on whether Caithin should come to Lyra's aid. Caplin voted in favor of providing military assistance, though his reasons were of a more personal nature. They weren't going to find Indigo while a war was going on. Most of the council members had been hesitant to get involved, though Serivar also supported the idea. The reasons behind that support still eluded Caplin.

The mare was breathing easier now, as were the other four horses. Caplin turned her and mounted, the guards rushing to follow his example, as though they feared being left behind. Squeezing his legs, he urged the mare up to a trot and left the clearing behind, driving for the city at a less intense pace for the sake of the horses.

•

It took no more than half an hour to get back into the city and ride to the Healer's Academy administration building. The woman who escorted him to the headmaster's office gestured for him to wait and stepped inside, shutting the door behind her. If he hadn't already known the office was protected against eavesdropping, he might have put his ear to the door. Instead, he waited patiently.

That he could wait patiently was a pleasant change from his earlier temper. Deciding to confront Serivar calmed him. The anger and frustration faded, replaced by the resolute determination that came with having a purpose he could act upon. When the woman came out and gestured him in, he smiled and entered the office, gesturing for his shadowing guards to wait outside before he shut the door.

Serivar stood behind his desk, his slender face an impassive mask. He bowed and Caplin acknowledged the gesture with a polite nod.

"Prince Caplin, I wouldn't have expected to see you the day before your wedding. You must have so much preparation still to do." There was the faintest, uneasy edge to his voice as he gestured to a chair.

Caplin sat and Serivar waited until he had settled to do the same, an uncommon show of proper courtesy from a man who often forgot to include titles for anyone short of the king himself. Was the headmaster trying to get on his good side for a reason? Maybe he suspected the purpose of Caplin's visit.

"Lord Serivar," he acknowledged the headmaster in as polite a tone as he could manage. "Given the coming festivities, I'm sure you can imagine why I might be avoiding the palace right now."

The headmaster smiled, pretending to commiserate, but his eyes narrowed a fraction, undermining the sentiment. "Certainly. To what do I owe the pleasure of your visit?"

"I wanted to thank you for your support in the council yesterday, though I'm still a little puzzled as to why you want to aid Lyra now. As I recall, you didn't support the alliance with Emperor Yiloch before and now he's back in charge of Lyra. Why show support for him this time, when he's been accused of such horrible crimes against Caithin?"

Serivar picked up a few scattered books from his desk and stacked them in one corner. Then he moved the inkpot and a few scattered quills to one side. He rested his elbows on the cleared surface and steepled his fingers, regarding Caplin over the peak.

"I am not supporting Emperor Yiloch specifically, but Lyra can be a powerful ally. If they fall, then we have an unknown entity to deal with. By all reports, it doesn't seem that these visitors from beyond the Rhuakine are all that friendly. Besides, if we come to the aid of Yiroth now, then we have another powerful bargaining point in our favor moving forward."

"Yes, I know all the political reasoning," Caplin replied with a dismissive wave of one hand. "What I want to know is what *your* motivations are in regards to Lyra and Lady Indigo."

Serivar sat back, his pleasant half smile vanishing the instant Indigo's name came up. The headmaster brushed at one sleeve as though some offending substance had appeared there. He finally met Caplin's eyes again, his warm brown eyes gone cold.

"Unfortunately, I have business to attend to, Lord Caplin. I really would love to discuss this more, but—"

"I'm only asking for a moment, Lord Serivar. I don't see why it would take more than that for you to explain your honorable intentions."

The headmaster's slight frame rose and fell with a heavy sigh. "This is absurd. I've given my explanation. Why must you persist in questioning me?"

Caplin tapped his fingers on the desk, meeting that cold gaze. "Fine. I'll accept your reasons for wanting to send aid to Lyra… for now. What about Emperor Yiloch and Lady Indigo. What do you think should be done with them when this new enemy has been dealt with?"

"This is council business—"

"No." Serivar flinched at the force behind the word and Caplin forced a pleasant smile. "This is nothing more than personal curiosity."

Serivar clenched his teeth, muscles in his jaw tightening. "Emperor Yiloch should pay for his crimes, by which I mean he should be put to death. Someone else in the royal line should ascend to the Lyran throne. There must be someone suited to the position."

"And do you think the emperor will get on the first boat across the Gilded Straight and put himself in our hands? That doesn't seem at all like the Emperor Yiloch I know. Besides, are you so certain he really is guilty? Lady Indigo didn't seem to think so."

"You yourself admitted that she is in love with the Lyran emperor. I'm not sure her judgement should be trusted."

Caplin frowned. "Yes. She also loved this school and she has always been very close to my family." There was an undignified grunt from Serivar, but Caplin ignored it and continued. "To my shame, I was willing to accept that love for Yiloch was what drove her at first. It took my father to make me realize that it just didn't make any sense. She wouldn't abandon everything that mattered to her to rescue him if she believed he was behind the assassination of the royal family. There is something more to this and I think you know something about it. Something you don't want to talk about."

Looking like a cornered animal, Serivar stared at him for several minutes, his hands dropping to the arms of his chair and tightening. Then he shook himself, the fearful look giving way to irritation as he adjusted the stack of books again.

"Emperor Yiloch's adepts signed confessions stating

that he was guilty. There is nothing left to discuss."

"Yes, I know. None of it makes sense, does it? That is why I think we need to be very deliberate about trying to put the pieces together. If Lord Theron is able to bring Indigo back, I'm sure her testimony will help shed some light on the investigation. I also think it would help if you shared whatever information you're hiding."

Serivar's lip rose in a snarl. "I don't know what you're playing at, Prince Caplin, but don't think you can manipulate me with your petty political games. I am not a mere lord. I am headmaster of the Caithin Healer's Academy and head of the King's Order..." Serivar trailed off, his eyes narrowing when Caplin shuddered.

Now why did that proclamation send a chill through him? The King's Order were the only adepts in Caithin other than the Ascard Watchmen who used ascard for anything other than healing. They worked in dedicated service to the king.

Or did they? Who gave them their orders, really? His investigation into the Order once he was in a position to be aware of their existence revealed that all of their activities were coordinated through Serivar. Even the few creators and adepts on duty in the palace answered to him as head of the King's Order.

Something Caplin had said to Indigo came back to him then. *We don't train such skills in Caithin, we smother them. It only makes sense that the assassins would be foreign.* If only that were true, he would have so much less doubt and fear spreading through him now like some malignant disease.

Somehow, Indigo had known the truth before he had. He had seen argument building in her eyes when he said those words, though he had dismissed it when she didn't put voice to it. She had already known about the King's Order, which suggested, given the secrecy its members were sworn to, that she must have spoken with Serivar about it, and the only way the headmaster would have divulged that information to her was if she were a member of the Order. But, shortly after learning about it, Caplin had indulged his curiosity and read through the roles for the King's Order, a created document that a select few people were given the ability to read. Indigo wasn't on that document. All adepts of the King's Order were supposed to be on those roles, even the ones in training.

Another thought occurred to him while Serivar regarded him with a disturbing expression of increasing calm. As someone with no functional connection to his inner aspect, he wouldn't know if someone was using ascard against him. If there was something sinister going on here, the headmaster, with the wide array of adepts following his orders, could be a powerful and dangerous man. He wasn't well equipped to deal with such a threat and, while he doubted that the headmaster would do anything to him now with the royal guards standing outside, he wasn't willing to take the chance.

Standing, Caplin nodded to the other man.

Serivar stood as well, that growing calm breaking all of a sudden. His quarry was making an escape.

"Lord Serivar, perhaps we can talk more about this later. I have a wedding to prepare for and you, as you said, have business to attend to."

Serivar's gaze turned inward, losing focus and Caplin decided not to wait for a proper farewell. Instead, he hurried to the door and let himself out. Serivar was starting to speak when he shut the door behind him.

He no longer cared what the headmaster had to say, he didn't want to be alone in a room with him. Perhaps he was being paranoid, but Serivar had a distinct advantage over him in his ascard power and his connections. If he was hiding something and wanted it to remain hidden, how far might he or one of his many adepts be willing to go to keep it that way?

One way or another, Caplin promised himself as he strode down the hall with the guards falling in step behind him, *I will find the truth in this, even if it means proving Emperor Yiloch innocent.*

Yiloch snapped awake. Sitting up in his bed, his nerves crackling like fire in his skin, he listened, one hand already holding the dagger he kept under his pillow. He waited.

Nothing.

Why had he woken in such a state of alert then? It was still dark outside the crystal windows, whitecaps in the ocean below picking up a scant luminescence from the sliver moon. A nightmare might have woken him, though he couldn't remember the last time that had happened.

He waited a few more minutes in the calm quiet darkness.

Calm. Quiet.

Suddenly he realized what was wrong. There was nothing, and that was the problem. The constant mental assault, the barrage of ascard intimidation that had been radiating out from the Grey Army for the last two days, had stopped. That could only mean one thing. The warlord was through playing games, now he was ready to make his move.

Yiloch pulled on his boots. He had laid down to rest without getting out of his clothes. It would be folly to put comfort above readiness at a time such as this. If luck were with him, Lady Auryl would still be sleeping.

There was no need for her to go through the stress of knowing they were under attack right now and he didn't need the irritation of her questions or the distraction of trying to keep her from harm. Someday he would have to address the resentment he harbored toward her for not being Indigo, but he had much bigger problems right now.

He strode through the halls, moving with quick, eager strides. Action was something he understood. The waiting was tortuous. For better or worse, the time for fighting had come.

A servant darted around one corner and leapt sideways, slipped on the floor, and caught himself on a hallway table. The vase in the center rocked to and fro, but settled upright at the man's touch.

He blew out a relieved exhale and turned, bowing deeply.

"Emperor Yiloch. Lord Captain Adran requests your presence." He paused a few seconds to catch his breath before rushing out with the rest of the message. "He and Commander Hax are waiting on the outer wall by the main gate."

"Thank you." Yiloch acknowledge the message and dismissed him with a quick nod of appreciation then hurried on, breaking into a jog in empty halls where no one was around to be worried by his urgency.

The door attendant at the main entrance hall spotted him the moment he stepped out of an adjacent hallway and opened one massive door, allowing him to pass outside without a break in stride as though he had been expected, which he probably had been if the messenger had done his job well. The serving staff within the palace always worked together well that way, each one alerting the others to the things that might affect them for maximum efficiency. Many of them were from families that had worked within those halls for generations. They were yet one more reason he wasn't going to let this army destroy his home.

The waiting night was black and tense with a sense of anticipation. Torches lit around the vast courtyard by the barracks, stables, and other buildings, offered a moody, flickering illumination for the constant movement of soldiers. The activity level told him that many of his officers were already aware of the change in the enemy army and were well into the process of getting mobilized for confrontation. In the midst of the bustle, a young man came trotting toward him, drawing Tantrum along behind him in full battle gear. Irritated by the relentless tugging, the stallion jerked back his head, yanking the youth back several staggering steps. The youth's gaze turned inward and he shook his head, perhaps reprimanding himself for allowing his own impatience to interfere with his ability to perform his duties. He placed a hand on the stallion's neck to calm him.

Yiloch covered the last bit of distance to spare the young man any further conflict with the particular stallion. The youth held out the reins, bowing as he did so, and stepped out of Yiloch's path.

"Your majesty. Lord Captain Adran sent word that your horse should be made ready for you."

He took the reins, appreciating Adran's forethought. For a few seconds, he considered asking the youth how long he had been waiting with the stallion in order to see how far behind his captain he was, but the boy looked tense enough to burst in his own skin already. It would be cruel to further rattle his nerves with unexpected and ultimately irrelevant questions, especially when Yiloch really didn't have time to worry about such things.

"Thank you," he acknowledged, letting the youth take care of punishing himself for yanking on the sensitive horse. "You may go."

The youth's face flushed bright in the flickering torchlight and he bowed deeper before turning to hurry back to the stables, his abrupt departure drawing a snort from Tantrum. Yiloch swung up on the dappled grey stallion and turned him toward the inner gates, stroking his neck to sooth him. Mounted, he had a better vantage and could move around the considerable inner courtyard and the city itself much faster. The inner gates stood open for now, allowing for the quick movement of troops into and out of the city.

He urged Tantrum up to a ground-eating trot, passing fast through the gates. Unless things went horribly wrong, the battle would stay outside the outer city wall.

As he moved out into the city, he spotted a number of adepts, marked by the symbol of an eye with a star pupil embroidered in silver on the shoulders of their grey and blue uniforms, moving about amidst the soldiers and the few civilians not holed up in their houses. Most of them looked bone-weary and tense. The ones who looked the worst were those with the strongest connections, he suspected, the ones most sensitive to the Grey Army's intimidation tactics.

I hope you are all stronger than you appear.

Most of them had seen some level of conflict when he took the empire from his father if not before then, but the Grey warlord had introduced a few new challenges already. It would be foolish not to expect more.

Yiloch experienced a puzzling blend of excitement and dread as he considered the prospect of facing off against this new and challenging foe. It was thrilling to have a worthy opponent. His father hadn't been, not really. His destructive behaviors had made it easy to gain allies within the imperial army and therefore easy to turn the tides once he was dead. With Indigo there and the timely arrival of others, even Myac hadn't proven that hard to overcome, though he was still out there somewhere wreaking havoc on their lives. The many recent trials with Ferin's loss and his estrangement of Indigo made him hungry to lose himself in fighting this enemy, despite the risks. He would have to be careful not to make any mistakes as a result. Arrogance had a sharper edge than any blade.

A blue light flared on the outer wall to the right of the main gate, drawing the figures of Adran and Ian out of the darkness. Yiloch turned Tantrum toward the nearest stairs and pulled the stallion up at the bottom, leaping off before he had fully stopped. He took the stairs two at a time and hurried over to join the two men. Hax was there as well, eyes narrowed as she leaned on the wall, peering out into the darkness. Yiloch scanned the lands beyond the wall. Movement was discernable in the dark, but only if he focused hard.

"Ian, can you create a light out there, just for a moment. I want to see what we're facing."

Ian nodded. A pinprick of light appeared in the sky halfway between the outer wall and the line of trees that followed the river. Then the light burst outward, illuminating the entire expanse for several heartbeats. A mass of mounted warriors filled the open fields. They were statue still, aside from the few horses that spooked at the flash. In the brief light, he saw that they carried no shields. There was nothing obvious to protect them from arrows launched from the wall. It was a disconcerting statement of confidence in their barriers. The scene exuded an ominous calm. The warriors waited like patient cats, ready to pounce the instant their prey let down its guard.

I will not let down mine, Yiloch thought with a satisfying burn of defiance.

"Have you had any luck breaking through their protections?"

Ian glanced along the wall. A group of adepts was gathered there. One twitched and turned to face Ian, responding to some silent summons from the creator. She gave a slight shake of her head, her distressed look conferring all the information Yiloch needed. He emitted a soft growl of frustration as he glared out into the darkness. Ian, recognizing that Yiloch already had his answer, wisely held his silence.

There was no order issued, no battle cry from the fields, but suddenly the wall shuddered beneath them as if struck with a massive wave. A few cries of alarm rang out along its length and an almost feral snarl came from Hax.

"Fire your lead archers when the light appears," Yiloch commanded, glancing from Hax to Ian.

Hax gave the order the moment Ian illuminated the opposing army and a volley of arrows whistled through the night. The arrows stopped several feet short of the lead riders and clattered to the ground, useless. The light vanished again.

Yiloch cursed, pounding one fist against the cold stone of the battlement. The wall shuddered again as another wave of power struck it. At least he understood now why the army carried no torches. They didn't need light for an attack like this and the darkness concealed them from the Lyran army. The lack of sight would put the defenders on edge, but he wasn't willing to waste his ascard resources on illumination. He had a feeling they would need every resource they had in the days ahead.

"Ian, if your adepts haven't figured a way to break their barriers yet, then we need turn our attention to finding some way to block their attacks or this wall will come down." Ian nodded and turned, jogging over to the adepts. Yiloch turned to Hax. "Get some units working to move people back behind the inner walls. Be discrete, we can't fit the whole city."

"Yes, my lord," Hax replied, her lip curling as though his orders had come with a bitter taste. She headed down the stairs then, calling out orders with every step and soldiers jumped to carry them out.

The hint of predawn light was beginning to spread across the scene. Yiloch ground his teeth as he looked out over the attacking force. There were thousands of them. Like a vast colony of fire ants, they would swarm in when the wall fell and begin a similar attack on the inner wall.

Another violent tremor shook the wall then. It would go down if the adepts didn't figure something out fast. The cracking and grinding of stone rang out around the front portion. Time stretched while he waited to feel the wall tremble again and the city behind him was silent, as if its residents waited with him, holding their breath in fear and anticipation.

Ian trotted back over to him.

"We've managed to block an attack by combining

the power over the group into a shield of sorts, but it's going to take a heavy toll on energy to keep it up," he reported.

Yiloch nodded. "They shouldn't be able to sustain these attacks without draining their adepts as well."

Ian's apologetic grimace wasn't comforting. "Because they're used to working this way, they won't be burning through as much power as we will because of our inexperience. They have a lot of adepts out there who are clearly trained in this kind of unified defense and assault."

"Set a group to blocking the attacks for as long as they can. I don't want you to be one of them. I may need you for other things later. When the first group starts fading, we'll decide whether to start a new group on that task or retreat. In the meantime, if you have any ideas for bringing down those barriers, they would be very welcome."

Ian nodded, his silence on the matter expanding the hollow dread in Yiloch's chest, and returned to the team of adepts.

Yiloch shoved despair to one side and faced his advisor. "Adran, tell Hax we need our soldiers ready to retreat on a second's notice. I have a powerful feeling things aren't going to go the way we would like them to."

Adran nodded. He looked tired, but Yiloch envied him his inability to feel the power that was going into the Grey Army's attacks now. The earlier intimidations had been unnerving, but these waves of power were stunning in their force and seamless perfection. If only they could break down those protections. Even then, the battle would be a hard one. Every mounted warrior for as far as he could see was armed and he suspected all of them, adept and soldier alike, were skilled with their weapons. At least physical combat would be an improvement over the growing feeling of helplessness.

He pounded the wall again, snarling in frustration.

•

The sun had been up for a few hours when Theron joined them on the wall. The first group of defending adepts was fading. They sat against the inside edge of the wall now, more than one of them with their eyes closed as they focused all of their attention on blocking the attacks. Each one looked exhausted, their faces ashen, their lips pressed tight together. Several of them winced on occasion and, given the timing of the reactions, he suspected they were responding to attacks against the wall, each one a little harder to stop than the last.

Beyond the wall, the Grey Army remained patient and unmoved by their feeble resistance. They knew as well as he did that this was only a delaying tactic.

Before acknowledging the emissary, Yiloch turned to Ian.

"How long has it been?" he asked with a deliberate glance toward the group of adepts.

"Less than four hours," Ian answered.

"How many groups do we have to throw at this?"

"Based on skill set and strength of connection needed, I can probably come up with about five more effective groups."

Yiloch leaned on the parapet, scowling out at the invaders. "That only gives us about seventeen hours of defense assuming every group holds out for about the same amount of time. Maybe a bit more if their adepts start to weaken. How much time will the first group need to recover?"

Ian chewed at his lower lip for a moment and Yiloch took advantage of the pause to nod to Lord Theron so the man would know he had been noticed. Theron offered a slight nod in return, his attention on Ian.

"We could swap out the last group with the first and rotate them through that way, but after this much exertion the groups may not be as strong the second time around."

Yiloch shook his head, his lip lifting in a silent snarl as the wall trembled. "Get another group ready to take over and come back. We need to discuss our options."

Ian nodded and hurried back to the group of adepts.

Yiloch met Adran's worried gaze. "Adran, get word around to Commander Hax that we should move at least two-thirds of the army behind the inner wall now." The wall trembled again. This time, he did his best to ignore it. "The rest should be ready to retreat..." He trailed off when he saw Leryc coming up the near stairs, taking them two at a time as he himself had earlier.

The young captain strode up to them, giving Theron a curious glance then catching Adran's eyes in a gaze rife with longing and fear before bowing to Yiloch. "My lord, Cadmar sent a messenger in via the port. There are reinforcements in the valley just to the north. About 2000 strong. They await word from you before making a move."

Cadmar was no fool. An outright attack while the barriers were up would have resulted in the slaughter of those 2000 soldiers. In sheer numbers, the Lyran force was greater than the Grey Army now, but unless they figured out how to destroy those barriers, it gave them no real advantage.

"Send word that they should remain hidden. I'll have an adept send out a blue signal over the palace if we get the opportunity to attack. If an orange signal goes up, they should retreat to safety."

Leryc lowered his gaze and drew a deep breath. After a few seconds, he released it and nodded. "Yes, my lord. I will see that the message is sent."

Ian joined them again as Leryc departed and Adran went in search of Hax. He nodded once to indicate that the next group was busy blocking attacks. The bleakness of his expression wasn't encouraging.

Turning away from that discouraging look, Yiloch's gaze lit upon Theron who was staring out at the Grey Army with a look of intense concentration.

"There must be some way to fight them."

"If you have any ideas, I'm open to hearing them. Our adepts simply aren't strong enough or practiced enough at working together to bring down those barriers or continue fighting this assault for long," Yiloch admitted with a tight edge of anger in his voice. "If you're going to leave, now would be a good time. I suspect we will be evacuating some others before the day is out."

Theron shook his head. "If this army was up against Caithin, I'm afraid we would have even less chance of fighting back. I have an interest in seeing them defeated here. I think I'll stick around for a while. Learn what I can and hope for a breakthrough."

Yiloch nodded and gazed out over the untouched enemy army.

Less than three hours later, the next group of adepts broke down.

CHAPTER FIFTEEN

The last few days of travel were miserable for Indigo. All the Kudaness warriors kept their distance from her, giving her dark looks for the way she had dared to use ascard in front of them. For that, she would not apologize. The man had died far more peacefully by her method than he would have by theirs, though she continued to fight the ache in her chest at having forced his end when his body refused to let go on its own. What gave her that right? What gave any of them that right?

Suac Chozai still held on to his anger over the sucar incident. Adding this new infraction to the mix only served to increase the tension between them. His anger wasn't as easy to ignore given that she did still feel a nagging remorse over taking the sucar without asking. In the end, though, she didn't care if they all ostracized her, so long as they continued to march north toward Lyra.

They were getting close. Less than a day at the current pace and they would be at the gates of Yiroth, or at least as close as they could get with the Grey Army in their path. It was almost eerie how well she remembered this area from when she passed through with Yiloch's army not such a long time ago. A lot had changed in such a short time. She no longer felt like the same person. Her ability with ascard had grown considerably, though it still failed to gain her what she wanted most. Mostly it had helped her become a murderer and an outcast. Even here, where the Kudaness had accepted her as a priest, that power was making her unwelcome.

Still, she did appreciate many of the advantages it offered.

She spread her ability throughout the army of dark-skinned, tattooed warriors. When she touched Suac Chozai, she narrowed it to a guiding thread of ascard and began to weave her horse through the bristling warriors, their spears making a field of spikes from her vantage. At the end of the thread, she found the Murak suac walking with the other suacs. She bowed her head in a show of respect as they glanced up at her and, although there were numerous frowns of disapproval, they opened a path for Chozai to move over beside her.

"Suac Chozai, may we speak?" she asked in Kudaness, pausing only a little as she struggled with the right words.

The suac gave her a dark look, but he nodded. "We speak already. What do you wish to say?"

"We are close to Yiroth now." Despite the uneasy jitter of her nerves, she pressed on, reverting back to the Lyran trade dialect for expediency. "Perhaps it would be wise to ask the gods what lies ahead."

"You wish to use the sucar again?"

The tension in his tone discouraged her. Still, she wasn't about to let him cow her now, not when she had gained so much ground through being stubborn.

"It makes no sense to charge in blind when we have the means to look ahead at what waits for us." Chozai said nothing, but she could feel a tangled web of emotions warring within him. "Do you disagree?"

He shook his head. "Your words ring true, but the last time you searched, you did not find what you were seeking."

"Then perhaps you should be the one to walk. It isn't necessary for me to go."

His brows went up and he turned a shrewd gaze on her. "That you are willing to let me go alone speaks well of what you have learned, but this is still your spirit journey. When we stop again, I will come and guide you."

She inclined her head in a nod to express respect for his decision and moved back out to the edges of the army where she could more easily ignore the bitter glances so many of them cast her way.

When the army stopped for their brief midday rest, Chozai sought her out with the sucar skin in hand. The urgency in his manner gave her a small twinge of satisfaction. Now that she'd brought it up, he was as eager as she was to learn more. They found a secluded spot on the edge of the clearing and sat facing one another. Chozai held the skin out to her. She hesitated. He had never offered it to her first. Was there some significance to the gesture? Perhaps he didn't really intend to follow her. He had tried to kill her before. After all their confrontation in the last few days, might he be hoping to incapacitate her to rid himself of the burden? The others certainly wouldn't hold it against him.

He frowned, the movement of muscles in his face bringing the tattoos to life for a few seconds. "This is your walk," he said in Kudaness. Then he shifted back to the trade tongue. "This time, you will lead. I will watch and guide if needed."

She nodded, a warm flush infusing her cheeks when she realized her hesitation was only perpetuating the mistrust that had built up between them. After all the progress she made before in gaining acceptance with him, it was foolish to keep pushing things back the other direction. She accepted the skin. Her eyes met his dark copper ones as she tipped her head back to drink. Despite the horrid taste, she had trouble making herself swallow the foul liquid sitting on her tongue. What did her eyes look like now? Were they becoming like his, like the eyes of all the suacs?

She forced the swallow, fighting a blast of nausea. He took the skin from her as the sucar rushed through her system. Their surroundings spun out of focus, sinking her fast into blackness.

"You know what you want to see."

She glanced to her side, finding Suac Chozai standing there, swaying to the odd rhythm of the poison. Around them was blackness, an empty void. Frustration pulsed through her, passing out from her in the form of an orange haze that dissipated into the darkness. Chozai struggled to hold back a grin that finally won out and she scowled at him.

"I knew what I wanted before, but I never found him. I only—"

Chozai cut her off with a sharp hiss. "That is between you and the gods. Perhaps you did not want to find him as much as you believed."

She scowled at him and her irritation now became a red haze in the darkness around them. The suac chuckled for a second then his gaze gained an almost palpable weight.

"You have great power, Indigo un Ani. Your mood alone molds this experience. Focus that power. Use it. I cannot teach you to control the walk as we do without a great deal more time. You must use those skills you already have."

"But… you don't believe in using ascard in that way. I've been reminded of that time and again. Now you want me to use it," she questioned with an edge of exasperation, though she was already opening up the connection within her to begin probing about in the darkness for something that might guide her.

"The gods have not chosen to strip you of this power when you walk with them. It seems that they must want you to have it. If that is true, I think they will let you use it to find what you seek. If you die using it here, then we will know I was wrong."

She rolled her eyes at him, but she was only partially paying attention to his words now. The ascard around her was completely malleable, formless on its own without any distinguishing signature. Closing her eyes, she thought of the city of Yiroth, as she had seen it from the outside with Yiloch's army. She thought of the city itself and the walls, of the magnificent palace nestled within.

"Impressive."

The tightness in Chozai's voice made her open her eyes. They now hovered above the city and surrounding land. Below them, thousands of Grey warriors were gathered. The glow of an orange sunrise filled the sky, which meant that what they were seeing had either already happened, or had not happened yet. A large section of the massive outer city wall was reduced to a pile of rock and mortar. More of the fierce warriors were within the city already and numerous buildings burned unchecked.

Her stomach twisted into a cold knot. Bile rose in her throat and she forced it back down. Trying to hold her focus, she moved over the city to where the defenders had retreated behind the inner wall. Yiloch stood on the wall near the main gate, his silver hair blowing in the wind, his pale eyes flashing. He was engaged in a heated discussion with Hax and Adran. One hand toyed with the hilt of his sword, hungry to put it to use. He was magnificent, but ineffective in his rage against this enemy, a state that would only make that rage burn hotter. A little further down the wall, Ian stood amidst a group of adepts, his face full of concentration, desperation, fear. As they watched, the inner wall trembled with an assault from the adepts within the mass of Grey warriors sitting bold on their mounts outside the wall.

She heard a moan of anguish and realized it came from her own lips. The anguish morphed to desperation, and then fury burst to the surface, drowning everything else. The scene vanished, returning them to the blackness, but this time the dark, again reflecting her emotions, flashed with bolts of light like lightning.

Chozai met her eyes for a few seconds, his expression unreadable, then he vanished. She pulled herself forcibly from the sucar's hold.

Leaning to one side, she retched, then turned to Chozai, wiping her mouth with the back of her hand. She took a mouthful of the water he offered to rinse her mouth and spit.

"We must move, now," she demanded, handing the water back to him.

"It will take a good four hours for our warriors to reach the city, and they will need to rest and refresh before they attack," Chozai said. "What we saw takes place at sunrise, more than likely this coming sunrise. The gods rarely show what has already passed."

She ground her teeth. Looking around, her eyes came to rest on her horse and she nodded, resolute.

"I'm going to go ahead. Join me as soon as you can." She stood and he rose with her, his hand closing on her wrist.

She met his eyes, drawing on ascard to push him away with force if necessary. He released her arm, seeing the determination in her gaze.

"It doesn't matter how strong you are, Indigo un Ani, you cannot fight them alone."

"No, but I might be able to bring down their barriers or at least figure out how to buy the time you need to arrive."

Chozai held her eyes for a long moment. Finally, he stepped back and nodded his head once. "The gods be with you. We will follow as soon as we are able."

She returned the nod and strode to her mount. Swinging up in the saddle, she turned him toward Yiroth and kicked him up to a canter, fast leaving the Kudaness behind. From there, she drove the gelding as hard as she dared. She had no desire to injure the horse, but the images of the collapsed outer wall and the inside wall shuddering under their attack pressed her on.

Fear and worry created a painful lump in her throat and twisted her stomach in knots that resisted her healing skills. With the Grey Army protected behind their barriers, Yiloch's soldiers and adepts would be unable to fight them. They might be able to hold them off for a time, but the power necessary to overcome those barriers wasn't going to be found among the adepts Yiloch had available to him.

Barriers and masking were things she had a natural aptitude for and, with her power, she didn't doubt that she could find a way to bring them down. She had to. After this last use of the sucar, her connection to her inner aspect felt stronger than ever. Still, the Grey Army's controlling adept was skilled at his work and powerful in the sheer number of adepts whose power he had feeding into his own. It would take all of her strength to overcome them, perhaps more, and if she did succeed in bringing down the barriers, she would be weak and vulnerable to any adepts or warriors that chose to come after her. The Grey warlord had been aware of her before when she tested the barriers. There was no reason to believe that he wouldn't be aware of her when she tried to bring those barriers down. She would have to be very careful.

She was familiar with the landscape on this side of the city, but not infallibly so. As night fell and she suspected the road was bringing her close to the open fields outside the city, she reached ahead with ascard. When her power touched the river no more than four or five miles ahead, she drew it back and slowed her mount. The animal required little encouragement, stumbling to a walk, his head swinging low as his sides heaved. They proceeded at a more measured pace while she scanned the area, wary of stumbling upon scouts from the Grey Army.

The gelding dragged his feet along wearily enough that she finally dismounted. She could lead him from here as fast as he would walk on his own and he needed the break. A twinge of guilt pierced through her when she noticed sweat running in rivulets down his legs. Droplets spattered to the ground from his belly, shimmering in the light of the rising moon.

She spared a tiny fraction of power to ease the animal's distress on a mental level so he might recover faster physically. It wasn't much, but it was something, and she might need him again soon.

They hadn't walked for long before she could hear the river. She pulled the weary horse along, forcing herself not to reach ahead and search out the Grey Army now. There was no point in wasting the energy and risking detection. This time, line of sight would have to do for information gathering.

She skirted through the woods around the river town, not wanting a close look at what the army had left behind there. A small side stream that flowed toward the river offered some guidance and provided a spot where she and the horse could drink without fearing contamination from potential carnage up the river. From there, they followed the stream to where it joined the river and she searched out a calm, narrow spot where they might cross without much exposure.

This close to her objective, she began to consider the possibilities. The first time, when she had breached the army's barrier to learn more about them, she had detected hundreds of adepts in their midst, their power funneled through one adept. If that adept focused all of the power on the barriers, then it would be a much greater struggle to bring them down. The assault on the walls, however, had to require a fair bit of that power. If that assault were in progress when she went after the barriers, she would have a better chance of succeeding. There would be a strong link from the barrier to the controlling adept and, through him, to the other adepts, which presented another appealing opportunity. If she could bring down the barrier in such a way as to send the power surging back through that adept and along those connections, she might be able to disable a large number of the Grey Army's adepts in the process.

You might even kill them.

Jayce, lying dead on the floor of her apartments, swept to the forefront of her mind, his blank eyes staring up at her. She pushed the image away. Now was not a time for guilt. There were too many lives at stake.

Before proceeding beyond the river, she checked again to make sure that her connection to Ian was blocked off the same way her connection to Yiloch had been for some time. That link alone, if left active, might be enough to warn the warlord of her presence. The thought of letting Ian or Yiloch know of her presence through that link before she began work on the barrier, of giving them reason to hope, was tempting, but not worth the risk of discovery.

After the river, she remained in the cover of the trees to avoid attracting the attention of anyone in the fields beyond. She could see the besieging army before she heard much. There were none of the usual noises or smells of war. This was a silent, insidious siege. Under the light of the moon, she could see that the outer wall still stood. In the fields between the tree line and the outer wall the Grey Army appeared to be patiently waiting. If not for the power she could feel being directed at the wall in waves, she might have believed they meant to starve Yiloch's people out.

She wasn't going to get any closer without someone spotting her. Her attack would have to happen from here unless she wanted to try to work around to the port side where she might be able to get closer, but that would take too much time. Time she was sure they didn't have.

Indigo wrapped the gelding's reins on a tree branch, leaving enough length for him to forage and keeping the wrap loose enough that he could work free if she didn't return. The animal stopped and hung his head, lipping halfheartedly at the ground in a weary attempt to find food. She took the ring she had given Yiloch off and put it in a saddlebag in the unlikely event that someone who knew them both would find it if things went wrong.

Walking a short distance away to put herself out of range of the horse's feet if he moved around, she found a smooth spot next to a tree and sat, leaning back against it. The trunk was strong, a solid living presence to support her physical form. Sight didn't matter for this and would likely be more distracting, so she closed her eyes, knowing it might be dawn or later before she opened them again, if she ever did. With a small bit of ascard, she forced calm over herself. Then she took the time to investigate her own shields and barriers, testing their strength and tying them fully into the ring that Yiloch had given her so that she would not have to maintain them actively while she worked. The draw on the ring would push its limits, but she hoped to be done before it weakened too much.

The simple tasks of securing her protections calmed her more and her heartbeat began to even out, her breathing becoming slow and deliberate. When she felt ready, she refocused her inner aspect using it to gather ascard from the air, earth, and even the trees, drawing in as much as her environment could give. When it felt like the power gathered in and around her might be enough to destroy an entire city, she channeled a small thread toward the army, masking it meticulously as she sought their protective barriers. Her pulse and breathing sped up when she encountered the extraordinary creation. Pausing, she spared a moment to calm herself again. She was only going to get one chance at this, it had to be done right.

When she was ready, she continued, her working slow and deliberate, meshing her power into that of the barrier rather than pushing through it, making her presence simply one more in the hundreds of ascard signatures already integrated into it. The barrier protected the army from physical weapons as well as from direct ascard attacks, but this wasn't a direct attack on the army or even a direct attack on the barrier. It was a joining. The barrier itself had no safeguard against the subtle way she was insinuating her power into it. Even with that lack, it was a beautiful thing, like an immaculately woven gown. It felt almost criminal to destroy such artistry, but they had used it to destroy so much. They would continue to destroy things she loved if she let them go on unchallenged.

When her meshing was complete, she moved through the barrier, finding the primary connection to it that marked the lead adept. Inching along that connection, she felt her way to the adept himself, stopping every few minutes to be sure that he hadn't noticed her actions. The necessary caution was maddening in that it made progress slow, but it was the only way she could hope to succeed. When she touched his inner aspect, she created a discreet link that would guide the backlash of power released when she destroyed the barrier. That backlash would certainly kill him, but it might not harm the other adepts in the army.

With the utmost caution, she began reaching power out along the binding links through which the lead adept drew power from all of the other adepts in the army. Taking them a few at a time, she tied the inner aspect of each one into the guiding link so that the backlash would affect them all. It would weaken after it passed through him, but any level of harm it caused the other adepts would help Yiroth.

Time was ticking by, the wall getting closer to collapse with each assault, but impatience would destroy the delicate web she wove. She would need to dissolve each point of the web immediately after the power surged through the connections or the destructive force of the backlash would rebound along it and hit her as well. Better that though, than failure.

Her physical body stiffened when she recognized the ascard signature of one of those adepts. Turning all of her attention to that one point for a moment, she followed the link and found the clear signature of Myac's inner aspect. She reached in to his inner aspect and investigated the link that bound him to the lead adept. The nature of the binding was invasive, forced, leaving Myac only enough connection to ascard that he would be aware of the way the other adept used his power. It was a cruel torment and she could hardly imagine a more deserving victim. He had come after her and now he was the one imprisoned. There was a certain justice to it and yet she felt no joy. Knowing his power was at the Grey Army's disposal only brought fear. She had to succeed.

With even greater resolve, she tied a strand of the web into his inner aspect before moving on to the next set of adepts.

•

The wall shuddered, dust rising as cracks formed. Adran grabbed the stone parapet to keep from falling. Yiloch did the same, his face twisting with rage again, before he closed it off, forcing calm once more. He wasn't the type to take defeat easily and Adran could only imagine the black vortex of fury boiling inside him now. All day long, they had tried different attacks, both with physical weapons and with ascard, to no avail. The enemy's shields were impenetrable. The emperor's storm-filled eyes turned to where the adepts were working. Adran followed his gaze to see Ian walking toward them, his expression grim.

"What's going on?" Yiloch asked, the barest edge of frustration apparent in his tone.

Ian's voice was thick with disappointment. "They're putting more power behind the attacks now and our defenders aren't that strong. They must have had more adepts in reserve. Their barriers are as strong as ever," he added at the flicker of interest in Yiloch's eyes.

Yiloch closed his eyes and shook his head. Adran swallowed, trying to ignore the growing pit of despair hollowing out his gut. When those pale eyes opened, they still burned with a fevered determination that made him almost believe they stood a chance.

"A few more solid hits like that and the wall will come down. Do you have a group you can put to work behind the inner wall so this group can move back?"

Ian glanced back at the adepts. The struggle they were putting up was plain in their pained expressions. The young creator sighed as though the fate of the world rested in his hands. Too much responsibility for one so young, even someone as strong as Ian. Turning away from the adepts, his eyes swept back past them and came to rest on the Grey Army, nearly invisible again in the fallen dark.

"I have a group that can manage long enough," he answered.

Yiloch nodded. "You've done well, Ian," he said, trying to counter the defeat in the creator's voice. In these dismal circumstances, the fact that the other man even put out the effort to be supportive made Adran love him that much more.

Ian ducked his head in an evasive semblance of a nod and turned away. "I'll get the others going so we can retreat."

Theron cleared his throat as Ian walked away and they turned to him.

"I have a few adepts on the warship that might be able to add their strength. They have the right skills in their repertoires."

"Will they work with our adepts?" Adran asked.

Theron met his gaze, recognizing the issue. His eyes were full of steely determination that Adran had to work not to flinch away from. It must be worry for Indigo that drove him to offer up his own resources to their cause. Strange how she managed to bring help to them, even when she was miles away. Jealous as he might be of Yiloch's love for her, he had to admit that it had proven beneficial at times.

"They will if I tell them too," Theron replied.

"Captain Leryc," Yiloch called to the young captain just down the wall.

Leryc hurried over, his eagerness to serve Yiloch written plainly over his fine features. His gaze caught Adran's for a few seconds, a sad smile touching upon his lips before he focused on their leader. "What can I do, my lord?"

"Leryc, I need you to tell Hax to sound the retreat to the inner wall. Then gather an escort to take Lord Theron down to his ship and back."

"Yes, my lord." He gave a quick nod and turned to Theron. "Lord Theron, if you would come with me."

As Theron and Leryc started down the stairs, the wall trembled again. Loud cracking rent the air and dust billowed as stone ground together. Adran caught himself on the parapet and took hold of Yiloch's upper arm with his other hand to help balance him. Both Theron and Leryc were knocked off their feet, but managed to catch themselves before toppling down the stairs. When the dust cleared, the two men were already on their feet again. They both glanced up at Yiloch, perhaps to reassure themselves that he too was still standing, before resuming their hasty descent.

"Perhaps we should also head down," Adran suggested, releasing his hold on Yiloch's arm.

Yiloch turned and stared out over the night-shrouded fields beyond the wall. Behind them, the retreat sounded. Adran balled his hands into fists, hating the sound, hating the meaning behind that sound. Yiloch turned away from the field and stared down at his retreating troops, a small force still waiting below to escort him in. In a motion so fluid and silent it was almost dream-like, Yiloch drew his sword, spun and swept it down. The created blade, backed by his ascard-enhanced speed and strength, cut into the pale stone and a large corner of one merlon dropped to the ground with a solid thud.

Whether he meant to take the first piece of the wall himself or the action was simply an outlet for his anger was unclear. Adran wasn't about to ask. He longed to help in some way. To save the city they both loved and ease the fury and anguish in Yiloch. Right now, it was ascard power that dominated the battlefield and that put it well outside of his expertise. Every soldier in the army probably shared his frustration at this point. Knowing that didn't make it any easier to deal with. Unless the adepts and creators back at the palace working to find a weakness in the barriers came up with something, the best they could do was try and get out of this with their lives.

Yiloch's ascard users were trying. Ian had been checking back with them all through the day and into the night to see if any of their ideas or discoveries would prove useful. So far, none had. The young creator was also working on the problem at all times, the glazed eyes and furrowed brow attesting to the fact that he was wielding ascard in some way every free moment. If only he could find an answer, anything at all to get them out of this hopeless position.

A hand rested on his shoulder and he met Yiloch's eyes. So much misery in those beautiful eyes. Adran had to fight a sudden painful tightening in his chest. There was nothing he wouldn't give to see Yiloch succeed, he'd proven that in the past, but this situation left him helpless.

Yiloch's expression changed, a gentle smile touching his lips and eyes for a moment. "Come, my friend, it's time to go."

Adran nodded and they headed down the wall.

Back inside the inner wall, they handed off their mounts and found Ian standing in the middle of the vast, crowded courtyard. He and the young woman next to him were both staring at nothing, their faces masks of deep concentration. They stood close enough that their shoulders touched. Hundreds of soldiers moved around them. Aware of the importance of their work, everyone left the two a buffer of several feet of open space so as not to disturb them. They all understood that their fate, the fate of all Lyra, was in the hands of ascard users at this point.

Adran followed Yiloch over to stand before the two and they waited, the soldiers widening their berth and offering respectful nods to their emperor as they passed. They were arranging in ranks and units as much as possible in the limited space. Their expressions were bleak, but determined. If the enemy protections came down, they would be ready to attack. Archers lined the walls, waiting for the sound that would signal them to let their arrows fly, hoping against the odds that it would still come. That determination filled Adran with a sense of pride, though hope evaded him. Glancing at Yiloch, he saw the emperor also scanning over the troops and the activity on the walls, his lips pressed in a grim line.

"They are strong and brave," he muttered. "I hate to let them down."

"I believe they feel the same way about you."

The two adepts before them animated suddenly, eyes regaining focus as they shifted a few steps apart. Ian seemed unsurprised to see them, though the woman's eyes widened and she inclined her head in a hasty show of deference, making the tiniest dip with her knees as though tempted to curtsy, but unsure if it was appropriate.

"My lords," she breathed.

With the faintest of nods to acknowledge the woman, Yiloch rested his intense gaze on Ian. "Any progress?"

Ian frowned, gazing at the woman for a long moment with a certain thoughtfulness in his regard. "Terea said she noticed a small change in the barrier, but there isn't anything now." The woman gave him a sharp look and he amended. "All I can sense is that the barrier seems a touch stronger. Perhaps they pulled another few adepts into the link."

Yiloch considered the woman for a moment and she held her head up as if trying to appear confident in defense of her observations, but her entire form leaned a touch back from him.

"What are your primary ascard skills?"

"I...," she trailed off, something in Yiloch's gaze making her glance away. She focused on Adran as though finding comfort there and he noticed that she had pale amber eyes that reminded him of Eris. "Masking mostly and some illusion."

"You're a creator?"

She nodded, her gaze still locked on Adran as she shuffled her feet back a fraction. Eris, with a wild smile and mischief flashing in her amber eyes appeared in his mind. He wished the woman would look away.

"Keep investigating, Creator Terea." Yiloch's tone was gentle now, suggesting that he had noticed the effect he had on her. "See if you can find the source of this added power."

Finally, she looked at Yiloch, her eyes not quite meeting his. "The masking on the new power is very thorough. I can no longer separate it out from what was already there. I'm sorry."

A flicker of a smile, laced with bitter hope, touched Yiloch's lips, the faintest upward turn at the sides of his mouth.

Following his thoughts, Adran asked, "You say it was masked?"

She looked at him again and he had to struggle not to turn away. "Yes, very well. I've never seen such superb masking."

"I'm changing my orders," Yiloch declared. "Don't touch the new power. Don't even acknowledge it. If you do, we may all regret it." Her eyes widened and she shuffled back another inch. "Keep searching for anything else, some weakness in the barrier. You've done well."

"Yes, your highness." She glanced at Ian who nodded once. Without another word, she bowed her head to them each and hurried away.

"Ian, why would they mask any power going into their barrier? Have they masked anything else that you've found?"

"I can't think of a reason and Terea would have noticed it if they had. She's very good. The guiding adept has done everything very openly, almost to the point of boasting." Ian's expression brightened the tiniest bit.

"You don't think?"

"It seems like a remote chance, but we haven't got many options left. If there is any chance at all that she's out there trying to do something, we don't want to be poking around drawing attention to her."

"Agreed. I'll see to it. I'm going to go check on the adepts up on the wall."

Yiloch nodded. "We'll come with you."

A group of riders charged in through the partially closed gate as they prepared to climb the stairs up onto the inner wall, Theron and Leryc among them, which meant that the three other Caithin men were the adepts. They waited at the base of the wall as the five riders approached and dismounted.

"Good work Leryc," Yiloch acknowledged. The young captain gave a tight smile and inclined his head. "Go tell Hax to make sure everyone is ready to move if we get a chance to fight."

"Yes, my lord." He glanced once at Adran, his gaze overflowing with longing. Given the uncertainty of their future, Adran shared his yearning. If only they could afford a moment to be together, but this wasn't going to be that moment.

Leryc trotted away and Yiloch turned to Lord Theron and his men, all of whom bowed.

"Emperor Yiloch, this is Adept—"

Theron broke off. A cry of pain drew their attention to the adepts on the wall as one slumped over, rendered unconscious with the efforts of his exertions. Yiloch took the stairs two at a time with Adran and Ian following on his heels. Before they reached the top, a loud rumble shook the ground and dust billowed out in a massive cloud at the far edge of the city as the front section of the outer wall collapsed. Ian sprinted to the slumped adept, then turned and motioned to Theron. The emissary went over taking his adepts with him and the group fell into intense discussion.

Adran stood beside Yiloch, staring out at the cloud of white dust beyond the city that glowed in the moonlight like a ghost of the wall. As the dust began to settle, they could see Grey warriors already moving in to clear the debris and make an easy path into the city. They were now at their last line of defense. The Grey Army would be in the city soon and they were running out of adepts who could block their attacks. One way or another, the waiting was almost over.

One after another, Indigo created links to each foreign adept, her physical body fading from her awareness as she moved along weaving an increasingly complex web of destruction through the Grey Army's ascard users. She was the barrier now, indistinguishable from the creation the adepts had made, and she was the web along which the power of that creation would blast back upon them when it was destroyed. When the links were finally all in place, she did a second pass through them and discovered, with a pang of disappointment, that the warlord had no connection to the lead adept and therefore wouldn't suffer with the others. Someone else would have to deal with him when she finished. Even if she survived, she wouldn't have the strength.

She moved her presence to the peak of the invisible barrier and drew on more ascard, pulling in as much as she could handle. When she had collected everything she could, she realized with a cold despair that it wasn't going to be enough. The creation of the web and the ascard she had been using to mask all of her activity drained her to the point that the power needed to bring down the barrier was now out of her reach. A scream rose in her throat, but the distance between physical body and awareness was enough to make the reaction dissipate.

Focus.

All she needed was access to another inner aspect. Someone else's strength that could help gather and hold all the ascard she needed for this to work. It seemed like such a simple problem. Power was all around her, with the hundreds of adepts in the web, but if she tried to force control of someone's inner aspect, they might resist and the lead adept was certain to feel the change. The only answer was to draw on someone outside of the army, but it would require a good supply of energy to make the reach into the city and mask it along the way. There was no one there, not even Ian, with the strength necessary to make up the difference. To make it work she needed someone within the army to willingly link with her along the connections she'd already created. If they worked together, they might be able to break the lead adepts binding and bring down the barrier before he could react.

Seeking out the proper thread, she moved cautiously back into Myac. Someone else controlling his power had to be driving him mad and he was no fool. He had to know that the death of the lead adept would free him. If only he would let her show him what she meant to do. The only real drawback was that, if she linked with him in that way, she would have to protect him from the backlash as well or suffer it through their link.

She touched upon Myac's inner aspect, careful to avoid the binding of the foreign adept. She allowed him to feel her presence, knowing he would recognize her power after all the encounters they'd shared. There was a ripple of tension through him that she hoped the strange adept wouldn't notice or would perhaps dismiss as a reaction to the assault on Yiroth. Pulling back a fraction, she remained still for a moment, when there was no change in the flow of the insidious ascard, she touched on Myac again.

Would he even figure out what she wanted? His own connection to his power was reduced to a whisper. Still, if he let her connect through that, she was sure she could use that connection to free him from the other adept and take advantage of his considerable power to help destroy the barrier before the man could do anything. If Myac fought her, however, the other adept was going to notice and everything could be lost.

First, she broke the link she'd created that tied him into the web. Then, tugging at that whisper of ascard that was still his, she drew him with her, letting him ride on her power so she could show him the web she had woven. He would have to translate what it all meant. The slow process of moving his restricted power picked at her patience. She yearned to move into her physical body and open her eyes to see how much time had passed, but she was too far removed and deeply enmeshed in the barrier to risk such a maneuver now.

Finally finishing the tour of her web, she moved them both back into his inner aspect and released him. She waited for a short time. When he didn't react in any way, she tugged at the thread of ascard again to try to prompt a response.

Myac! It must be now.

She tried to impart the urgency through the touch of her power. If he thought it over for too long, someone might notice the spider's web of destruction she had woven into the barrier. It would take very little to destroy the web that she had spent hours creating.

That small bit of power he still controlled embraced

her with sudden desperation and he opened his inner aspect to her power. Without hesitation, she wove her ascard into him, meshing their power into one force. Then she took hold and pulled on his inner aspect, ripping it from the other adept's grasp. Power akin in strength to her own flowed into her, the ascard signature of Myac blending perfectly with her own. So much glorious power.

Struggling not to be swept away by the intoxication of so much power, she used it to draw in more ascard from outside the barrier. The ascard that coursed through her now numbed her physical senses, bringing with it a feeling of elation and invincibility. Somewhere in the trees, her lips curved in a euphoric smile.

The moment was now.

Surging all of that ascard power up into the barrier, she blasted it apart. The ascard in the barrier itself and the ascard she had used to destroy it all surged through the web. For mere seconds, she let herself feel the backlash sweeping out, then she broke away, taking Myac with her. With the last little flicker of strength, she unwove herself from Myac and fell away, plummeting back into her physical body and continuing a spiral down into darkness.

•

Yiloch could see the group of adepts now blocking the attacks in the faint light of predawn. Dark circles formed under their eyes and the Caithin men were becoming almost as pale as their Lyran counterparts in their fatigue. Most members of the group were strong adepts with a good mastery of the necessary skills, but a distinct racial tension added stress to the blend. Even with that, they had managed to hold off the assault for over three hours. There were no more among their ranks with the skills necessary to block the enemy attacks. Those who had defended the previous day weren't recovered enough to pull off a long stretch of blocking and the wall wouldn't hold up to the army's unblocked attacks for long. This was their last stretch of defense for the wall and they still had no better plan. Whatever Terea had sensed before, nothing had come of it. The brief hope was gone and now rage and frustration pulsed through him like a poison.

He scowled down at the warlord who watched them with an eager, arrogant smirk. Very little of the warlord's army had entered the city. Perhaps 500 warriors at most waited in the streets. Arrogant was an understatement.

Nearly an hour ago, Yiloch sent Adran to lead Lady Auryl, her family, and several other important nobles and merchants to the port through the back trails along the rocky beach. He was to see them to a ship and secure additional ships ready to set sail at a moment's notice. Evacuation of as many people as possible was starting to look like their only recourse. The possibility brought with it an almost blinding fury, but he had taken Yiroth once, he would do so again if he lost it now.

All of a sudden, Ian and all of the other adepts and creators on the wall staggered as though struck. Adran, who was standing between them, managed to catch the creators arm before he fell from the wall. Even Yiloch felt a concussion much like that of a catapult stone sending a tremor through the ground, but this tremor went through the ascard and none of the archers along the wall were affected by it. There were anguished cries outside the wall and he watched in astonishment as numerous Grey warriors recoiled, some falling from their mounts, their faces twisting with agony.

There was a moment of confusion on all sides and he turned to Ian. The creator had one hand on Adran and another on the wall as though he needed help standing, but he was smiling. There was a maniacal sparkle in his pale eyes that gave Yiloch a faint chill. A bolt of power shot from Ian. It drove out above the main street, creating a line of blinding red light several blocks long, then molten rain sprayed down from it onto the warriors lining the street. Shouts of pain and panic filled the air as their hair caught fire, their skin and armor searing under the molten droplets, their mounts panicking.

"Fire on all targets!" Yiloch cried. "Prepare to open the gates! Send up a signal for the reinforcements!"

He wasn't sure who did the deed, but blue signal flashed in the brightening sky above the palace to signal the reinforcements. At the same moment, arrows flew and Grey warriors fell under the assault, their barriers gone. The ones who had fallen first must have been adepts whose power maintained the barriers, though they had been armed and dressed in the same fashion as the other warriors. The Grey warlords smile was gone and he had turned away, looking back into the city. The fire rain and arrows bounced away from him, suggesting that he maintained his own protections. He started shouting out orders in a strange tongue and led a retreat heading full speed out of the city.

Yiloch turned to Ian. "What happened?"

"Someone destroyed the barriers. They must have channeled the energy back into the adepts controlling it. I felt death all through the army out there."

"Who could have done something like that?" Yiloch asked. He knew the answer, but he needed to have it confirmed, to force himself to acknowledge the implications.

"Only two adepts I know of have anything near the kind of power that must have taken," Ian said. "Somehow, I don't see Myac rushing in to help."

Yiloch gazed out towards the forest. "Then she's out there somewhere."

"Yes," Ian replied soberly. "Somewhere, on the other side of them."

"She? You mean my daughter." Theron who had been nearby, watching over his adepts, stepped up to the wall now and stared out in earnest.

The slip, calling Indigo his daughter, warmed Yiloch toward Theron even as cold dread made a knot in his stomach. He lowered his gaze and saw the Grey warriors pulling out of the city to rejoin the army beyond the remains of the outer wall. Fathoming the kind of power she controlled was beyond him, but he doubted she could have much left after that performance. Dozens of Grey adepts lay dead outside the inner gates. If Ian was correct, there were many more dead beyond the outer wall. If the Grey warriors found her now, she wasn't going to survive the encounter.

"Hax, gather the units. We're going out now." He turned to Theron. "Get inside the palace. If things should go badly, I expect you to get to your ship."

Theron narrowed his eyes and Yiloch braced for the argument. Then the man glanced out toward the trees again and nodded.

"Yes."

Lord Terral was at the gate already, riding at the head of his soldiers. Yiloch wondered at his uncommon eagerness to enter battle, unless he hoped to atone for his crimes. There wasn't time to question it now. He rushed down the stairs, leapt on Tantrum, and moved him into place as his army prepared to charge. When the gates were open, the army surged through. Most of the Grey warriors had already retreated beyond the ruins of the outer wall seeking to rejoin the main body of the army where they would have an advantage. Many remained in the city as well and Yiloch broke Lord Terral and Captain Leryc off with units to run a sweep. They would kill any Grey warriors and save who they could among those residents who were still in the city.

Yiloch knew he needed to give the Grey Army as little time as possible to regroup. Right now, they were unprotected and disorganized. The panicked response was enough to tell him that this turn of events was completely unexpected and unplanned for. This was the moment to come down on them with all of his force and try to crush them as one might a horde of ants invading the kitchens.

Lyran soldiers, on foot and mounted, rushed through the main streets of the city in pursuit of the Grey warriors. Adepts and creators went with them and some reached ahead, using ascard to sweep more of the debris from the wall aside and create a wider path for his army to pass through. Within moments, they were surging out through the destroyed wall. Their anger and the power of their pent up frustration charged the air, carrying the feel of a violent storm approaching out upon the field. The sensation lifted Yiloch, pushing him to a height of bloodlust that was exhilarating. He let out a war cry that his soldiers echoed as Tantrum leapt a portion of the fallen gate that was missed in the sweep.

Meeting the eyes of the first Grey warrior he spotted, Yiloch smiled and raised his sword. Steel met steel with a satisfying crash, the physical impact jarring through him, real and brutal. He turned Tantrum and the stallion struck out mid-spin, catching one leg of the warrior's horse with a steel shod hoof. The other animal shrieked. It staggered and the rider fell forward into Yiloch's thrust sword, blood gushing over the blade as it sank into his throat.

After so much time spent waiting for his city to fall before this unstoppable force, seeing their blood spill drove his hunger for battle to a fever pitch. Steel clashed all around him. Voices cried out in pain or anger. Hooves pounded the earth. The music of conflict played on all sides. A murderous grin on his face, Yiloch spun Tantrum around again and they quickly found another partner to dance with.

CHAPTER EIGHTEEN

Myac reeled, the world spinning around him while he kept a death grip on the saddle. Despite the growing light of dawn, blackness threatened at the edges of his vision and he heard the screams of dying adepts all around him. The backlash Indigo had unleashed upon the army's adepts with the destruction of the barrier was violent and lethal, a maelstrom of wild power. All that saved him from that power was her protection, something he imagined she wouldn't have given if it weren't necessary. Now it was up to him to get out of the middle of an army that was about to engage in full scale battle. The trickle of strength he had held back from Indigo the instant she broke Ini-jnai's hold over him would have to be enough to keep him safe.

All around him, the warriors were in confusion, trying to grasp what had happened as adepts intermixed within their ranks collapsed from their mounts, the majority of them dead before they hit the ground. He couldn't tell if Ini-jnai was alive or not since Indigo had broken that binding. The foreign adept still had his key stones, but he had ridden with Ksa-jnai into the city. They left Myac out toward the back of the army where he wasn't going to be noticed. Perhaps they feared the defenders would make annoying rescue attempts if they saw one of their own. Little did they know that most of those behind the city walls would be more apt to try to kill him than save him.

Beyond a desire for revenge, Ini-jnai's fate was unimportant. He was free. It was the time to make his getaway and regroup. Before Indigo unwove their ascard—that magnificent storm of power they created together—he had managed to track her location through their temporary link. He knew where she was when she destroyed the barrier, though he could no longer feel her.

Struggling against lightheadedness and nausea, he gathered his focus enough to turn his horse toward the woods. He kicked the animal hard, steering it through ranks of warriors as the sounds of thundering hooves and battle cries rang out from the city. Real battle was about to begin, the kind where blood stained the ground and people bled out from non-lethal wounds or were trampled to death in the melee. The kind of battle he wasn't interested in being a part of in the best of circumstances.

As though someone had called them by name, the warriors turned toward the sounds of impending attack and drew their weapons. A few tried to block Myac, swinging at him with their short-hafted spears, but it took very little ascard to knock those attacks away. Minutes later the horse was diving into the trees and he steered it haphazardly in the direction he had sensed Indigo, still fighting to hold his seat with the ongoing dizziness.

If not for the horse tethered loosely to a tree, he might have missed her, might have even trampled her. At the last second, he managed to pull his stocky mount up and turn him. The abrupt twisting stop in combination with his distorted sense of balance sent him sprawling to the ground a few feet shy of her. Pain lanced through the injuries Ini-jnai had poorly healed and through the older wound that she had inflicted on him. Tears sprang to his eyes and he lay there on his back for several moments gasping for air and waiting for the treetops to stop spinning.

He could hear the sounds of fighting now. Steel clashing. Cries of rage meant to bolster courage. Screams of agony. Sounds that chilled him and helped clear his head. This wasn't a safe place to linger. Rolling over, he got to his feet and stumbled to her side.

For a minute, he could only stare at the still figure leaning against the foot of the tree. She was dressed in Kudaness clothing and he could see that she was still breathing, albeit shallowly. He knelt down beside her and brushed her hair away from her face, exposing a dark tattoo on one cheek. He sucked in a breath, his heart skipping a beat when he recognized it as an elegant rendition of the symbol of the Kudan priesthood.

They had taken her, a Caithin, a woman, and an adept, into their sacred priesthood?

"What a remarkable creature," he murmured, tracing the lines of the tattoo with a finger.

She looked calm, peaceful, as though the task she had accomplished had lifted all the weight off her shoulders. Perhaps it had. Where Myac had been doomed to watching the army tear down Yiroth and many of his hopes with it, she had managed to intervene against odds that appeared insurmountable. Odds that would have driven so many people to simply give up. She had drastically improved the chances of victory for her beloved Yiloch and his city and she had saved Myac's life.

Whether through necessity or some sense of mercy didn't matter, though he suspected it was the former. His ability was his again. When he fully recovered from the power she had drained from him to take down the barrier, he might even be able to fix some of the damage Ini-jnai's less than precise healing had left.

He reached out to her with his power, curious if she had suffered damage from the backlash and scowled. Her elaborate shields and maskings blocked him, as strong as ever. In her unconscious, weakened state, she should be completely unguarded. He traced her figure with his eyes, enhancing his vision with ascard until he detected an anomaly at her left hand. It was the ring, the elegant pearl ring Serivar's wife had admired over dinner. As he probed at the object, he finally broke into its myriad protections. The piece was as magnificent in its hidden purpose as it was in its external design. A considerable amount of ascard had been worked into it, mostly protections, and her barriers were tied neatly into the mix. He couldn't stop a grudging smile in admiration of this creation that had undoubtedly caused him difficulty in locating her more than once.

He leaned down, intending to take the ring, and stopped as the sound of fast moving horses reached his ears. Given the direction, there was little doubt that enemy warriors were coming in search of her now, which suggested that at least some of their adepts had survived to track her.

He hesitated, brushing her cheek again with his fingers. So soft. So vulnerable. He could kill her now or he could leave her for them to kill. Somehow, both options were inadequate. Inadequate and so much less than she deserved. There was no true hatred for her left in him, not like the hatred he harbored for Yiloch or Ini-jnai. She was a beautiful and worthy opponent, someone he would prefer to defeat with his own skill and ingenuity. With his plans falling apart around him, their rivalry was one of the few things he had left worth savoring.

Myac leaned close, pressing his lips to hers in a soft kiss as he slid the ring from her finger and dropped it into a pocket. She was beautiful and worthy, and far too powerful to be allowed such advantages.

Rising, he turned toward the sound of the approaching riders, walking forward to place himself between them and Indigo. He could see them through the trees now. A quick search with ascard revealed nine individual riders, two of them adepts weakened by the power backlash. He shook his head in disappointment. Ksa-jnai expected her to be too weak to fight and he wasn't wrong. Too bad, he assumed she was alone. Even as weak as he was, he was still far more powerful than anyone in the approaching group.

Smiling pleasantly, he waited until he was sure they had seen him, then he lashed out with several blades of power. Nine heads rolled, some of the bodies falling instantly, others staying with their mounts as though prepared to continue the attack for several strides before they slumped over and fell. Indigo's horse only flinched as the confused mounts bucked and bolted around it.

He leaned against the tree, feeling the drain of that effort after everything else that had occurred. The kills were quick and simple, but he delighted in the thought that Ksa-jnai and Ini-jnai, if they still lived, had probably felt the abrupt loss of those men. It was worth the heavy drag of fatigue.

Now he had to decide what to do with Indigo before more came.

When he turned back, he started, his gut churning with dread. They were no longer alone. A Kudaness high priest stood next to the tree now. His copper eyes bored into Myac, as though they could see to his soul. Myac doubted they really could or that gaze wouldn't be so steady. Would it?

"She is not yours," the high priest declared in the trade dialect.

His deep voice and his presence radiated power despite the fact that he had no active connection to the ascard that Myac could detect. He hesitated. The odd power the suacs controlled made him uneasy, but this was only one priest. Gathering his power, he prepared for an attack, fighting the growing weakness, then faltered. In the trees beyond the priest, he saw more coming. There were Kudaness warriors moving through the trees as far as he could see with several more suacs at their head. White-hot rage ignited within him, but he suppressed it. A mistake here, as worn down as he was, could prove fatal.

"Time will tell," he growled.

He bowed with mocking respect to the suac and turned away. As soon as he was mounted, he glanced at Indigo once more.

Kill her?

He should kill her and bolt before the others had time to react. More of Ksa-jnai's warriors were coming from the other direction now. He could hear them and feel them. A lot more.

Not like this.

Myac turned the horse away, aiming deeper into the woods in a direction that would take him away from the fighting, then he urged the animal to a trot. Let the Kudaness deal with the coming warriors, and with Indigo, for now.

•

Blood ran in thick streams off Yiloch's blade. He spun Tantrum with leg cues and blocked an attack, then urged the stallion forward and rammed the attacker, sending the warrior reeling back onto a waiting Lyran blade. His eyes met the Lyran soldier's eyes for an instant before he wheeled the stallion back around and charged another Grey warrior on foot. The warrior's eyes narrowed and he ducked under Yiloch's blade at the last second. When he spun Tantrum for a second attack, another Grey warrior leapt from his mount, slamming into Yiloch. Tantrum went over and Yiloch threw himself clear, bringing his dagger around into the vulnerable point under the other man's arm as he fell. He landed heavy on his back with the warrior dead on top. For a few seconds, his world was a flurry of feet and hooves. Then he was on his feet again. The man he had attacked initially lay on the ground with scorch marks around his lips and eye sockets, burned out from the inside with ascard.

Another Grey warrior turned to face him. Yiloch shifted his blade for a block. A strange guttural cry rang out and the Grey warrior checked his attack, backing off suddenly. Glancing around, Yiloch watched as a group of Grey warriors drove back his soldiers, leaving an open space around him. A hole opened in the mass of bodies around that space and the Grey warlord entered. His black eyes blazed with fury. His lip rose in a silent snarl and he lifted his spear-like weapon to point at Yiloch.

A string of angry words came forth that meant little to Yiloch, but he thought he could guess at the general intent.

There was little doubt, judging from the way the warlord handled himself and his weapon, that he faced a capable opponent. There was no room for uncertainty here. Yiloch stepped into a fighting stance. Whatever went on beyond this circle was of little import now. He got the impression the Grey warriors would not interfere with their leader given the speed with which they had backed off and created a space for this confrontation. His own soldiers would intervene given the opportunity, but that wasn't something he dared count on now.

The Grey warlord attacked, his charge low, swift, and fierce. Yiloch had watched their style enough to expect such an attack, though the speed with which the man moved caught him by surprise. The point of the blade snagged a joint in his armor, digging into the flesh over his ribs before he could spin away. The pain made his breath catch.

Backing off, he eyed the warlord with new respect. The man's movements were unnaturally fast, fast enough they had to be enhanced by ascard. He faced a warrior adept like himself, someone who used ascard to boost his ability in combat. The thought brought a thrill of anticipation with it as well as a touch of dread. This fight would be a true challenge.

The next attack Yiloch evaded at the last second with a touch of extra ascard speed. He spun back and his blade missed the warlord's right arm by a small fraction. This time the warlord backed away. Now he understood Yiloch used the same methods and his expression turned thoughtful. After a moment, he gave the slightest nod, then smiled and charged. Yiloch swapped himself with the ascard in the air behind the warlord, but when he reappeared, the warlord was already facing him and Yiloch barely deflected the blade, the edge cutting a shallow gash in his thigh.

Frustration blasted through him and he attacked. Holding on to the power to speed his movements, he charged in on the warlord with a flurry of strikes, catching the blade deep in the biceps of the other man's right arm before he managed to predict and block the rest of the attacks. The warlord reeled back and glared, pain twisting his expression as he switched arms with his weapon. He attacked fast, the blood that soon ran down Yiloch's sword arm showing that he used the weapon proficiently with either hand.

They engaged again and again and Yiloch drew blood several more times, but his own wounds were increasing in number faster than his opponent's and his sword arm was growing heavy. Pain, the general loss of blood, and the fatigue of using ascard were all starting to tell on him and none of his own soldiers had managed to breach the circle yet, assuming they even realized what was going on amidst the chaos of the fighting. The odds looked less favorable with every passing moment.

The warlord swept in again, his attack high this time. Yiloch moved himself into a new space, but his reaction time was slowing. He backed away again with a deep cut along his jaw. Warm blood streamed down his neck and under his armor to mix with his sweat. With the mass of fighting bodies around them, direction became confused and a grey haze now threatened at the corners of his vision. The warlord was weakening as well, but all his stumbles meant was that Yiloch had barely enough time to block his attacks. The attacks themselves were still stronger and faster than he could manage in return.

Lightheaded and dizzy, Yiloch staggered. The warlord lunged, his cruel smile hinting that he expected this to be the end of their fight. Yiloch lifted his sword. Too slow. Much too slow. Something struck him from the side and knocked him out of the line of attack. He hit the ground, the churned earth grinding into the gash in his arm. The impact and pain stunned him. Before he could recover, the warlord hit the ground in front of him. The man's black eyes stared into his without expression. Blood gushed from a long gash that ran down from the edge of his jaw on the left to his collarbone on the right, laying his throat open.

A dark hand moved into Yiloch's line of sight, offering assistance. Fighting dizziness, Yiloch followed the arm up with his eyes to find a familiar face hovering over him.

Suac Chozai.

There was a distant sting of wounded pride as he realized the other man had finished the job for him, that he had been unable to defeat the warlord alone. Too weary to care for long, Yiloch accepted the hand. It would take far too much time to struggle to his feet alone. The strength in the grip was reassuring. The suac had a shallow gash across his chest just below the collarbone, but appeared otherwise unharmed. Moving slow so as not to worsen the lightheadedness he felt, Yiloch looked around them.

Kudaness warriors surrounded them, fighting with the savage intensity that made them such feared opponents. Even the Grey warriors seemed stunned by their ferocity. A young Grey warrior shoved his way into the circle, dodging attacks with surprising agility and Yiloch tightened his grip on his sword. The man looked down to the body of the warlord lying at Yiloch's feet with a pained expression. Turning away, he let out a hoarse cry. More warriors picked up the cry and it gained momentum fast, spreading through the rest of the Grey army. The sounds of steel clashing faded as the remaining Grey warriors knelt and placed their weapons on the ground in apparent surrender. With the Grey warriors kneeling down, Yiloch saw that there were as many dark Kudan warriors on the field now as there were pale-skinned Lyran soldiers. More perhaps.

He offered a tight smile of gratitude to the suac and instantly regretted it for the resulting pain and the surge of fresh blood running from the wound on his jaw.

"I thought you predicted that my empire would fall," he said, grimacing as more blood ran from the wound, soaking the collar of his undershirt. How much of the moisture he felt against his skin was his own blood? More than was good, that much was certain. He leaned on his sword in an effort to appear steadier than he was.

Chozai shrugged. "It turns out that there are some things in this world that can change prophecy. Things the gods do not always show us."

"Like what?" he rasped.

"Like Indigo un Ani," Chozai replied, a flicker of amusement shinning deep in his copper eyes.

A flood of relief made Yiloch's head spin and he caught the stabilizing arm Suac Chozai offered him.

"Is she all right?"

Chozai answered him with a chastising scowl. The moment seemed to stretch for eons as Yiloch struggled against the darkness at the edges of his vision. Around them, there were still lingering cries, the sound that appeared to declare surrender for the Grey Army. He didn't know exactly why they had given up, though the sudden loss of so many adepts and the arrival of the Kudaness had certainly put them at a disadvantage. Steel still clashed in a few places, but a familiar cry rose up from his own people now. Victory. The sound made him feel a little stronger, even with blood running from his many wounds sucking away his strength. His people had won. Lyra was still his.

Chozai glanced toward the woods and said, "She is at least as well off as you are."

That wasn't extremely comforting given that he felt as though he'd been trampled by a herd of horses, but at least she was alive.

"My lord."

Yiloch turned toward the call, staggering like a drunk despite his cautious movements, and saw Lyran soldiers and Kudaness warriors parting to make way for Hax. Another soldier rode alongside her, leading Tantrum behind him. He could only vaguely remember when he had lost the stallion at this point. He took the offered reins and leaned against the sweaty animal.

"My lord, you look dreadful."

Yiloch chuckled weakly. He could imagine how he looked, bleeding from myriad wounds and struggling to remain upright. Hax was flushed, her hair soaked with sweat and a fair amount of blood in evidence, though he couldn't tell how much, if any, of it was hers. He closed his eyes for a moment and the ground lurched beneath him. He snapped them open again.

"Your wounds need attention," Hax stated, her firm tone telling him she would drag him to that attention if he resisted. "Ceryn will accompany you back to the palace. I can manage things here."

He wanted to argue, but he knew he didn't have the strength to. With a slight nod, he turned to Tantrum. Chozai stabilized him with a discreet hand as he pulled himself into the saddle.

"I need to see her," he said, giving the suac a hard stare once he was settled.

Chozai nodded. "There is much to discuss. You will receive us this evening. If she is ready, I will bring her."

Yiloch hesitated. The evening was still so far away.

"Go, my lord, or you won't be receiving anyone this evening," Hax prompted, her voice tight with sympathy, but unyielding.

Yiloch nodded and turned Tantrum toward the palace. The Grey warrior who had initiated the call to surrender met his eyes for an instant and then bowed low, touching his head to the ground. The frustration of not being able to understand the gesture fully only made his head spin more, but he managed to sit straight in the saddle. No one who saw him would know how much effort it took to stay astride the big stallion. Blood continued to run unchecked from his wounds and each step Tantrum took made the world swim in his vision. The ride to the palace took an eternity. Once there, he slid from the saddle with none of his usual grace. With the first step toward the doors, the world spun. His gut spun with it and someone caught him as his legs gave out.

CHAPTER NINETEEN

The usual elation and relief of victory evaded Adran. Physical, mental and emotional exhaustion had all taken their toll on him. The fear that Yiroth would fall and that Yiloch might not escape in time after he had only just returned had twisted him into thousands of knots of tension. Every muscle in his body taut with anxiety. Now the fear began to fade, leaving behind a painful mess of fatigued muscles and frayed nerves.

The soldier who came to the docks a short time ago with word of the battle's end had consented to escort the Lady Auryl and her family back to the palace in his stead. Adran assured them he would follow soon, insisting that he must first collect the names of the many captains who were in a position to suffer losses as a result of having their ships commandeered for evacuation purposes. They had to be swiftly and adequately compensated, so he had gathered his list. Then he took a few minutes to lean against a building and appreciate his ability to breathe again.

Yiloch was home. The enemy was defeated. Leryc was safe and alive and busy helping Hax. There was hope for a return to normalcy or whatever passed for such in this life.

There had been no good end in sight for this battle.

The destruction of the barrier, which took down most of the Grey Army's adepts with it, and the arrival of the warriors from Kudan were both unexpected. Without those things, they would have suffered an ugly defeat. However, neither event had actually ended the battle. According to reports, the Grey Army had surrendered the moment Yiloch killed their warlord. At best guess, it was some rigid battle protocol, perhaps founded in religious beliefs, that led them to surrender upon the defeat of their leader. Given the language barrier, guesses were all they had at this point.

The soldier said Yiloch suffered numerous injuries in his fight with the Grey warlord, but nothing that was life threatening now that he was receiving proper treatment. Many other wounded were being tended and the Kudaness were helping round up and contain the remaining warriors of the Grey Army until they could figure out what to do with them. There would be negotiations with the Kudaness after the enemy was satisfactorily contained. That kind of help never came for free. There would be some price. Still, with Yiloch injured, negotiations would have to wait for a while.

Adran took a deep breath, pushed away from the wall, and began his trek back to the palace to see how he could be of service and visit the coffers. He had promised immediate recompense to one captain who had been ready to set sail when they boarded his ship and started unloading cargo to make space for passengers. Most importantly, he needed to go see for himself how Yiloch was doing.

The soldier who came to the docks in search of him hadn't known how the barrier came down, but Adran had his suspicions. None of Yiloch's adepts had that kind of power. If he were right, would she be there when he arrived, tending to Yiloch? From the sounds of things, the emperor could use a healer's care. Then again, after such a feat, it was more than likely that she wouldn't have the strength left to help anyone. Perhaps she would be lying next to the emperor receiving treatment as well.

Somehow that possibility made him smile. No matter how or why she had wronged him, Indigo had, in his opinion, proven her love for Yiloch.

What he found in the palace entry and main halls was a wild flurry of activity. Those soldiers who weren't rushing around with the intense looks of men and women fulfilling important duties were standing watch over the many nobles and merchants who hadn't yet returned to their homes. Palace servants scurried about seeing to the needs of the soldiers and civilians both. All had a glow of relief in their eyes. Young noblemen and women were flirting and laughing to settle their nerves while the politically inclined nobility postured amongst their peers as though it were intended to be a political gathering of some kind. Already, they were trying to put the events behind them.

Adran huffed at the noise and bustle while he waved down a harried looking servant. The young woman, stray wisps of brunette hair that had escaped from her tight bun creating a halo around her flushed face, altered her course toward him. Brushing a strand away from her mouth, she bowed, her eyes never actually focusing on him. He suspected she was running through a list of things she needed to do in her head. She looked distressed enough that he almost apologized for bothering her before he reminded himself that it was part of her job to deal with this kind of thing.

"How can I help you, my lord?"

"I need to know where Emperor Yiloch is being tended."

Relief lit her eyes at the prospect of something she could take care of quick and painlessly. She nodded once and pointed to a hallway at one end of the room. "Down there. Second door on the right. You can probably still follow the trail of blood. We've cleaned most of it up, but we've not made it down that hall yet."

It chilled Adran that the room she sent him to was the same room Yiloch had kept his father's body in for a few days after he had killed the man. Why, of all the rooms in the palace, had they chosen to tend him in that one? It was no better suited to medical treatment than so many others were. Then again, it would probably appeal to Yiloch's sense of ironic humor that they were using the same room for him.

As she had indicated, there was still a smeared trail of blood running from the end of the hall to the door. Stepping to one side of the grisly mess, Adran knocked twice and walked in without waiting for an answer. The attendant who had been coming to answer took a quick step back out of his path. Adran left him to shut the door and walked to where Yiloch lay on a narrow bed on top of several layers of bloodied linens. His eyes were closed and his face ashen, but his breathing was steady. A woman was carefully stitching a long gash along his jaw while another surgeon, this one an elderly man, sat stitching a deep wound in one arm. Several other wounds had already been tended and still another man was holding pressure on a wound in one thigh.

Adran winced, resisting the desire to touch him, to feel the warmth and the pulse that would prove he was alive rather than relying on the faint rise and fall of his chest. There was a peculiar twist of disappointment that Indigo wasn't there. Had she been the one to take down the barrier or had someone else figured it out? And why was Yiloch unconscious through this process? If he had simply blacked out from loss of blood, shouldn't the pain of the stitching have woken him?

The three working on Yiloch ignored Adran. They were very intent on their work, so he turned to a young man seated at the foot of the bed. It appeared that he was only watching at first glance, though the inward focus suggested more.

"How is he?" he asked in a whisper, trying not to jar any of them from their work.

The young man stirred as though waking and his pale lavender eyes flickered to Adran with a flash of irritation. Then recognition lit his eyes and his face warmed with a welcoming smile.

"Lord Captain Adran," he greeted. "Emperor Yiloch will be fine. He's lost a lot of blood. Some of those wounds were very deep, but it will all heal. Have a seat." He gestured to the bench he was sitting on.

Surprised by the warm reception, Adran accepted the seat. From here, he had all too good a view of the wound on Yiloch's jaw and he pressed his lips together with concern. Such a scar marring those perfect features would not please him when he woke.

The young man seemed to read his thoughts. "Don't worry. Lerana's very good. The scarring will be minimal."

"Yes, well, that's minimally comforting to hear," Adran returned wryly. "Why doesn't he wake?"

The young man chuckled softly. "Because I won't let him."

Adran shifted his seat to look at the youth. Pale, elegant features and long silver-blue hair tied back in a tail attested to strong Lyran heritage, though something in the strong brow hinted at a little bit of mixed blood. His focus was intent on Yiloch. Adran followed his gaze to the still figure on the bed and grimaced. How he yearned to do something more than watch. He envied the young man and the surgeons the skills that allowed them to help their emperor.

"Are you a healer?"

"Not at all. I grew up in a bad part of Tunsdal—"

"I didn't know there were any good parts," Adran interrupted.

The youth chuckled again and continued. "I learned at an early age that finding a way to use ascard to put thugs and thieves to sleep rather than killing them outright got me into a lot less trouble. Turns out the skill has other uses too." He indicated Yiloch with a wave of one hand.

"So it would seem."

"I'm Adept Ryn," he glanced at Adran, offering an encouraging smile. "I promise you, Emperor Yiloch won't only come through this fine, but he won't feel any of this pain."

"Thank you," Adran murmured.

He stayed there silent for a long time watching Yiloch breathe. His breathing was slow and even, suggesting that he really didn't feel any of the pain of their ministrations. That was comforting at least. He wasn't going to wake in a good temper though. If Adran hurried out to the docks now with the compensation for the one captain, he should be back in time to help the emperor when he woke. "I'll leave you all to your work.

Take good care of him."

Ryn smiled. "We promise."

Adran nodded. Yiloch was in the best possible hands for now. "Thank you. If Emperor Yiloch wakes up before I'm back, tell him I went to the docks to settle some things."

He left the room reluctantly and collected the necessary funds before heading back along a different meandering route to the docks. It took some time to focus past his concern for Yiloch and the pleasure of knowing he would be all right. The sight of several building fires being contained brought him back to the reality of the situation. Worry over Yiloch had kept him from thinking of the other lives they had stood to lose in this conflict. So many dear companions had been lost over the last few years. Ferin had joined the list that included commander Dalce and his sister Eris. How many more close companions had nearly died in this battle? How many people whose names he would never know had been lost?

By the time he arrived at the docks again, an ache of loss filled him.

Leaning against the corner of a building, he closed his eyes and drew in a deep breath. The smells of the sea and the pungent aroma of fish were comforting. The city suffered a brutal blow, but Yiroth would recover. They would all recover. Even he would eventually recover. Lingering on the things he had lost did no one any good. He was no good to anyone, especially Yiloch, in that state.

Adran opened his eyes and considered the ships rising and falling on gentle waves. Pushing away from the building, he walked out along the dock to the Gilded

Dancer. Someone else was on board talking to the ship's captain. Perhaps he should wait. Then again, this would only take a moment of the captain's time and the man was probably eager to be on his way. It would be rude to hold him up any longer.

Adran ascended the plank onto the ship and started toward the two conversing men. When he was only a few strides away, the captain glanced at him and nodded respectful acknowledgement. The man speaking to the captain turned also and shock froze Adran. Though his hair and eyes were now a pale, more natural color, Adran knew his face.

A glimmer of surprise flickered in Myac's eyes, but he smiled as though spotting an old friend.

"Lord Captain Adran," Myac greeted, adapting to his arrival with chilling ease. "I hoped you would join us soon. Good Captain Lachard is ready to set sail. Are you prepared?"

Adran opened his mouth to say one of the many hateful things running through his mind. Instead, he said, "Yes." His stomach knotted, fear curdling in his gut as he spoke the word and his lips curled up in a smile, an expression far opposite of what he intended.

The glimmer of cruel satisfaction in Myac's eyes before he turned back to Captain Lachard made Adran want to scream and run and yet he could only stand and watch. Control of his body, of his voice and expressions, had been taken from him. How? Why? What had the evil bastard done to him?

"You're going also?" The Captain lifted one thick eyebrow in curious inquiry.

Adran found himself nodding. "Yiloch has unfinished business in Demin," he answered.

"Very well. If you have my compensation, we'll get moving."

Adran nodded again, handing Captain Lachard the pouch of coins. The captain opened it, dumping them into his palm. Myac shifted his weight from one foot to the other, showing a hint of nervous impatience while the man counted. When he looked closer, Adran could see that Myac had deep circles under his eyes and there was a new scar on one side of his face. Whatever hardship he had endured, he still seemed to have enough energy to wreak havoc.

Dumping the coins back into the bag, the captain nodded satisfaction and said, "Tal will show you to your quarters."

"Thank you." Myac's smile was polite, masking his apparent exhaustion for a moment.

Help me. Adran hoped the desperate message would get through somehow when he met the captain's eyes, but the other man only nodded once and turned away to manage his ship. The adept touched Adran's elbow and they followed the indicated crewman, heading for the steps that would take them below deck. His mind raced, panic screaming below the calm surface. At least above deck, there was a chance someone would see him and wonder where he was going, someone who might come to question or at least take word back to the palace. Below deck, even that small hope was gone. Adran struggled for control of his body, but it ignored his every effort.

Myac leaned close and murmured in his ear. "Don't bother," he said. "You have no chance against me." Leaning away again, he spoke at a normal volume. "I'm so very glad you could join me, Lord Adran. This little trip promised to be quite dull alone."

Adran felt a shiver run through him, but it was only in his mind. His body refused to respond even to that.

Despite being held asleep for two hours having his wounds tended, Yiloch's concern for his city, his people, and for Indigo, wasn't enough to fend off the natural sleep his body needed. After assisting him to his personal rooms, the surgeons left him and he drifted into an exhausted slumber. The fight with the Grey warlord haunted his dreams. In those dreams, Suac Chozai didn't arrive on time. Each time the warlord's final blow struck him, he woke with a start, then exhaustion would drag him down into sleep again and the dream would start over.

Yiloch started awake yet again, though this time it wasn't the dream that stirred him. Pain shot through every wound. He ground his teeth against it and struggled up to sit on the edge of the bed. There was another knock at the door and he got slowly to his feet. He limped to the door, trying not to pull the stitches in the wound on his thigh. When he opened it, a young, unfamiliar page was lifting his hand to knock again, his brow furrowed with lines of anxiety. Jerking his hand back to his side, he knelt and bowed his head.

"My lord."

"What is it?" Yiloch asked, unable to keep the strain of weariness from his voice.

"My lord, the surviving Grey warriors are fully contained and under guard. The Kudan suacs have requested an audience."

"Demanded it, I imagine."

"Yes, my lord," the page confirmed, his voice faltering.

"Thank you." Yiloch rubbed at his temples, struggling against a threatening headache. "Have them brought to the throne room in thirty minutes."

"Yes, my lord." The page rose and bowed before turning to leave.

"Wait." The page stopped, turning back with his head bowed as though he feared to look upon his emperor. "Is there a woman with them?" If she were with them, it would be worth the hassle of dealing with them immediately.

"I do not know, my lord."

Yiloch waved him away. The possibility of seeing Indigo set his nerves on edge. Their last encounter had involved death threats and much hostility on his part. He dreaded the reception he might get from her, especially now that he owed her a considerable debt for coming to Yiroth's aide. Why had she come? Had she convinced the Kudaness to help them? It seemed inconceivable that one woman could have done so, but they were here. Something had driven them to this action.

Where was Adran? He remembered someone saying something about Adran at the docks. What about Terral and Lord Theron? He cursed the injuries that left him in this state of pain with little awareness of what was going on outside his rooms. Hax was alive, which meant the prisoners would be handled with the proper caution. He had no doubts about her abilities. Someone had mentioned Leryc helping her. There was still Ian though. He hadn't seen the young creator since the fighting started. Was he injured? So many questions he didn't have answers to.

Yiloch grimaced and regretted it when sharp pain blazed through the wound on his jaw. Walking to the mirror, he wiped away a trickle of blood and pressed a linen to it until the bleeding stopped. Then he considered his reflection. The long gash marred smooth pale skin, a glaring red wound that would heal as a thin white scar. He had to fight back a scowl to keep from making the wound bleed again.

He summoned attendants to help him get into clean clothes, something appropriate for the coming meeting. Even with help, the process was a painful struggle. He pondered his sword. Someone had cleaned the weapon and placed it back on the stand in the sitting area of his chambers. The light of a late afternoon sun passed through the faceted crystal windows and lit the blade in fragmented rays. The weight of it would pull on stitches over his ribs, but he almost never went without the weapon. With a cautious exhale, he turned away, leaving the sword in its place.

To his considerable relief, Ian was waiting outside the door now, leaning against the opposite wall. The young creator had circles under his eyes, but he managed a weary smile that mirrored Yiloch's own. The simple comfort of Ian's supportive presence bolstered him, giving him a little more confidence for the coming audience.

"Have you slept?"

Ian shook his head as he fell into step with Yiloch, his stride checked to accommodate his leader's injuries. "Not really. There was too much to do managing the wounded and controlling the Grey warriors. Though, to be honest, they have actually been rather cooperative. Since I wasn't hurt, I felt like I should help."

Guilt twisted in Yiloch's chest. There would have been little point in him trying to stay out on the field though. His injuries wouldn't have allowed it.

"Has Adran returned?"

"Not yet." Ian started to walk at his normal pace then checked his strides again with an apologetic smile. "Hax has been managing quite well though. Adran sent word that he was staying at the docks a while longer to wrap things up with the ship captains. One of the adepts who helped with your healing said Adran stopped in to check on you before heading back out to the docks.."

Yiloch nodded. Adran was attentive to such things. Everyone always got the consideration they needed with him around. The man was a priceless asset, though he would rather have him by his side for this audience.

"And what about—"

"She's here," Ian interrupted. He glanced an apology at Yiloch then, his cheeks picking up a pink flush. "Sorry, what were you going to ask?"

"You already answered it. Have you seen her?"

"No, but I can feel her through the link now. I..." Ian trailed off, blanching when he looked at Yiloch this time.

Yiloch forced an easy tone though he felt like someone had stabbed a dagger into his chest. "I wouldn't expect her to re-establish the link with me after our last encounter. I am glad she is well, though."

Ian nodded and fell silent, his shoulders hunching as he drew into himself. They continued the walk to the throne room without speaking. Once there, Ian took his customary spot flanking the throne. Hax wasn't there, but several ranking soldiers were, including Lord Terral who sported a dark bruise over his right temple and a split lip. Theron was also there, standing near Lord Terral, his calm facade broken by the worry in his eyes. Yiloch took his seat on the throne, relieved to take the stress off his leg.

The waiting commenced. Yiloch had to focus to keep from fidgeting as he sat. He must greet the twelve suacs representing the Dursik un Kar properly in respect to their status and the aid they had given Yiroth. What he wanted to do was discard the formality and go to see Indigo. He needed to see for himself that she was alive and well. The wound across his jaw throbbed, the stitches pulling with every slight change in expression. Focusing on that pain helped him keep his regal, calm veneer when the suacs finally entered the throne room. Each suac brought only one warrior from his tribe, a silent commentary to their confidence in their position, a confidence they had earned.

When Suac Chozai entered the room last, Yiloch wasn't surprised to see his head held high and proud, a hint of smugness in his expression as those copper eyes stabbed into him. Then another figure entered, walking a step behind the tall suac and Yiloch's heart seemed to stop. The group halted inside the door. Each Suac and warrior stepped off to one side or the other, creating an aisle for Suac Chozai and Indigo, who continued forward. They both stopped at the head of the group and Chozai leaned closer to her, saying something soft in Kudaness that Yiloch couldn't quite make out. After a few dragging seconds, Indigo nodded and continued forward alone.

As she approached, he was shocked to see a delicate tattoo on her right cheek. Not any tattoo either, but the tattoo of the Kudaness priesthood. A vague recollection came to him of Suac Chozai referring to her as Indigo un Ani on the field. At the time, he'd been too disoriented by pain and blood loss to acknowledge it. When he looked into her eyes, he noted that they were a little different than he remembered. She looked confident and strong if perhaps a bit tired. She didn't need someone to support her. She certainly didn't need him. The realization was disheartening somehow. Then he saw a flash of teeth as she bit her lip, betraying her nerves, and his heart began to pound in his chest.

Curse this propriety. He was the emperor.

Yiloch rose and strode down the steps towards her, limping as little as he could in an effort to hide the extent of his injuries from her. A few of her steps faltered, her eyes widening, then she continued, stopping when they were only a few feet apart. He looked into her eyes and a protective anger rose in him when he noticed the flecks of copper within that beautiful blue. How dare they risk her life with the sucar.

His anger melted when she stepped forward, placing her hand tenderly over the gash on his jaw. He felt the wound healing, the stitches falling away. For a moment, he could see her as she had been their first night together in the prison, kneeling on the dirt floor before him to heal the cut in his arm, her eyes focused on the injury then as they were now.

Yiloch placed his hand over hers. She looked up at him, her copper flecked eyes brimming with hope and a shimmer of unshed tears. Relief flooded through him and he pulled her to him, wrapping his arms around her and closing his eyes while he breathed in her scent. She wrapped her arms around him in turn, squeezing tight. The pain the embrace caused in his wounds far eclipsed by the pleasure of holding her. He felt her trembling and realized he was trembling as well.

Everyone would be watching them now. Opening his eyes, the first face Yiloch saw was Suac Chozai's. The insufferable man was grinning like a fool. His expression turned stern the moment he met Yiloch's eyes and Yiloch grinned at him without pain.

He pushed Indigo gently back and looked into her eyes. There was so much he wanted to say. Instead, he leaned in and she rose onto the balls of her feet to meet his kiss. He kissed her tenderly, savoring the feel of her lips against his, the taste of her. It was hard to believe she was here, that she still wanted him despite all that had passed between them.

Suddenly he felt her within him. The link she had created so long ago, she reestablished now. The feel of her coursed through him and all of his wounds began to heal. Intense pleasure passed through the link, a happiness that warmed him like a fine wine. He had no interest in letting her go. Not ever.

"Indigo un Ani un Yiloch, if you might disentangle yourself we would like to hold council with the Emperor," Suac Chozai said in Kudaness, his tone soft with affection and pride.

They parted and Yiloch fought off a desire to cling to her. She was his to love, even the Kudaness priest had labeled her his. They had also bound her to them with the title un Ani and the tattoo on her face. Reluctantly acknowledging that she was not really his, he released her. Her faced was flushed when she stepped back and turned towards the Kudan priests.

"Of course," she replied, also in Kudaness to his surprise. "My apologies. I…"

She hesitated then and Yiloch followed her gaze. In a doorway near the front of the room, Auryl stood staring at them. By her shocked expression, it was clear she had been there for several minutes at least, long enough to see their intimate reunion. Auryl met his eyes for a few seconds, then tears broke from her eyes and she spun, running from the room. Indigo glanced at Suac Chozai. Yiloch felt a surge of distress through her link to him then a cold nothing. The dagger twisted in his chest again and Indigo flinched as if responding to that pain. Her voice was strained when she spoke.

"You do not need me for this, Suac Chozai. I will leave you to your politics."

Yiloch waved to a page standing near the door. The youth trotted quickly over, bowing his head.

"My lord."

"Please show Lady… Please show Indigo un Ani to a room where she can rest and refresh."

"Certainly. Follow me, my lady."

Indigo refused to meet his eyes, but she followed the page. He watched her go, itching to follow. He needed to speak with her before she bolted off on her own again. Would she wait?

As she passed through the doorway, Lord Theron met his eyes for an instant, and then hurried after her. Yiloch sighed inwardly, wishing he could do the same. At least Theron might keep her from running away.

"Indigo un Ani will need to be privy to our conversations going forward. She is to act as our ambassador in Yiroth. She will stay in the palace and protect the interests of the Kudaness," Suac Chozai stated as he too watched her walk away.

Yiloch struggled against a smile at the thought of Indigo staying in the palace. It wasn't his decision to make. Then the smile faded. Right now, he doubted she would even consider such an idea.

"I gather she doesn't know this," he remarked on a hunch.

"She will not disagree," the suac countered, confident.

"Are we speaking of the same woman?"

The fond smile curved the suac's lips again and Yiloch marveled that she had weaseled her way into this stern man's heart against all odds. At least she gave them some common ground. With her power and her charm, she was a considerable asset. If only she really would stay. He swept his eyes over the group of Kudaness, spotting several treated injuries.

"Come, I imagine we would all prefer to discuss things sitting down." He nodded to Ian who joined them as he led the way to a council chamber off the throne room.

CHAPTER TWENTY ONE

I ndigo, wait."

She turned in the doorway of the room the attendant had taken her to, recognizing the voice and the man behind her with a start.

Theron.

So much had happened and she was still so exhausted. It was hard not to believe she was imagining things. Her focus in the throne room had been so completely on Yiloch that she hadn't noticed her uncle. Relief burst through her and with it, all the stress, exhaustion, and hurt came crashing down. She threw herself into his open arms, tears flooding down her cheeks as she buried her face against him. With her ability active, she felt the adoration and relief surging off him when he wrapped his arms tight around her. She was so much more than some burden his brother's treason had pushed upon him. That sudden certainty made the tears come faster.

Theron stroked her hair, murmuring soothing words as he held her, moving her through the doorway into the room with a gentle guidance.

The attendant cleared his throat. "Would the lady like a warm bath?"

She was still crying too hard to respond, but she felt Theron nod. A door opened and closed, leaving them alone. When her tears subsided, Theron backed her away with a hand on each shoulder. He eyed her face and wiped at her damp cheeks with a soft linen.

"There. That's a little better. A strong woman like you shouldn't be drenched in tears."

She answered with a tremulous smile. "I suppose I don't look so strong now."

His warm smile brought the sting of fresh tears to her eyes, but she clenched her teeth and drove them back this time.

"Even the strongest of men would break down after everything I know you have been through, and since I probably don't know half of it, I'm more than impressed that you have held it together this long." He considered her in silence for a moment, concern joining his other emotions. His gaze lingered on the tattoo. "When I hoped for an ambitious child, I didn't expect The Divine to take me so seriously."

She sniffled and smiled. "Neither did I."

Theron laughed, but the furrowing of his brow warned her that the conversation was about to change. "You do love Emperor Yiloch. I find that a little hard to figure out, but I can't deny what I saw out there. I have to ask you to set aside all of that and answer me truthfully."

She had no trouble meeting his serious gaze now. This was a subject of great importance to her and those she cared for.

"Did he play any part in the assassination of the Caithin royal family?"

"He did not," she stated. "I know who is responsible..." She trailed off when he raised a finger to her lips and shook his head.

"Nothing is going to change tonight. Tomorrow, we will talk more. Right now, that answer is enough for me. You need rest and food, and a bath is certainly in order," he added, wrinkling his nose and giving her a teasing wink.

Unable to express her gratitude in words without bursting into tears again, she settled for hugging him. Theron kissed her forehead. Then he stepped back and brushed his thumb across the tattoo on her cheek, looking over her face as though hoping to etch it into his mind. He smiled, but there was a hint of sadness in that smile now.

"Get some rest. We'll talk again in the morning."

She nodded and watched him leave. There was a great deal they needed to talk about, but she had many things to consider now. Theron was highly respected in the Caithin high council, but she needed much more than the support of one man if Yiloch was to be exonerated of this crime. If she chose not to do things his way, would Theron forgive her?

She couldn't stop a bemused smile. It was probably a little late now to start worrying over what other people were going to think about her choices.

When the attendant came back through the servant door in one side of the lavish bedchamber, she followed him eagerly to the waiting bath. He showed her the waiting robe and offered to send food and drink. Without guilt, she requested that he send the finest Lyran wine in the palace along with the food. Yiloch owed her something for helping save his kingdom and for letting her think, even for a moment, that she really mattered to him.

She reclined in the hot, scented bath, wondering if some of the steam might not be rising from her own anger with him, rather than the heat of the water. The feelings she had read off him had felt deep and sincere. Was there some way he could deceive her ability that completely? She doubted it. Perhaps her own longing had deceived her, causing her to misread his emotions.

No. The emotions had been real. He might be skilled enough to deceive her in other ways, but he wasn't capable of lying to her ascard ability. In which case, he did love her. He did want her. And yet…

An ache of sympathy for the woman she had seen in the throne room brought the sting of tears back to her eyes. When Yiloch had seen the woman, there had been no sense of guilt from him, only a hint of resignation that touched her ability like a heavy sigh. The only hurt she sensed from him was in response to her own upset. How could he be so cold? The woman—so young, and beautiful, and dressed in attire befitting royalty—had been hurt by what she saw transpire between them. She must be his fiancée. Who else could she be?

Indigo rose from the bath and wrapped the soft robe over her shoulders. She eyed the bed.

Less than an hour ago, Suac Chozai had woken her. It would take a great deal more rest to restore her true strength, especially after exerting enough to heal Yiloch's many injuries.

She rubbed the spot on her finger where Yiloch's ring had been. When she woke, the ring was gone and Chozai's explanation for its absence haunted her still. He had informed her, in a somewhat disinterested tone, that a Lyran adept had been standing over her when they found her. He had been strong enough to take out a number of Grey warriors who came searching for her. This man must have taken the ring, he said. His description of the individual wasn't a good match for anyone she knew, but after the way Myac had disguised himself in Caithin, she was only willing to give so much weight to a physical description.

She sighed and walked over to sit in a chair beside the fireplace. There was far too much to think about for her to go to sleep now. Instead, she gazed into the flickering flames, prepared to consider all that had passed in the last several hours and how it might change things going forward.

A knock on the chamber door startled her awake. A serving woman, who had brought a tray of food and some wine while she was sleeping, and who was now tending the fire, met her eyes. When she nodded, the woman walked over to answer the door. Indigo couldn't see who was there from her vantage.

"I wish to see the Caithin woman," a woman's voice snapped in the elegant dialect of the Lyran aristocracy.

Apprehension spiked within her. Was she up to having this confrontation now, because it didn't appear that she was going to get an option?

"Yes, my lady."

The serving woman opened the door and bowed out of the way.

Bitterness preceded the Lyran woman into the room, bitterness that formed a thin shell over a core of hurt. Her perfect, refined features were cast in a mask of aloofness when her pale eyes fell upon Indigo. Indigo forced herself to her feet, her bare feet, and pulled the robe more completely around her as the other woman dismissed the servant. She was all too aware of how inappropriate her attire was for such a meeting, but she'd been given no warning. This would have to do.

The door closed, leaving them alone in the dancing light of the fire. Absently, Indigo used ascard to light candles around the room, wincing when the woman started in surprise at the casual display of power. Well, perhaps the small demonstration would keep things civil.

The woman's anger flared again, chasing away the moment of fear.

"I am Emperor Yiloch's fiancée, Lady Auryl Vyram," she introduced in a tone that could freeze a river.

Indigo kept her expression impassive despite the ache those words opened up within her. *You knew this had to happen*, she reminded herself. The ache remained.

"I can't imagine what he sees in you," Lady Auryl said, eyeing Indigo with a grimace of disgust. "A Caithin woman, of all things, and rather unremarkable looking at that."

"I can't imagine," Indigo snapped back, her calm disintegrating before the degrading tone. Did the woman think she could chase her away with petty insults? She felt a brief flare of jealously in response to the other woman's beauty. What did he see in her compared to this gorgeous, delicate creature? "Perhaps you should ask him what it is I have that you apparently lack." Temper flared, and pain, such a deep, aching pain. Indigo held up a hand to stay Auryl's retort. "I'm sorry, Lady Auryl. That was wrong of me to say."

The sudden apology undermined Auryl's rage, and tears sprang to her beautiful eyes. "He loves you. How can he love you?" Auryl's voice cracked and her proud shoulders sagged forward as a sob shook her.

"Please don't," Indigo soothed her with ascard, manipulating her emotional pain with a touch of calming sedation. The effort sapped her, proving how much rest she still needed even now. "Please, Lady Auryl, sit with me."

Auryl dabbed at her tears and nodded, her regal façade broken by the power of her sorrow. At least she appeared unaware of Indigo's manipulations. Indigo waited while the other woman crossed the room, and then sat when she did, hoping to suggest an equal status. Lady Auryl wasn't the empress yet and Indigo was, if nothing else, a Kudaness priest and a powerful adept.

"I'm Lady Indigo Milan un Ani," she offered in the ensuing silence, resisting the brief wicked urge to add *un Yiloch* to the title.

Auryl stared into the fire. She had come here, judging from her initial words, to cut Indigo down and perhaps even chase her away. Now she appeared lost and frail, closed in on herself in the big chair across from Indigo.

"Yiloch and I…" An eyebrow lifted, a flicker of the earlier temper flashing in those eyes because she used his name so familiarly. Indigo continued, refusing to change the way she referred to him for the other woman's sake. "We should never have had this relationship. We should never have had the chance at it. Life is a strange thing. I can't really explain how it all started, but I do love him. I can't change that. Perhaps he loves me—"

"He does. It was in the way he looked at you, in the way he held and kissed…" her voice cracked and she fell silent.

"We can't be together. You and I both know that, and so does he," Indigo felt the long-standing wound of that truth breaking open and bleeding fresh within her as she spoke. Turning away, she stared into the fire and tried not to hate this woman who could have everything she so desperately wanted.

"That should be enough really," Auryl murmured into the silence. "When I learned I was to marry him, I didn't think I would care if he loved me. I would bear him heirs, as duty required, and then find my emotional pleasures elsewhere. I'd met him as a child and remembered being rather intimidated. When I met him again as an adult, I was captivated by how handsome he was, but even then, I didn't think it would matter. Anyone of such status is expected to have lovers. Most of us do. It wasn't until I saw the two of you…" She paused, collecting herself. "I expected him to have lovers, but I did not expect him to actually love them."

She put her face in her hands and silent sobs shook her shoulders.

Despite her exhaustion, Indigo got to her feet and walked over, kneeling next to the other woman's chair. Tentatively, she rested a gentle hand on Auryl's arm.

"I'm so very sorry," Indigo whispered. "I envy you more than you can imagine that you can have him as a husband, for what little that is worth."

Auryl looked up. Her pale eyes followed the path of a tear as it ran down Indigo's cheek. Reaching up, she brushed away the next tear that followed it, but another quickly took its place.

"Such beautiful skin," she murmured.

Indigo took her hand and held it. It was soft, as her own hands had been once, though the long days on the road had roughened them some.

Auryl smiled, a tremulous curving of her full lips. "Why couldn't you have been horrible," she sniffed. "I could have hated you. I could have thrown you out of the palace without another thought."

Indigo let out a soft laugh that held little mirth. "I'm leaving before dawn, if it makes you feel any better."

"Not really."

Indigo released her hand and returned to her seat, brushing away her own tears now. Silence reigned, broken only by the serving woman who poked her head in. Auryl sent her to get another glass for wine and they sat watching the fire in silence until sometime after they had each finished their first glass and dark had fallen outside. Without prompting, the serving woman had a full supper delivered to them. Indigo found it ludicrous, but somehow fitting, that she was here supping with Yiloch's fiancé.

"You've *been* with him?" The emphasis on the word *been* made Indigo shift uncomfortably in her seat. "Sorry, I suppose that probably offends your Caithin sensibilities. I am less upset by the thought of you having sex with him than I am with knowing that he loves you."

Indigo held her silence, unsure of what she was supposed to say to that.

Auryl filled their glasses. She took several sips of the wine before she spoke again. "I suppose there are worse people to share him with."

Indigo sighed. "I told you I'm leaving. You won't have to share him with me."

Auryl gave her a level look. "I saw the two of you together. Whether or not you are here, I will always be sharing him with you. Regardless, I am sure you will be back. You love each other."

And I have nowhere else to go, she thought. A deep, empty ache swelled within, filling every corner of her being.

"What is it?"

Indigo brushed away a fresh tear. "It's nothing. Nothing I can't handle."

"Everyone needs a little help sometimes." Auryl smiled, a warm encouraging smile. When Indigo remained silent, she said, "The tattoo is rather stunning. I like the effect."

Indigo started to explain the symbol and Auryl shushed her.

"I know what it means, but I like it for more than its meaning. Now," she paused to take another sip of her wine, "what weight rests on your shoulders that it brings such misery to your eyes, and do not play strong with me. We are women. It is our privilege to comfort one another."

Indigo gazed into the fire and took a long sip of her wine. She swirled the glass, holding the liquid in her mouth for a moment to appreciate its complexity. A faint touch on her links told her Ian was soundly sleeping down the hall. She envied him the rest. Yiloch was still in the council chamber off the throne room. He too, needed rest, and more healing. Sometime in the night, he would get it… the healing at least.

She met Auryl's eyes and nodded, pushing away a twinge of guilt. Relaxed by the wine and warmed by it as much as by the surprising welcome in the other woman's eyes, she began to speak.

CHAPTER TWENTY TWO

Lady Auryl left a few hours later. She had listened to Indigo talk for much of that time and was now the only one who knew the truth about how Indigo had met Yiloch. As strange as the circumstances were, Indigo felt she had gained a friend and ally in the other woman. Midnight was drawing near. Yiloch, his weariness resonating with her own through their link, was in his chambers now. Like her, he was still awake, troubled by worries and plagued by pain from a body that needed more healing.

She could help him, but after spending so much time with Auryl, it was hard to go to him without feeling as if she were betraying the other woman. For a short time, she paced the room, determined to resist. Acutely aware of his need and of how much she wanted to see him in spite of everything, she finally slipped from the room, using ascard to ensure that she went unseen as she traversed a few hallways to his chambers. Outside his door, she hesitated, feeling ahead for the signature of anyone else in the room. He was alone and still very much awake.

She pushed open the door. The room was dark, dimly lit by the light of a moon filtered through wispy clouds and faceted crystal windows. He reclined in a chair, gazing out toward the ocean.

"I hoped you would come," he said without turning. Perhaps he feared what he might see in her eyes after the way they had parted.

"Hm." She closed the door, listening to the soft click of the bolt as she locked it, and walked up behind another chair, resting her hands on the back, the solid object offering a sense of stability. His long silver hair gleamed in the moonlight, pale features statuesque and perfect. She ached to touch him. If only he would look at her, but then, she wasn't sure her resolve could withstand that gaze. "I spent the last several hours talking to your fiancée."

Regret rose up in him.

She scowled at his back. "I would be less angry if I thought you felt at least a touch of guilt for what you're doing to her."

He snapped to his feet and she could feel the pain of his injuries, of his stiff and bruised muscles, through their link. Despite that pain, he moved over beside her. She turned away from the chair to face him and he placed a hand against her cheek, staring into her eyes. His gaze was demanding and filled with a desire that sent blood rushing through her in a wave of heat, but there was a much deeper emotion beneath that. Something that made her heart soar and ache at the same time. His touch was so warm, so wonderful, she struggled against an urge to close her eyes and forget all the things she wanted to say.

After a few seconds, she managed to pound the desire back down. She needed to keep her head clear and speak to him. There was so much she needed to say, but too much wine still fogged her thoughts and his touch only made it worse.

"Do you feel guilty?" His voice was a soft growl, desire mixed with anger. "Do you feel any shame for coming here?"

I did not come here for that. She met his pale eyes in the darkness. Need coursed through her, giving lie to the thought. Passion and longing surged up so powerful she swayed beneath the force.

"How could I not come?" she asked when he steadied her with a hand on her arm.

His kiss banished all her thoughts. She wanted him, all of him, his emotion, his passion, his bare warm skin pressed against hers. Pushing ascard through him, she found and finished healing his wounds, then leaned into him, struck by a sudden rush of fatigue. Yiloch lifter her into his arms and carried her to his bed, laying her down with care.

"It seems you're now at my mercy," his eyes lit with mischief.

"In more ways than you know," she breathed, inviting him with a smile. She shivered with pleasure at his touch and he kissed her again, harder this time, his hands moving aside her robe to seek out her bare skin in the darkness.

•

He drew her hand to his lips and kissed the fingers, drawing her up from satisfied slumber.

"Where's your ring?"

Myac. A chill swept through her. She pressed herself against him, trying to cling to the lingering remnants of drowsy bliss.

"Someone took it when I was unconscious after I brought the Grey Army's barrier down."

Anger stung her extended ascard senses and flickered across the link. He set her hand back on his chest. Then his fingers traced her jaw and stopped at her chin, turning her face so he could look into her eyes.

"Who took it?"

She sighed, lamenting the loss of the sated calm that now slipped away from her. "Is Myac in Lyra?"

His muscles tensed against her. "He did return. He came to the palace in disguise and spoke to Lord Terral. Apparently, he went out searching for you, assuming he would find me wherever he found you. He hasn't been heard from since he left here. We found evidence that he'd clashed with the Grey army at one point, but no sign of him after that."

"Lord Terral knew it was him?"

"Lord Terral is his father."

She lifted up on her elbow to gaze down at him, making no effort to hide her surprise.

A grimace tightened his features. "Myac planned to get rid of me and put his father, and ultimately himself, on the throne."

She sensed reluctance in him. There was more to the story, but she would have to trust that he would tell her if it was important. "I believe he was the one who took the ring."

"Why wouldn't he have killed you?"

"Perhaps the arrival of the Kudaness interrupted him," she said, though there was probably more to it than that. He had tried to seduce her in Demin, perhaps there was some sincerity to his efforts, and she had freed him from the Grey adept. Maybe there had been some honest feeling behind his attempted seduction or perhaps simple gratitude for his freedom stayed his hand.

The most disturbing thing about it all was that she could have learned to care for the man she thought he was in Demin. Never could she have loved Edan as she did Yiloch, but a lesser kind of love perhaps. Myac on the other hand. She couldn't love him, but the weaving of their power to bring down the barriers had been intoxicating beyond anything she had ever experienced. He was right. They were similar in some ways. There was no reason to trouble anyone else with such thoughts, however.

Yiloch pulled her close, a hint of protective fear flickering across the link as he kissed the tattoo on her cheek. She shifted away, meeting his eyes.

"Does the tattoo…"

He cut her off with a finger to her lips. "You are beautiful. You are exotic and strong, and you possess a charm that no one can seem to resist. This…" he ran a finger over the tattoo so lightly it tickled, "…is a physical representation of those traits, one you should wear with pride. I love every inch of you."

He held her eyes and his fingers moved down her body. When they reached the area just below her ribs, she writhed and laughed. Grabbing his hands, she straddled him, pinning his wrists over his head and lowering her lips to his.

"I love you," she whispered.

She kissed him hungrily and felt his body respond to her. With a wicked smile, she backed away a bit, licking his lips teasingly with the tip of her tongue while she held him down with a touch of power. Then she opened their link more, letting him feel her desire. His erection became hard against her and she moved herself onto him.

•

Sometime later she woke on her own, her body pressed close against him. She was content, laying there in his arms. Even the pang of guilt she felt over Lady Auryl wasn't enough to drive her away, but dawn would be upon them soon. There were important things they still needed to discuss, preferably without succumbing to other desires this time.

His hand moved to caress her cheek and he kissed her forehead.

"Good, you're awake," she murmured.

His hand returned to his side. "That sounds ominous." His tone had turned wary now.

She searched out his hand and brought it up to her lips, kissing each finger in turn before pressing it against her cheek. She closed her eyes for a moment to fight back the sting of tears.

"I must leave in the morning."

He shifted, moving her head gently from his chest to the pillow then lifted up on his elbow to peer down at her this time. "Why? You're here now. Stay."

She sighed and lit a nearby candle with a flick of ascard power then sat up, facing him cross-legged on the bed, all the while finding it remotely interesting that her nakedness didn't bother her in front of him. "I have to go back to Caithin."

"No. I won't let you go back. I can't protect you there."

"You mean I can't protect you if I'm there." She gave him an indulgent smile, hoping to remind him how doubtful it was that he could stop her from doing what she wanted. His dark scowl told her she had succeeded.

"Then I'll ask you again. Why? You know they'll arrest you. Stay in Yiroth and send Lord Theron to deal with the High Council." When she opened her mouth to argue, he added, "You're the Kudaness ambassador to Lyra, you can't just abandon your position here."

She could only stare at him for almost a minute, trying to figure out if he was being serious. When his somber look didn't change, she gave a small shake of her head. "Suac Chozai should have discussed that with me. Regardless, Caithin will not rest until someone pays for the death of the former king and his family. I don't think Theron alone will be able to convince them. I can persuade Serivar to confess and I think I can get Caplin to side with me. Those things in addition to Theron's assessment should be enough to clear both of our names."

"You've risked far too much for me already. Stay here. Adran and Ian can go to Caithin with Lord Theron to help clear things up."

"They don't have the information I have or the knowledge needed to motivate Serivar," she protested.

"Tell them what they need to know."

"What would I do here?"

"Lyra needs healers, Indigo. Who better to train them?"

The suppressed ache within her, the longing for somewhere to belong, expanded into a searing flame. She could do what he asked. Teaching healers and acting as a representative of the Kudaness, with those things she could belong here. It would also allow her to remain close to Yiloch. It was so tempting. Then again, it might be more than she could bear to see him, to be near him every day, and not be able to have him. It would not be fair to any of them, Lady Auryl especially.

She kissed him, leaning into him so he had to lay back on the bed. His hand took hold of her arm, pulling her down with him. How she wanted to give in and be with him once more. With a delicate touch of ascard, she eased him back into sleep, feeling his lips relax against hers, his hand dropping to his side. When he was in a deep slumber, she climbed out of the bed. It would have been nice to linger a little longer, but she had an idea and very little time to act upon it. She would need Ian's help though.

With a brief search, she found her robe lying on the far side of the bed. Wrapping it snug around her, she poked her head out the door to see if anyone was around. A tiny squeal of surprise escaped her when she came face to face with Ian. His eyes widened then a knowing smirk flitted across his features before he managed to school it away. She did her best to ignore his obvious pleasure at seeing her emerge from Yiloch's rooms. There were other, more important things on which to focus.

"Ian," she whispered, reaching out with her ability to search for any who might overhear them. "I was about to go looking for you."

"Yes, I know."

"How…" She trailed off, realizing that she had unintentionally projected her need of him through their link. With a flush of embarrassment, she wondered what else he might have felt through that link. "Oh. I'm so sorry, Ian."

"Please, don't be. I can think of few people I'd rather be summoned by at this hour of the morning," he said, his curious expression offering no insight on how much else he had felt.

She laughed softly and clicked the door closed. Taking his wrist, she started down the hall, probing ahead for anyone. Ian followed along without question, even mimicking her stealthy poise so that it began to feel like a child's game, sneaking through the halls after hours, trying not to wake their parents. Back in the room, her things still lay on the bed, the bed itself, unused. She drew the ring Yiloch had given back to her in the desert out of her packs. It still hung on the chain he had worn around his neck for so long.

She cradled it in her palm, aware that Ian was watching her with a reverent intensity. She remembered the moment Yiloch had first taken it from her. He slipped it from her finger in his prison, her engagement ring, and she made no protest. So much had changed since she met him. What a storm he had created in her life. Her fiancé, who had given her this ring, was dead by her hand. Perhaps it had been justified self-defense, perhaps not, but neither option made him any less dead or made her feel any better about it. The ring was hers though, and she would give it back to Yiloch now infused with protections like the ring he had given her. This way, even if she died, she could still help him and be with him in some way.

Swallowing the knot in her throat, she glanced at Ian. "I would like you to help me place some protections in this."

Ian lifted the chain, letting the ring dangle before his eyes. He smiled. "Like the one we did for you. I would gladly do this for you, my lady, especially if it's to his benefit. He seems to attract trouble almost as much as you do."

She smiled, pushing a wash of affection through their link. Ian blushed and focused pointedly on the ring dangling from his fingers.

"What kinds of protections were you wanting?"

She proceeded to explain what she wanted to do and they pooled their considerable power into the work. When it was done, she thanked him and left him with a fond kiss on the cheek. She returned to Yiloch's chambers, using a touch of power to hold him in sleep. She placed the chain around his neck, laying the ring on his chest where it had rested once before, and touched her lips to his in a light kiss. That done, she invaded his wardrobe and took one of his mother's simpler dresses that still hung there. He'd given her another once, so she knew it would fit.

Once dressed, she kissed him a last time and slipped away. The effect of her power would fade when she was far enough away and he would wake refreshed. Refreshed and furious with her for leaving him this way, but she couldn't allow him to talk her out of it or try to stop her some way. There was too much at stake if they didn't clear things up with Caithin quickly. Caithin could easily declare war if they continued to believe Yiloch was behind the assassinations. Lyra couldn't withstand such a war right now. The information she had was the key to clearing Yiloch's name. It was time to make his innocence known and make the guilty parties pay for their crimes.

CHAPTER TWENTY THREE

Sleep released Yiloch, easing him up to the light of a bright sunrise. He'd slept hard after his evening with Indigo. Not surprising since they had burned every ounce of energy they had left. He smiled at the memory. If she would only see sense and stay with him in the palace where she would be safe.

Prepared to start the battle fresh, he rolled over in the bed to find that he was alone.

In seconds he was on his feet, surprised to find the old familiar weight of her ring, absent since he had pulled it off in the Caithin Serroc prison, bumping against his chest. It was changed. He could feel that immediately and didn't doubt that she had intended for him to notice the protections woven into it.

That could only mean one thing. She was gone. Not just gone from his bed, but gone from Yiroth as well. The ring was a gift of apology, a token of her love to assuage him. He remembered their last words, discussing her future, trying to convince her not to go back to the den of wolves that waited across the Gilded Straight. His last recollection was her warm kiss igniting a surge of arousal, and then sleep had come over him. It hadn't been a natural sleep either. She had used her healing skills to sedate him so she could depart unchallenged.

He threw on clothes, not bothering with attendants, and stormed through the palace, worry feeding into his anger. How could she have gone? How could she have manipulated him that way? She hadn't even given him a chance to insist on sending someone with her at least, for her protection. She hadn't even bid him farewell, not in a traditional sense at least.

Lord Theron would have gone with her. He wanted to curse the man for encouraging her rash behavior, but they both knew how stubborn she could be when she put her mind to something and Theron would at least try to keep her safe.

A young guard danced out of his path in the hall and bowed, wary of the intensity in his manner, and Yiloch made himself nod in acknowledgement. These were his men. No matter how crazy Indigo might make him, he needed to treat them well.

He almost stopped to question the youth, someone had to know something, but she wouldn't have confided in a stranger. She might have told Ian or Adran of her plans, perhaps Auryl whom she was apparently having extended conversations with now.

He stopped in his tracks when he spotted Theron walking down the hall in the company of a servant. When the other man saw him, he frowned.

"Emperor Yiloch. When I couldn't find Indigo, I was worried that she might have gone to be with you. Now, I must confess, I am suddenly more afraid that you're going to tell me she isn't with you."

Yiloch reigned in his temper. Theron was not at fault if Indigo had chosen to leave him out of her plans. "She was with me. She snuck away sometime in the night and I have a feeling she's headed back to Caithin."

The furrows in Theron's brow deepened. "I must get back there before something happens to her. I don't suppose there's any chance of you coming along to your defense?"

"I'll send Lord Adran with the next merchant ship. I can't risk leaving here right now. There's still the Grey Army to contend with and the damage done to my country and my people needs my attention."

Theron nodded, an unexpected sympathy softening his expression. "I understand. I'll gather my things and head out immediately. As soon as I find her, I will send word to you and begin laying the groundwork for your defense."

"Just take care of her," Yiloch said.

"Consider it done, my lord." Theron bowed deep before hurrying off toward the rooms he had been assigned.

Fiddling with the ring that hung at his neck, Yiloch probed the protections in it to the best of his ability. One thing was certain, Ian's signature was in that work, which meant Ian would have more insight on when she had left. Stretching his ability to it limit, he finally came upon the young creator in the courtyard near the barracks. On his way, he searched for Adran with the same ability, but wherever his friend was, it was out of his range.

Outside, he found Ian talking to a woman he recognized as the creator, Terea, who had first noticed Indigo's presence in the Grey Army's barrier. Ian's gaze passed over Yiloch, then snapped back to him and locked there. His shoulders sank and the heavy exhale of resignation confirmed that he knew something.

"I need to speak with you," Yiloch growled, barely controlling the frustration and worry building up within him.

Ian dismissed Terea with an apologetic smile and fell into step with him as he started back toward the palace entrance. They had taken only a few strides together when he heard Hax calling after him. Yiloch stopped and forced himself to wait while she trotted over to them. She looked weary, as if she hadn't taken a moment to rest since the Grey Army first arrived. He would have to insist that she do so or she would go until she collapsed.

"My lord, I thought you might like an update."

So much going on and I've let Indigo distract me from my duties once again. He nodded. "Go on."

"I've set up a temporary encampment outside the gates to house the overflow of prisoners. We have several linguists working to understand their language so that we might come to some kind of accord, but it's going slowly. Their hierarchy is complex, but the new leader is a youth called Ini-jnai. He's a shrewd individual and cold, but he seems to be encouraging a few of those who appear to be captains to try and communicate. Captain Paulin is overseeing the guarding of the prisoners in the camp right now. Captain Leryc has a crew of laborers working on clearing out the destroyed wall so we can rebuild and Lord Terral has another crew assessing damage in the city."

Yiloch found his mood lifting as she spoke. Despite his injuries and the distraction of Indigo, things were moving along as they should. Part of being an effective leader was selecting the right people to serve under you. There was no doubt in his mind at this point that she had been the perfect choice to take Commander Dalce's place. He found a smile for her. "I could ask for no better. You've done very well. Thank you, Commander Hax."

"Thank you, my lord. It's good to see you up and about so soon after the injuries you sustained. I was a little worried you would bleed out before the surgeons got to you."

"Yes. Indigo finished the healing before she up and vanished again," he said, a hint of irritation coming through in his tone. "What's become of Adran?"

"The last I heard of him he'd gone down to the docks yesterday afternoon to deal with some captains in need of recompense. I haven't seen or heard from him since." Hax looked askance at Ian who shrugged.

"Emperor Yiloch."

Yiloch cringed inwardly. He hadn't seen Lady Auryl since she saw him with Indigo in the throne room. The two women may have come to some kind of understanding, but he doubted that would extend to him. The last thing he wanted now was to have an argument with her here. However, when he turned to face her, the alarm in her expression banished his dread at seeing her. Concern swept in to fill the space.

"What's wrong?"

"I was asking after Captain Adran and a soldier just arrived with word from Lord Terral that someone saw the captain depart on a ship yesterday in the company of a strange Lyran man. Lord Terral expressed concern. He said Myac might have been around the city and was worried that Adran could be in considerable danger."

Sudden nausea hit Yiloch like a blow to the gut. Adran had no power beyond that of a sword or bow to use against Myac. The adept, given a moment's chance, could easily overpower him. Killing a man like Adran alone would be akin to stepping on an ant for someone of Myac's power.

"When did the ship leave and where was it bound?"

"The ship left yesterday afternoon. According to the register, it was bound for Kilty."

"If Myac wanted him dead, why not just kill him here? Why go to the trouble of taking him away like that?" Ian asked, a distinct tremor in his voice.

Yiloch placed a hand on Ian's shoulder, both giving and taking comfort from the gesture. The creator had already lost one of his two cousins and Eris had been a lifelong friend to Yiloch. Neither of them was ready to lose Adran as well.

Hax answered the question for him. "Everything I know about Myac tells me he always has more sinister motives. Just killing someone is rarely entertaining enough."

Yiloch glanced at Ian, wondering if he looked as unnaturally pale as the creator did. "You spoke with Indigo. Where is she?"

"She left for the docks a little before dawn, after we finished with the ring."

"The..." He touched the ring under his shirt absently. They had worked the ring together just as Ian and Ferin had worked to create the ring he gave to her. Then she had gone, leaving him that token of her affection. A consolation prize in case she didn't return. Unfortunately, she no longer had the added protection from the ring he had given her. "I expect you to explain why you didn't think to question her clandestine departure later. Right now, I need to figure out what to do about Adran."

"Go after him," Lady Auryl stated. "Go find Lord Captain Adran... and Lady Indigo."

Yiloch frowned. If she only knew how much he wanted to do exactly that. If not for the Grey Army and the Dursik un Kar who were taking a chance to rest before starting the trek back to Kudan. If not for the damaged state of Yiroth, of Lyra in general, he might dare to go chasing after them. "I can't. There are things to be done..."

"You can," Hax interrupted.

He turned an irritated glare on her, which she met with an obstinate return glare before Auryl jumped into the silence.

"She's right." Auryl took his hand in both of hers, squeezing it in earnest. "Put Lord Terral in charge again." She shook her head to stop his objection and he held his silence, wanting to find a way to make it work. "If you promise to send him back to his manor when this is done, he will not disappoint you. He never shared his son's ambitions. I have spoken to him enough to be sure of that much. Your captains can keep an extra close watch over him if you feel it is necessary. Commander Hax can oversee military affairs without you for a short time. Whether you fail or succeed, you will not be gone long."

Yiloch started to protest then stopped himself. Regardless of whether what she suggested was appropriate or not, he believed she was right. He needed to do this. The two people he loved most were in danger. "You are a greater woman than you seem."

Lady Auryl shook her head, closing her eyes for a moment. When she opened them again, tears sparkled in them. "I do this for them. They both need you right now more than anyone here does. Yiloch the emperor is nothing if he is not first a man who cares deeply for the people around him. Get them and bring them back here where they belong."

"Might I suggest that you take Ian and a few guards with you," Hax commented, assuming that his departure was decided. "You can travel in disguise that way. Get into and out of Caithin without anyone knowing you were there."

Yiloch nodded. "Hax, send someone to summon Lord Terral and to secure passage across the Gilded Straight. Ian, find an adept or two who can speed the trip. I doubt either Myac or Indigo will have paid with coin when they can barter their abilities. We need to move fast."

•

Within an hour, Yiloch stood at the bow of a ship as it turned out across the Gilded Strait. Rain drizzled down on them, light, like a fine mist, but still drenching. It was warm enough and Yiloch wasn't about to go below. He wanted to see the Kilty docks the moment they came into view. Wanted to be ready to disembark. His mind raced with the many possible reasons why Myac would have taken Adran with him. None of them were good. The least horrible was that he meant to ransom Adran for something, but even that possibility came with no guarantee the captain would return unharmed.

Someone stepped up beside him. He didn't need to look to know it was Ian. The rain had stopped touching him and he was instantly dry, clothes and all.

"We'll need to find Indigo first. She'll be able to track down Myac faster than either of us can and she has the power to fight him."

Yiloch nodded. His hand came up to trace the shape of the ring under his shirt. "What did you two do to this ring?"

"We worked protections into it. Some powerful masking and a defensive barrier against ascard attack. Indigo figured out a way to make the ring absorb and reuse offensive powers so the barriers and masking will actually get stronger if you're attacked with ascard. It's quite brilliant," Ian said, admiration bubbling up in his voice.

Yiloch nodded, pride in her accomplishments warming some of the cold dread within him. If only she were with them now. They would have to risk her to find Adran, but he would do anything to save his old friend and Ian was right, she was the one person who might overpower Myac. They would have to outthink the other adept though. One mistake was all the opening the bastard would need to rain misery down on them.

"I remember the last time we made this trip," Ian said. "Despite the pending conflict with your father, the journey felt much less dire then."

Yiloch nodded. The weight that bore him down grew heavier with each moment that passed. "Yes. At least Adran was with us then."

"Yes," Ian murmured, his shoulders sagging under the weight of his own fears.

"And you were still afraid of me," Yiloch added with a sideways glance in an attempt to lift the mood.

Ian chuckled. "That hasn't changed. You still scare me."

They both managed to smile at that, but only for an instant.

The rain let up by the time they pulled into the docks in Kilty. The adepts Ian brought with them to speed the ship stayed aboard to await their return. They were both exhausted from their efforts and needed the rest. The captain, now well ahead of his planned schedule, agreed to wait one day for their return. Yiloch ordered the guards to wait with the ship. The fewer people who made the trip into Demin, the less attention they would draw and the guards were more likely than not to end up casualties in a confrontation with Myac. If something went wrong, the guards would return with the ship to notify Terral and Hax.

They secured a carriage to take them into Demin and Ian spent the journey focusing on his link to Indigo. Yiloch held his silence. He felt nothing of her through his own link, but he didn't have the knowledge nor the expendable strength to focus on searching for her. Ian shook his head in frustration. They were almost in Demin now and a decision had to be made.

"I can't reach her. She must be thoroughly shielded. Even the link is blocked."

Yiloch scowled. "She isn't expecting us so she's closed down all possible points of vulnerability. We'll go to the Healer's Academy. She's apt to be either there or in the palace and Myac is more likely to be at the academy with his fellow conspirator."

"You're probably right. I'll sneak in and feel things out. You stay out of sight. You're a wanted criminal here, after all."

Yiloch raised an eyebrow. He didn't like sending Ian into danger in his stead. "And if you need help?"

"I can use ascard to alert you if I sense trouble. I'll be careful."

Yiloch clenched his teeth. They didn't want to draw attention and he would draw a lot as himself. Even in disguise, two men wandering the academy at this hour might attract unwanted attention. Still, it felt like too much risk given what was already at stake.

"Perhaps you could continue to disguise me."

Ian shook his head. "I thought of that. It would take a lot of energy to disguise you and mask the working well enough that Myac wouldn't notice it. I don't think we can afford to waste powers right now."

Yiloch scowled, tracing the ornate crossguard of his sword with one fingertip. Lifting the curtain enough to peak out the carriage window, he watched the city approach. As they neared the outer guard post, the carriage came to a stop. For the purpose of getting into the city, Ian did disguise them, masking his working so the city's ascard Watchmen wouldn't be aware of it. The guards passed them through and the carriage driver called back to ask where he should drop them.

"The Caithin Healer's Academy," Yiloch called back out the window. He turned to Ian. "We'll do it your way, but be ready to send the summons. Myac isn't someone we want to underestimate."

"I know." Ian drew in a deep breath. His heavy exhale was rife with sorrow and dread.

"I won't give up on Adran."

"Yes. I know that too. It's one of many reasons I'm pleased to be in your service."

Caplin was weary. He was weary more often than not these days. He had spent the evening playing dice with several of the off-duty guardsman and his father. Gavin was as clever at the game as his servants were at filling empty mugs without being noticed and they all found themselves walking away empty handed and well liquored while King Gavin chuckled his way back to the palace with his winnings. For the duration of the game, Caplin's worries were reduced to distant naggings. Now, with alcohol numbing his body, he made his way back towards the palace proper and those worries emerged in sharp relief from the rest of his blurry thoughts.

What was happening in Lyra?

No further word had come from Theron. Would the next missive be a notification of victory or would they get a sudden rush of refugees from the fallen empire? It was maddening to sit here waiting. Indigo was over there, somewhere in that war torn country. What would happen to her if the invaders won? Why hadn't they sent aid to Lyra? The council remained too divided on the subject, but, ultimately, Gavin could have overridden their uncertainty. As king, the final word was his. As the king's son, perhaps he should have leveraged his position. Was it too late to influence the outcome now?

By the time he arrived in his rooms, he felt much too sober for the amount of drink he'd had. Andrea was already sleeping soundly. He stared at her for a moment. She was beautiful. Her lips parted a little in sleep, her brow furrowing with some dreamtime drama. He did love her. It wasn't the same love he felt for Indigo, but it was love.

Stripping off his clothes, he put out the candles she had left burning for him and climbed into the bed, careful not to wake her. For some time, he stared at the canopy over the bed and considered waking her for some pleasant distraction. But, his thoughts were still too wrapped in Indigo. It wouldn't be the first time he made love to her while thinking of the other woman, but he truly was trying not to make a habit out of it.

With a soft sigh, he rolled over and managed to drift off into a restless slumber.

Sometime later, he stirred in his sleep. Someone was calling his name in his head, like a voice in a dream, but more insistent. He tried rolling over, but the voice remained, pulling at him, asking him to wake. Irritated, he opened his eyes a fraction. Candles in the wall sconces on his side of the room flickered and someone now stood beside the bed.

What was Andrea doing awake at this hour... and wearing a traveling cloak?

Panic hit him like a punch to the chest and his eyes popped open wide. It wasn't Andrea standing there. Sitting up, he opened his mouth to call the guards, then stopped as the figure pulled back the hood of the cloak. He knew he must look a fool with his mouth hanging open, but he couldn't seem to help it. What he was seeing made no sense. Perhaps it was a very vivid dream?

A few blinks and a bite to the inside of his lip did nothing to change things. The figure standing in his chambers in the flickering light of the candles was Indigo. Her face stayed mostly in shadow, but there was no mistaking who she was. He'd known her most of his life.

I should call the guards.

He started to pull back the covers, then hesitated, glancing at the robe that lay pooled on the floor a few feet away. Following his gaze, Indigo reached down, gathered the fine fabric with one hand, and passed it to him. Then she moved away, going to stand in the sitting area by the fireplace with her back to him. His heart racing, Caplin stood, drawing on the robe and tying it tight before walking over to join her. As soon as he approached, she turned to face him and the fire crackled to life along with the nearest candles. He flinched, startled by the show of forbidden power, and glanced at the bed where Andrea was still sleeping.

"Don't worry, she won't wake so long as I am here. I'm glad you two went through with the marriage."

Caplin turned back to Indigo, his love for her a twisting ache in his chest despite the vast distance that had built up between them. He longed to hug her, to feel her soft warmth in his embrace, but so much had happened since she disappeared. She was a criminal. The initial impulse to call in the guards was the right one, especially considering that she had somehow managed to get into his private chambers unchallenged. He wasn't ready to do the right thing yet.

In the flickering light, he noticed the elegant lines of a tattoo on one cheek and there were three beaded braids in her hair. Braids were a mourning custom in Caithin, but these were different. They meant something in some culture, but his mind was still too foggy with sleep and drink for him to draw it out. He met her eyes and squinted, trying to determine, in the dim light, if something in those blue depths had changed as well.

What other powers does she have?

He glanced at the fire then considered the woman standing in front of him with a new, wary respect.

What else might have changed beneath the surface? She had killed Jayce. The ascard signature the Watchmen found in his charred body proved that much. She had stopped his heart with her power. He couldn't bring himself to hold that against her, though it did make him even more wary of her. She had also freed Emperor Yiloch and Lord Ferin, though the reasons for that were still unknown. What else might she have done since her departure? What events had led to the odd tattoo and the braids in her hair.

She met his eyes, letting him look at her. Undisturbed by his open scrutiny. "Much has happened since I last left you here, Caplin."

He took a step closer and brought a hand up toward her face, then hesitated. When she made no move to discourage the gesture, he caressed her cheek with his thumb, not quite touching the tattoo. "I can't say I'm fond of this. It looks…" he trailed off, still struggling to pull the reference from his clouded mind.

"Kudaness," she offered. "I am a priest of the Kudaness."

His hand dropped to his side and he took a step back, that initial sense of alarm sweeping back in with dizzying force.

"Much has happened," he agreed, placing a hand on the back of a nearby chair for support. He found it hard to look into those piercing eyes now. There was so much strength and confidence in that gaze. Had she always been this strong? Had he simply overlooked it in his arrogance? "I should be arresting you, you know. When no word came back from Lord Edan, we weren't sure if we should initiate military action. Then word came of another army invading Lyra and we decided to wait and see how that played out. We sent Lord Theron instead, and waited for his report. I didn't believe it when his message came back saying you were in Kudan. I guess it was true after all."

"I've spoken with Theron. The war has ended and Yiroth still stands. He will be back within the next few days, I'm sure."

"Why didn't you wait and come back with him? He could have protected you, assuming you should be protected."

There was a small tightening around her lips at his words, but she only shook her head and gestured to a chair with one hand. "Please sit, Caplin." The firelight illuminated flecks of flame in her eyes. "We have some things to talk about."

He nodded and, despite the sudden feeling that he had wandered unwittingly into the lair of a highly superior predator, he sat with her. This was not the woman he thought he knew, but then, Yiloch had said as much to him a long time ago. Now was he beginning to wish he had heeded the other man's words more carefully.

Forcing himself to meet her eyes, he said, "I'm listening."

•

Adran clawed his way to awareness. His head was full of a thick, sticky fog that caught and tangled his thoughts like insects bound up in a spider's web. He moved to rub his eyes only to discover that his hands were unable to obey him. For a few frustrating moments, his eyelids also refused to obey him. Then they crept open and he glanced around him into a deep darkness. Wherever he was, there were no lights to orient him, no glimmers of reality to ground him and assuage his fear. Tactile sense was painfully acute in the darkness. As his thoughts struggled to break through the fog, he tried to move again, but his arms and legs were bound to the chair he was sitting in and a rope around his chest held him so tight against the back of the chair that it restricted his breathing.

Adran shook his head, scowling at the persistent fog in his head. How had he gotten here? Where was here? Why was he tied up? He tried again to shift his arms, but the rough rope had no give.

"Awake are we?"

Adran tensed. His breath started to come in short, panicked gasps as he remembered boarding the ship, remembered Myac taking control of him. Despair flowed through him like a poison, twisting his stomach into knots, driving muscles to tense, pulling futilely against the bonds holding him. An image of Yiloch, a handsome and happy young prince before his mother died, popped into his mind and his throat constricted with the bittersweet memory of his beloved friend. He felt an icy certainty that he wouldn't be seeing him again. Of all the people he had ever known, Myac was at the bottom of the list of those with whom he wanted to spend his last moments. Too bad fate rarely paid attention to such lists.

Myac chuckled and a candle on a nearby table sparked to life, drawing him out of the darkness. His now pale eyes and hair brought out a traditional Lyran beauty in him that made him more terrible somehow. Adran yearned for the black eyes and hair that he had before. The strange contrast that made him look like the abomination he was.

"I wouldn't give up hope yet, Lord Adran. Someone might still save you." Myac took a few steps closer, his gaze dripping with disdain as he scowled down on his captive. "Then again, you have no ascard power or special trinkets to alert someone to your presence, do you? The odds may be against you after all. Of course, we could fix that."

"What are you doing, Myac?" His confidence boosted by the steadiness of his own voice, Adran managed to glare up at his captor.

Myac chuckled again, a sound that threatened to undermine Adran's fragile show of courage. "Playing."

Panic swirled up through the sticky web of thought again. He expected Myac to claim this was an act of vengeance or perhaps that he planned to ransom Adran for something. That one word, spoken with such dark pleasure, left him feeling chilled and nauseous. He searched within himself, seeking to rediscover that brief taste of boldness he had experienced, but it was gone, shattered and drifted away in the dark fog that filled his mind. There was only panic, nausea, and a terrible thirst.

"I need some water," he said, hoping to get a better feel for the situation through the adept's reaction. If Myac intended him for some greater purpose, than he would probably try to keep him alive. Although, even that prospect carried with it as much terror as it did hope. There were so many levels of alive.

Myac knelt on one knee by the chair and brushed his fingers across the back of Adran's hand with a lover's gentleness, but the light in his eyes was cruel. Adran tried to pull away from the touch, but he couldn't get any movement. The pale eyes sparkled with dark amusement.

"Savor it. That gentle touch will be a fond memory when I'm done with you." Myac reached into a pocket and withdrew a ring. The lovely pearl piece was unpleasantly familiar. Yiloch had given the ring to Indigo. How had Myac gotten it? A shudder went through Adran. "I see you recognize this. It's been tuned to Indigo's ascard signature. I could feel her coming through this. She arrived in Demin perhaps ten hours after we did." He slid the ring on Adran's little finger. "It is my hope that she will feel your suffering through it, but it will be faint, so we'll have to be sure your pain is truly exceptional."

"Why are you doing this?" Adran asked, hoping to stall him, or even make him reconsider. If Indigo was his target, then there was a chance, however small, that he might get out of this alive, assuming she arrived in time. The process of getting her there, however, didn't promise to be a pleasant one and, since he was only bait, Myac wouldn't be worrying about how much damage he inflicted on him.

Myac rested his hand on Adran's arm. He instinctively tried to flinch away again, but the tight ropes only made the movement hurt. The other man gave no indication that he noticed, or perhaps he simply didn't care.

"You see, I never wanted much. I only wanted to destroy Yiloch and take everything he had—his power, his empire, his happiness—from him. Not a lot to ask, considering what he took from me."

Adran started to protest, but Myac gave him an icy glare.

"Don't interrupt."

Hating himself for it, but afraid to do anything else, Adran held his silence.

"But all my plans kept falling apart, largely due to the intervention of a certain lady adept. At every turn, Yiloch has managed to keep everything and gain even more, including a few things I didn't realize I even wanted. I was prepared to tuck my tail and return to Caithin to sort things out. Then..." and his eyes sparked with an eerie pleasure that made Adran's stomach turn, "...then I saw you board the ship I was booking passage on and it all became clear. I've been trying to take too much too fast. I needed to narrow my scope and take a little at a time. So, I'll start with you, his dearest friend. Unfortunately, he isn't here to witness your suffering, but I think it will be even better if his beloved Indigo goes through it with you and is forced to break the news to him, don't you?"

So Myac planned to kill him regardless, only he meant to do it in such a way as to hurt both Indigo and Yiloch. Adran struggled against the terror churning his stomach. Bound in this position, all he would do was throw up on himself. He wasn't about to give Myac that satisfaction.

Myac smirked and stood. "Now…"

His pause made Adran look up. Myac's head tilted a fraction to one side, as if he were listening to something Adran couldn't hear. A slow, delighted smile spread across his lips and Adran broke out in a cold sweat.

"Even better. Your precious cousin, Ian I believe, is about to join us. You see, I left a working at the door of the building, something I came up with on my own to alert me of anyone entering or leaving. A clever little something I doubt even our darling Indigo will figure out."

Adran struggled to focus. Ian was strong, but was he strong enough to fight Myac when the demented adept was ready and waiting for him? Did Ian know Myac was here? He must know something or he wouldn't be in Demin. He ground his teeth, frustrated with the sticky fog that still tangled his thoughts.

Focus on Myac's words. His tone.

There had been something more than bitterness in his voice when he mentioned Indigo that time, something that whispered of spurned affection. Myac was walking away from him now.

Ian.

"You'll fail again. You always have. Why would this time be any different?"

Myac paused, turning just enough to glance at him and said, "I don't think so. Not this time."

"Indigo is stronger than you are. She will defeat you."

He turned around the rest of the way, a dangerous spark lighting his eyes. "Do you think so? Perhaps she is, but she has a weakness. You see, she cares about Yiloch and his companions. I dare say, she cares about you as well, and your cousin. What would she do to save you? Shall we find out?"

The index finger of Adran's left hand split open, blood surging out to hide the brief glimpse of white bone. Adran went rigid against his bonds. He screamed. Agony blasted through him. Myac walked over and put his hands over Adran's on the arms of the chair, his palm pressing down on the gaping wound. Adran tried to shrink away, terror and pain eradicating all coherent thought as he pressed his back into the chair. Myac leaned over him.

"Eager to get started, aren't you? I learned a few things about torture in my time with the Grey Army that I'm looking forward to sharing with you." Myac ground down on the damaged finger with the heel of his hand and Adran screamed again, pain stealing his dignity and dragging tears from his eyes. Myac leaned closer still, putting his lips beside Adran's ear. "Yes. Scream, Lord Adran. Scream all you want. No one will hear you outside of this room."

With those words, he walked away and Adran sagged against his bonds, his blood running down the chair leg. Tears streamed down his cheeks unchecked. Any glimmer of hope drained away with them.

•

"Serivar."

The headmaster hopped to his feet and turned. His eyes widened when he saw Myac standing by the open secret door in the back of his office.

"How? When did you…" Serivar ran a shaking hand through his short, dark hair. "How long have you been here?"

"It's good to see you too." Myac sneered at him. "I arrived yesterday. The journey was taxing, but not without reward."

"What of Indigo and Emperor Yiloch?"

"We'll talk about them later. Right now, Yiloch's young creator prodigy is on his way to your office." Myac walked over to the side table that always held a decanter of wine and four goblets. Reaching into his robe, he drew out a small pouch. With extreme care, he opened the pouch and tapped a tiny bit of the powder within into a goblet. "Stall him. Tell him you don't know where I am, but you can send for someone who might. Offer him a drink while he waits. Once he's had a bit of this, I'll handle the rest."

Myac walked back to the hidden door. He glanced over his shoulder at Serivar who was staring at the goblet as if it might attack.

"What is it?" the headmaster asked, tension rippling off him in such powerful waves it made Myac uneasy.

"It's a little mixture of some things from one of the store rooms. It's slow acting, but lethal. I strongly recommend that you don't mix the cups up," he added with a smile. Serivar was staring at him as though he had gone mad. Maybe he had. It didn't matter at this point. One way or another, Yiloch would suffer. "Oh, and don't come back to the training room tonight. I'm working on something important. I won't be forgiving if you disturb me." When Serivar blanched, he nodded his satisfaction and closed the door behind him.

Now it was time to see what it would take to get Indigo's attention.

CHAPTER TWENTY FIVE

You would have been wrong to attack Lyra," Indigo stated. "Yiloch didn't order the assassinations and the man you call Lord Edan is not who you think he is. Do you remember when we helped Yiloch take the throne? There was…"

She stopped speaking and winced when a strange pain speared through her. It felt distant, yet it came from within, as though someone had jabbed a needle into the core of her inner aspect. Worry boiled up from her gut and she turned her attention inward, to her links with Yiloch and Ian.

"Is something wrong?"

Concern flared. Following along her link to Ian revealed that he was in the city, but a closer investigation showed no signs of distress from him that might explain the pain. Yiloch was in Demin as well, though his presence was faint, partially blocked by the protections on the ring she had given him. She would have to adjust that if she got a chance, but she could tell enough to know that he wasn't in distress either.

Why had they come here now? They were needed in Lyra. Did they have that little confidence in her ability to deal with the situation?

But what if it wasn't about her at all? What if something else had gone wrong?

Scowling, she turned her attention back to Caplin. This was important and neither of them appeared to be in any immediate danger, so they would have to wait. "You remember Emperor Rylan's adept, the one who almost killed me when Yiloch took the throne?"

Caplin's jaw tightened and his mouth hardened into an angry line, his old protectiveness toward her overriding the new uncertainty for a moment. Though, whether it was anger with Myac for almost killing her or anger with Yiloch for putting her in the situation she couldn't tell. Perhaps both.

"His name was Myac, right? He escaped after Captain Adran shot him with a crossbow."

Indigo nodded. "Lord Edan is Myac."

Caplin shook his head, but Indigo could feel the reluctant trust born of years of friendship creeping up through his doubt. "But Edan is Caithin."

"Myac is a Lyran adept and creator, an incredibly strong one. He came here after he fled Yiroth and has been hiding behind the disguise of Edan, a young Caithin adept."

Caplin waivered. The doubt was still strong, reinforced by his wariness of the little power she had shown him, and there was something else there, worry perhaps, or fear. "What happened with Jayce, Indigo?"

She lowered her gaze and drew a deep, stabilizing breath. Now wasn't the time for a crisis of conscience. "I didn't want to hurt him, Caplin."

"You killed him."

She nodded. "He came after me with a dagger. I didn't know what else to do. I knew he would never stop trying to get back at me for escaping our engagement. I wish it hadn't ended that way, but I would be the one lying dead otherwise."

"You should have come to me. Burning down your residence made it look like you were trying to hide what you had done. Then you set free the people accused of assassinating the king and his family. The resulting picture isn't a good one."

She shook her head in earnest. "I know, Caplin, but the fire was my attempt to escape from Myac. Listen to me for a moment. Really listen."

He sat at the edge of his seat now, impatience in his posture, but he finally nodded.

"Myac was living with Serivar. They worked together to have King Jerrin and his family assassinated and framed the Lyran adepts for the crime."

Disbelief exploded with an almost tangible force. "Lord Serivar would never do such a thing. He's been a friend to the family for years."

"He's been a friend to your father, Caplin. He never got along with King Jerrin."

Caplin snapped to his feet, glaring down at her. "My father had nothing to do with this."

"Calm down." She held up a placating hand, resisting the temptation to calm him with ascard, and focused into him while he glared at her, sifting through his emotions. Deep in the mix, she found uncertainty. Something made him willing to consider her words and she needed to build upon that. "I don't believe your father was involved. He was merely a better option. Serivar always had marginal influence with King Jerrin. With your father on the throne, he stood to gain much greater influence because of their long-standing friendship."

Caplin sat down again, but his hands gripped the arms of the chair like he meant to tear them off, betraying his agitation. "If that's true, it hasn't worked out as well as he planned. It would explain some things about Lord Serivar's behavior of late, but..."

She nodded as his brow furrowed with thought. "I suspect Serivar grossly overestimated Gavin's trust in him. He hoped to gain political influence and guarantee his continued control over the King's Order. They framed Yiloch, counting on the fury of the Caithin people to force a quick and final judgement."

"And how does all of this help Myac?"

She could feel more willingness in him now. He wanted to believe her, either because of his lingering feelings for her or because of something he had seen in Serivar. Whatever it was, she needed his support and she wanted to gain it without using ascard power to sway him.

"The next in line for the Lyran throne would be Yiloch's cousin, Lord Terral, who also happens to be Myac's father."

Caplin's eyes widened and she could almost see the puzzle pieces slipping into place behind his eyes. She swallowed a smile.

●

Most of the academy buildings were quiet at this hour. Only the two medical buildings remained relatively well-lit and active to care for existing patients and deal with emergencies. The administration building between them appeared mostly dark, but the doors through which Ian had entered were unlocked, hinting at some presence.

The situation didn't feel right. Tension built within Yiloch like a growing bonfire. It consumed his patience, burning away at his nerves as he waited. There was no change in his link to Indigo that he could tell. Anything could be happing to Adran or to Ian while he sat here deaf and blind to them or as good as. His ascard ability simply wasn't strong enough and trained in the right skills to help him out in these circumstances. He hated feeling useless while people he cared about were in danger.

He reached for the handle of the carriage door, then hesitated. It would be foolish to risk being seen. Even the carriage driver might recognize him without any of Ian's workings in place. Ian assured him that he would send an alert with ascard if there was trouble. Still…

What if he can't send the alert off in time?

A pulling sensation struck him, as though someone were trying to drag him toward the building by his guts, then it went away as suddenly as it had come. Was that Ian's summons? Then why had it gone away so abruptly? Perhaps it was a false alarm. Alternatively, the creator might be in such grave circumstances that he couldn't maintain the contact.

Yiloch ground his teeth and clicked open the carriage door. He could see the entrance to the building from here. It was a good distance away, but he had conserved his strength so far. Drawing on his power, he swapped himself with the ascard in the air by the door. Without hesitation, he stepped quickly and quietly into the building before anyone could see him. A hallway stretched off to either side of the entrance and another continued forward with additional halls branching off further in. The halls were sparingly lit with an occasional wall sconce and nothing offered a hint to where he might find Ian, Adran, or Myac.

Cautiously, he reached into the building with tendrils of ascard, searching for the signature of Ian or either of the others that might point him in the right direction. He found nothing. Wherever Ian was, the room was either protected or too far away for his ability to detect him. Given the nature of the building and those who tended to spend time there, he was willing to bet on the former. Either way, it left him lost like a hound with no scent trail.

With no other options, Yiloch cursed under his breath and chose a direction at random to start his search, knowing that every second wasted might cost one of his companions their life.

•

Indigo lost track of what Caplin was saying. The odd sense of pain that had spiked within her earlier, that pain that appeared at her core and yet was somehow not hers, returned with far more force. She flinched, her stomach churning in response to the unpleasant stabbing pain, and Caplin trailed off.

"Are you all right?" He finally asked.

She held up a finger for him to wait as she searched in earnest this time. Yiloch and Ian were still in the city, but neither was in any obvious pain. The link to Ian had become faint, however, as though some kind of barrier had risen between them.

She ground her teeth in frustration.

There was something else. Something she was missing.

The strange pain came again and this time she latched onto it, tracing the sensation to its source. It led her back to the academy. She ran up against several strong barriers there and used more ascard to drill past them, following the sensation through to a familiar object. With a sinking sensation, she recognized the ascard signature of the ring Yiloch had given her. Forcing more power along the thread, she extended her ability to reach out beyond the ring and encountered another familiar ascard signature.

Adran? It was his pain she felt through the ring. What was he doing here and why did he have her ring? Using the ring to anchor the thread of power for a moment, she stretched her ability out from that point, moving several tendrils of power into the room beyond Adran. She touched another presence and recoiled. Surprise and horror took her breath away.

She put a hand to her throat, gasping as the pain flared again, stronger this time because of the ascard she had anchored into the ring.

"Indigo. What is it?"

"I have to go." She stood, bumping over a side table in her haste. A vase shattered on the floor. "I'm sorry. I can fix that later. If I convince Serivar to confess, will you listen?"

"Yes, I will, but…"

"Someone needs me now. I *will* be back. I promise."

She hid herself from sight and left Caplin behind. She made it to the carriage she had arrived in, all the while bombarded by increasingly intense flashes of pain, the last strong enough to trip her up. The driver accepted her urgent direction to the academy and moved the horse out at a fast trot. Then another chaotic mess of sensations struck her, pain, fear, and panic, but it was all coming through her link to Ian this time. A moan of dread escaped her and she reached out with ascard, using it to drive the horses faster. The carriage driver shouted at them to slow and she put a tendril out to calm him in turn. When they stopped outside of the academy there was another carriage parked out in front. She placed both drivers into a deep slumber and hurried inside.

The pounding of her heart was almost enough to deafen her as she moved cautiously through the building, her palms damp with the sweat of fear. If someone saw her here, they were very likely to recognize her. Now, more than ever, she couldn't afford delay. Ian was dying. She could feel his life ebbing through their link, though she didn't know why yet, and the pain response from Adran was growing weaker. Terror tightened her chest, making it hard to breathe as she followed the sensations to Serivar's office.

When she stepped into the office, Serivar was pacing behind his desk. His eyes widened, but he didn't have time to react beyond that before she put him to sleep as well. The heavy thud when he struck the floor made her wince. She would have to hope no one heard. Hastily, she shut the door and hurried to the hidden one at the back of the room. The pungent tang of vomit stung her nose as she entered the training room. The room was dimly lit with a few candles placed on the one table that had been moved to the center, just past a figure slumped in a chair with his back to her.

Forgetting caution, she ran to the slumped figure, noticing the ropes that bound him to the chair and the dark liquid pooling around the legs. Reaching out with ascard, she lit the candles in the sconces around the room and stopped abruptly, only a few steps from the figure. The dark liquid was blood, and it covered the figures clothing and skin as well. A gentle touch with ascard confirmed that it was Adran.

Stepping reluctantly around in front of him, she let out a cry of horror. If not for his ascard signature, she wouldn't have recognized the man sitting there through the blood and open wounds that covered his face. Every part of him was riddled with deep open cuts. His chest barely moved, but it did move. He was still alive, though fortunately unconscious. Struggling against an urge to throw up, she made herself step closer. She reached to touch him, but couldn't see where to do so without causing pain. She spotted the ring then, placed on Adran's little finger, sticky with blood. She reached for the item, not sure what she meant to do with it.

I must help him. She continued to reach for the ring, horribly mesmerized by the glint of white pearl still visible amongst the red of his blood.

"I'm pleased you could join us."

Her head jerked up, her hand snapping back to her side. Myac stood watching her. His pale hair and eyes brought out his resemblance to his father. While she indulged in her horror, he had placed himself between her and the door. A chill swept through her, creeping cold fingers up her spine, but anger quickly incinerated it.

"What have you done?"

Myac smiled. "I was only having a little fun."

Rage blasted through her and she almost lashed out at him, but she caught herself. Adran needed immediate help. He was far enough gone that it would take nearly everything she had to save him, assuming she could still do so. She sent ascard into him to assess the extent of the damage and had to fight the rising bile when she discovered broken bones and other internal injuries in addition to the obvious external wounds, all of them inflicted with ascard bearing Myac's signature.

"You don't think I'll sit by quietly and let you heal him, do you?"

She tensed and withdrew, leaving a tendril of power in Adran to monitor him.

"Oh," his smile deepened, "and aren't you forgetting something."

"Forgetting something..."

She realized then that the pain and panic she'd felt from Ian was gone now. There was only silence in the link. She swallowed and she followed the link to its end only to discover the young creator was in the room with them.

Myac stepped to one side and she saw Ian lying in a heap by the wall to the left of the door. The stench of vomit came from there. A quick assessment confirmed her fears. Myac had poisoned him. Like Adran, he was either unconscious or too weak to do anything. His heartbeat was faint and stressed, his breathing shallow.

"When you meshed our power to bring down the Grey Army's barrier, I got to see exactly how strong you are. I know your limits now as well as I know my own and I can tell by your expression that you've already realized you can't save them both. It really is a shame. Oh, and you have me to deal with as well. You could perhaps save one of them in time, but could you do it after defeating me? Do you think they'll even be alive long enough to find out?"

The pleasure in his voice made her anger almost as strong as the helplessness and terror she felt, but not quite. She reached out with ascard. She needed help. Her reach struck a wall of power. The barriers around these rooms were strong and old, protecting the secrets within, but she had breached them earlier, following the touch of the ring. From the inside, however, they were stronger than ever. Someone had enhanced them considerably not to keep magic out in this case, but to keep it in.

"No, you won't be calling for help," Myac said, correctly translating her change of focus. "The barriers have been cleverly fortified by an adept who specializes in such things. I did make a little modification in the hopes that you would feel Adran's suffering through your ring, but it is mostly flawless."

She made herself breathe deep and slow. Despair was welling up inside her. She couldn't afford to let it overwhelm her. Perhaps she could manage something through the ring if he'd made an exception in the barriers for it.

"Wasting time, aren't you? I don't think they can hold on much longer."

She glared at him. "What does it matter if you won't let me help them?" She hissed the question, fury burning molten within her even as defeat loomed up like a dark shadow in her mind.

"Well, I suppose it doesn't, though I am curious who you would choose to help. Would it be your beloved emperor's best friend or the young creator you seem so fond of? Tell me."

Despite the desire not to let him see her cry, she felt tears begin to escape down her cheeks. Through her power, she could feel both men growing weaker. Neither had much time left. She began to work the ascard in both of them, trying to find a way to stabilize them at least. To buy a little time.

Adran's body jerked when a fresh wound opened along his neck, his eyelids fluttering for a second. She screamed frustration, balling her hands into fists.

"You're not playing the game right."

"Why are you doing this?" Her demand rang hoarse and desperate in her ears. She yearned to help Adran, but Myac was too well tuned to her ascard signature after their blending of power in Lyra. Anything she did, Myac would feel and he would make Adran suffer for it.

The amusement in Myac's eyes faded and he frowned. A deep inner pain flashed across his face then. It was a pain for which Indigo could feel no sympathy anymore.

"Yiloch destroyed my life. I thought I would pay him back. I would take everything he held dear away from him. His empire, his companions, ultimately, his life, but my efforts always goes awry. Often thanks to you, it seems," he added with a bitter smirk. "And he just gets more and more. He gets his empire. He gets you…"

A chill passed through her as his voice trailed off. "How did he destroy your life?" Her voice trembled, almost as much as her body did now, feeling the agony of the two men dying. He was right, she couldn't save them both, and the longer they delayed the less chance she would have of saving either.

"Did you know he killed my mother? Beheaded her right in front of me and left me for dead. That is the man you love. A heartless murderer." His expression was cold, dark with hatred. "But you knew that. You saw him kill his father. Blood spattered on his face and in his hair. His eyes gleaming with savage pleasure. You know the monster he is."

"*You* would speak of monsters," she snarled. Adran's heartbeat was slowing, failing. It couldn't work much longer given the amount of blood he had lost and the extensive damage his body suffered. She wasn't sure how long Ian could last either. It depended on what poison had been used.

"If I am a monster, it is only because that is what he made me."

"Stop this, please." Her voice broke in a desperate sob, but she didn't care. Let him see her breaking. Maybe he would find some inkling of pity within and have mercy.

Myac sneered, dashing the faint hope. "Pick, Indigo. Who would you save?"

A flicker of movement in the hallway beyond Myac caught her eye. A flash of silver reflected in the candlelight. The silver moved and she realized it was the blade of a sword. For a second, Yiloch's face appeared then vanished again in the deeper shadows of the hall. Why hadn't Myac sensed him? Why hadn't she sensed him? Had they both been too distracted?

No. There was a perfectly logical reason neither of them had detected him. It was the ring she had given him along with the barriers around the room working together to hide his presence. Hope flickered back to life within her and she struggled to focus, tried to remember what Myac had just said. If she did anything to betray Yiloch's presence now, she would be trying to rescue three men from Myac's clutches.

Meeting Myac's eyes again, she saw them narrow. A glimmer of suspicion rising at her brief distraction.

I would save you.

"It doesn't matter who I would choose," she protested, recalling his question. She didn't try to fight the trembling in her hands or the tears that still ran down her cheeks. No matter what happened now, she was going to lose at least one of them.

"If I told you I would let you save the one you chose, would that change things?"

"Then what," she hissed. "You'd stand aside and let us leave?"

"I owe you something for freeing me from the Grey adept in Lyra. I would let the one you saved leave. Not you though. You can't expect me to let you go that easily."

Adran's heart stopped. Indigo spun toward him, sinking to her knees next to the chair in the thickening pool of blood.

"No!"

A gasp from Myac drew her attention and she turned to see a silver blade thrust out through his chest. Yiloch grabbed him around the throat, pulling him close. He released the hilt of his sword, leaving it punched through Myac's chest, and drew a dagger. The dagger he ran across Myac's neck, slicing deep with a speed and strength that required ascard power.

"If I created you," he whispered, "then it is my place to destroy you as well." He let go of Myac and the adept slumped to the floor, the shock in his eyes already fading as blood gushed from his wounds.

She turned back to Adran, checking all his vitals, using ascard to assess him. There was nothing to do. He was already gone beyond her reach. Still knelt there in a pool of blood and defeat, she withdrew her power and thrust it into Ian, filtering the poison from his system as fast as she could. He was on the edge, moments from joining Adran, but there was still a chance. Silent sobs shook her as she worked and she felt Yiloch move around her to where Adran was, still bound to the chair. She continued to focus on the task while he cut Adran free and laid him out on the table, anguish pouring off him in staggering waves.

In time, Ian's pulse steadied and his breathing began to even out. He would live, though he needed more care. She sagged forward, catching herself with her hands on the blood-soaked floor, her strength nearly gone, and wept, vaguely aware that the ends of her hair were trailing in Adran's blood.

Yiloch's silence finally drew her out of her misery. Glancing around, she found him sitting beside the table on which Adran lay. His elbows rested on the table, his head in his hands, silver hair creating a curtain that hid his face from her. The surging anguish was gone, replaced by a hollow misery. She longed to comfort him, but what could she say or do? Adran had been with him his entire life. How did one help with a loss of that magnitude?

She struggled to her feet. The weight of the blood that had soaked into her skirt made it drag heavy at her waist, pulling down her weary body and her breaking heart. Adran's blood, everywhere, on everything. Myac's blood coated the floor now too. So much blood.

She took a few tentative steps closer to Yiloch. "Yiloch?"

He lifted his head from his hands, but he didn't look away from Adran. He held out a hand to her.

"I believe this is yours," he murmured, the emptiness in his voice drawing more tears from her tired, painful eyes.

He opened his hand. On his palm rested the pearl ring he had given her, still smeared with blood.

"I'm so sorry," she managed to choke out around the painful tightness in her throat. "I tried."

His hand closed on the ring and withdrew. When he spoke again, it was barely more than a whisper. "I believe you did. I know you did, but I need someone to blame right now, someone I can still hurt. I don't want that to be you."

She winced as her heart fragmented again, breaking more than she would have thought possible.

You've proven you can hurt me before.

She turned away from him and walked slowly, weary in more than flesh, over to where Ian still lay. Kneeling, she placed a hand against his neck, finding his pulse without ascard this time. It was weak, but steady.

"By The Divine!"

She turned her head to look at the newcomer. The motion felt slow and unsteady, as though even that effort was almost more than she could manage. She was hollow inside. Broken.

Caplin stood in the doorway, staring at the carnage around the room, looking as though he might be sick. Given his battle experience, she thought that was a considerable testament to the horror of the scene. Yiloch made no move to acknowledge him, so she made herself rise and took a few steps toward him. Several guards waited in the hallway behind him. She knew how she must look with blood in her hair, on her hands, soaked into her skirt, so it didn't surprise her when most of them narrowed their eyes in accusation and disgust before looking away. Only one of them met her eyes, a middle-aged man who might have been attractive if not for the poorly healed scar across the bridge of his nose.

She held his gaze. "This man was poisoned," she said, indicating Ian with one hand. "I've cleared the poison from his system, but he still needs attention. Take him to the west building and ask for a master healer."

The guard with the scar moved to do her bidding then hesitated, looking to Caplin for approval. Drawing on ascard, she prepared to manipulate him if necessary, but Caplin met her eyes then nodded to the man. She stepped aside, releasing the extra power as two of the guards lifted Ian between them. The creator moaned as they carried him from the room. The sound, a confirmation that he was indeed alive, comforted her. She watched them until they passed out of sight. Part of her wished Ian had been the one to die. She loved him, but it would have hurt Yiloch less to lose him. A vile sting of guilt came quick on the heels of that though, making her wince.

"Are you hurt?"

She looked down at the skirt of her dress, at her bloodied hands. How should she answer that question? Physically, she was unharmed. Emotionally, she would feel better if she had been soaked in lard, mauled by a pack of dogs then thrown in salt water.

"It's Adran's blood," she said finally.

Caplin glanced at the figure on the table with open-mouthed dismay. He'd spent some time with Adran in the campaign against Yiloch's father, though not as much as he'd spent with the captain's late sister, Eris. The mess on the table was hardly recognizable as the same man.

"That's…"

She jerked a hand up quickly and he fell silent. The last thing she wanted was a crass comment that might set Yiloch off. There were now more people in the room for him to take out his rage on and most of them were ill equipped to deal with him.

"I should be arresting him," Caplin said in a low voice, his eyes darting to Yiloch.

She looked over at the Lyran emperor. He hadn't moved from his position, bowed forward beneath a misery she could feel all too well through the link, but never truly *feel* as he did. His beautiful hair still obscured his features. His hand, however, balled to a fist around her ring, betraying the molten fury she could feel coming off him now, the defiance. The emotions warned her that he was hungry for conflict, any outlet for the pain and hopeless rage with him. Myac called him a monster. Whether she agreed with that assessment or not, right now she was willing to bet he would be capable of monstrous things.

"Let's not," she said. Relief washed through her when Caplin allowed her to direct him back down the hallway with a hand on his elbow. "Why did you come here?"

"You said something about convincing Lord Serivar to confess. I figured you might have come here and I was concerned given the way you left." In the Headmaster's office, several guards stood around Serivar's prone form looking uncertain. Caplin nodded to the still figure. "Was he also poisoned?"

She scowled, a refreshing hatred burning up through a small fraction of her sorrow. "No. I put him to sleep. I needed him out of the way." *Even if he were poisoned, I wouldn't tell you. Not until he was good and dead.*

She turned to stare back down the hallway. Yiloch still hadn't moved. She could feel his every black emotion; hatred, despair, anguish, even fear. Perhaps he feared going on without the one companion who had always been beside him. Struggling against more tears, she faced Caplin.

"You need to understand, Prince Caplin." There was a slight stiffening in his shoulders at her formal address, but she couldn't bring herself to feel bad for him. He had chosen not to trust her back when it mattered most. They couldn't be the friends they had been once. Not now. Too much had happened. Too much had changed. "Adran has been by Yiloch's side his entire life. Myac tortured Adran to death to make Yiloch suffer. The Lyran emperor is a lethal man when angry and this would not be the best time to test him. Leave him with me and I will see that he doesn't leave Demin until things are resolved."

"I should be arresting you as well, Lady Indigo."

She met his eyes, but she didn't need to see the remorse in them to know he wouldn't argue the matter, she could feel him yielding, melting under a mountain of regret.

"Arrest Lord Serivar. It's near sunrise. I will be at the palace with Emperor Yiloch before nightfall tomorrow to go before the king. This situation will be resolved, but first, there are the dead and those who survived them to attend to."

Caplin nodded. "Is there any way I can be of help?"

She considered the offer. There were so many complications to deal with and Yiloch himself was apt to be the greatest. There were some things Caplin was in a unique position to help with though, not the least of which was their criminal status. "I could use a temporary pardon for Yiloch and myself, or at the very least, permission to move about the city as needed. A few guards to help move bodies and to act as escorts or speak in our defense should we need such would also be welcome."

Caplin nodded. "It will be done. I can also provide you quarters in the palace for the time being so you can both have some privacy in which to rest before you see my father."

She narrowed her eyes, wary of the offer.

"As guests, not prisoners," he clarified, understanding her hesitation. "I will arrange for proper guest quarters to be prepared for you when you're ready and I will see that you are provided clean clothes."

She closed her eyes and took a deep breath. It was good to have his support, at least as far as this. It relieved a small bit of the burden that weighed her down. "Thank you, Caplin."

He nodded to Serivar. "Can you wake him? It would make transportation easier."

"I'd really rather not."

Caplin narrowed his eyes at her and she shrugged.

"I tied off the ascard working. It will wear off in a few more hours. Given his ascard ability, I think it would be best if he were in custody by then."

"Take him and put him in the carriage," he ordered with a nod to two of the remaining guardsmen. He set a hand on her shoulder then and gave it a gentle squeeze. "Please be careful, Indigo."

She nodded, resisting the urge to pull away, and watched in silence as he left, leaving four more guardsmen behind with orders to assist her as needed. He didn't specifically tell them to follow her orders, however, a lack that emphasized the distance built up between them. When Caplin was gone, the men turned to her. Their regard was openly skeptical, but they would do as their prince commanded, though she had no doubt they were here to ensure she made no escape attempts as much as anything. Still, she had their assistance and protection. That was all she could ask.

"Wait here a moment."

Without waiting for their response, she returned to the training room. Yiloch hadn't moved and the turmoil of emotions creating a storm around him hadn't improved.

"We should move him." The sudden blast of searing anger shocked her. She took a step back from him. "Eventually," she added more to herself.

Turning, she walked back to Myac and leaned down, taking the hilt of the sword in her hands. When she pulled the body shifted, but the blade stayed where it was. Glancing down the hall, she considered asking one of the guardsmen for help, then realized Yiloch might not take kindly to them handling his sword. Biting her lip in frustration, she used some of the little ascard power left in her to free the weapon from the ribs it was wedged between and drew it free, swallowing a rush of bile at the sensation of the blade sliding through flesh and bone. After sweeping it clean with more ascard, she walked over and set it on the table alongside Adran.

Returning to the office, she sent one of the guards to retrieve blankets from the medical buildings in which they could wrap the bodies to move them. It made sense to send both bodies back to Lyra so that they could be dealt with according to the customs of their home country. However, there was still much to do here, so she would move them to the dead rooms in the west building where healers could maintain the bodies until they were ready to accompany them home. She would talk to the healers herself when they took Myac's body to the dead rooms. That way she could express in person the need for careful preservation and respectful handling, especially in Adran's case. Yiloch, she would give a little more time alone with Adran.

Sinking down in Serivar's large chair, she rested her head back and closed her eyes. She was so weary. If only she could rest for a few minutes, then perhaps things wouldn't seem so terrible.

"My lady, the blankets."

She opened her eyes and stared up at the guardsman. Had he been gone more than a few seconds? She must have dozed off. Part of her hated him for disturbing her, but none of this was his fault and there was still work to be done. She forced herself to rise again.

"Yes. Thank you. Come with me."

She supervised their work, placing herself between the guardsman and Yiloch to eliminate any risk of them disturbing him. They rolled Myac over and his head twisted unnaturally, lolling so that his pale eyes stared at her even when his body faced away. The ascard enhanced slice of Yiloch's dagger had cut more than halfway through his neck, leaving little to hold the head in place. Her stomach lurched and she covered her mouth with one hand as a guard reached over and straightened the head.

"Are you all right, my lady?"

She nodded hastily, averting her gaze. "Just cover him and we'll take him to the west building."

The guardsman raised an eyebrow at that, but refrained from questioning further. She followed the two who lifted Myac at a distance as they carried him from the room. The other two followed close behind her. When she continued out of the office, the two remaining guards hesitated. She looked back at them and understood the problem. They weren't about to leave one of the fugitives unguarded.

"Both of you will stay here. Do not go back into the training room until I return and do not let anyone else go back there either. Understood?"

They nodded and took up positions inside the office door.

It took a few hours to give a satisfactory account of her situation that didn't reveal too much information to the master healers on duty in the west building. Eventually, and with the slightest touch of emotional manipulation, she convinced them to care for the bodies until the return trip to Lyra. Throughout that time, she maintained awareness of Yiloch through her link to him and the ring he still held, hoping he wouldn't get a sudden urge to go somewhere. A quick touch along the link told her Ian had received more of the needed care and was resting quietly now. Sinking further beneath a load of physical and emotional exhaustion with every passing moment, she trudged back to the other building. The hard part was only starting.

This time, when she entered the training room, she shut the door behind her, leaving the guards in the office and taking a few seconds to check the barriers still protecting the room making sure they would hear nothing.

"Yiloch?" She accepted the twitch of one finger as adequate acknowledgement. "We must move Adran to the west building where they can care for him until it is time to take him back to Lyra."

There was no hint of response, not even a flare of emotion. She chewed at her lip. She wanted to yell at him, to strike him even, but that was her own tiredness and misery driving her. If they both gave into the storm of emotions, the results wouldn't be pretty. A strong temptation to manipulate him with her ability nagged at her, but she resisted. If he realized what she was doing, it would only make things much worse and she was growing too exhausted to risk it.

"Please."

Yiloch stood, his movements slow and deliberate. He picked up his sword, absently wiping the blade on pants that were already stained with Adran's blood without noticing that she had already cleaned it. He sheathed it then stepped up alongside the table and carefully lifted Adran's body. His gaze fell upon her like a splash of icy water.

"Where?"

CHAPTER TWENTY SEVEN

When they finally arrived at the palace, Caplin welcomed them himself, his manner solemn and wary. He escorted them to the rooms they could use. He never had learned to make full use of the serving staff at his family's home. It didn't surprise her to learn that his habits hadn't changed now that he was prince. The rooms he escorted them to were the same extravagant rooms Yiloch and his entourage had used when they came to make an alliance with King Jerrin what felt a lifetime ago now. There were a number of guards stationed outside the exits to the common area, but the common area itself and the bedchambers were empty. She appreciated that he was at least treating Yiloch with the respect due his station even though the Lyran emperor hadn't yet been cleared of the assassinations. The resentment and mistrust she could feel directed at him, Caplin kept hidden under a gracious facade.

Yiloch took no notice. He hadn't spoken a word since asking her where to take Adran's body. As soon as Caplin offered him use of one bedchamber, he walked in and shut the door behind him.

Indigo grimaced as the lock clicked into place.

Caplin offered her a sympathetic look. "I have a key if you want it," he murmured.

She shook her head. "No, he needs some time alone. I won't worry about it just yet." Besides, she could open it with ascard if she wished to, though she wasn't about to mention that to Caplin right then. His trust of her was deeply shaken already. She turned and walked toward the neighboring room. "You must give him a chance. He played no part in the murder of your uncle and his family."

"That remains to be proven, but he still stole your heart away. I can't help resenting that. I would have been much less trouble."

She laughed, though it sounded weak and hollow, dampened by sorrow. "Possibly, but I would have been a terrible political match for you and it isn't his fault I fell in love with him."

Caplin smiled. The expression looked forced.

I can't deal with this right now. She sighed. "You do love Andrea, do you not?"

"I do, but not…"

He trailed off when she held up one hand. "That's all that matters now. I need some rest."

Caplin nodded. "I can see that. We'll deal with other things tomorrow."

She glanced out through the opening to the terrace that overlooked the center courtyard. The sun was already below the level of the opposite roofline. The birds chattering on the roof peak were silhouettes in the spray of light that still peeked over. Where had the day gone?

"Yes, tomorrow. Thank you again for your assistance today."

He walked over to take her hand and squeezed it. "We were the best of friends long before any of this madness. I haven't forgotten that."

She found a smile for him, weak, weary, tempered with sadness, but a smile nonetheless. "I'm glad those memories still hold a place in your heart. No matter what comes, those memories are still ours."

She pulled her hand away and entered the neighboring room, shutting the door on Caplin and the world outside. A selection of clothing options waited for her, draped over the back of the couch in the sitting area. She could look them over later. Now she longed for nothing more than to strip off the blood soaked dress and crawl into that soft, enticing bed. When that was done, she closed her eyes and moved her awareness into the next room.

Yiloch lay stretched out along the couch, she could feel him staring at the ceiling, his emotions a thick ball of darkness roiling around him. With the lightest touch, she incrementally enhanced his fatigue until he finally drifted off to sleep. Drawing back into herself, she used the last of her failing strength to tie off a working of ascard to ensure that she would wake at the proper hour and finally relented to the need for rest that had been dragging at her for hours.

●

It was an hour after midnight when the light tug of her own power pulled her awake. Stretching her senses, she found little activity in the palace. Quickly, she chose the darkest item among the clothing options and dressed. Adding a cloak of ascard to hide her, she moved out into the palace.

I'm getting good at this sneaking about. Perhaps there is a future for me in thievery... or politics.

There was morbid humor in the thought. Pushing such things from her mind, she focused on tracing Serivar's presence to the ascard shielded prison cells under the barracks. The shielding prevented use of ascard from within the cell, but tracking from outside was easy enough. Getting into the barracks would take a bit more masking, but she was reasonably refreshed after her rest and more than strong enough to manage the task. Now, with Myac gone, there was no one she knew of who could rival her ascard strength. What place did someone with such absurd power have in the world?

She heaved a sigh, finding she needed to refocus herself again on the task at hand. The night outside the palace walls was cool, pleasant, and very dark. The last worked in her favor, reducing the amount of power she needed to use to hide herself. There were several soldiers standing near the front door of the barracks talking heatedly about something. A moment's eavesdropping told her they were discussing whether Caithin should make a move against Lyra now. Word of the Grey Army's attack and Lyra's weakened state had made it across the Gilded Straight, as one would expect of two so closely placed nations. From what she could tell, they didn't know Yiloch was in Caithin, which was all for the best.

This was her task, to stop any military action against Lyra before it could start. Not only stop it, but also open the door for trust to build again between the two nations. That required clearing Yiloch's name and exposing the guilty parties, though one of those parties had already faced his punishment. The path that had led her to this point was long and confusing, not a path she would have necessarily chosen for herself or even considered possible in the beginning. Now that she was here, there was little point in not going forward.

She insinuated a tendril of thought into one man's mind, giving him a restless urge to walk. The man shifted his feet, glancing around as though searching for something.

"Come on. All this talk of war has me itching to fight. I need to walk off some energy."

The other three agreed with his sentiment, with a tiny touch of outside intervention, and they walked past her out toward the practice rings. She frowned after them. That kind of mental meddling gave her an unclean feeling, but it was terribly handy.

Reaching her power beyond the door, she checked for any presence in the main room. Other than several soldiers asleep in their bunks, the room was empty and it would be easy enough to hold them in sleep. Moving quickly, she made her way into the sleeping quarters and down between the rows of beds, most of them occupied, then stepped through the open door into the room above the prison.

Two men sat in the small musty room. A dice set lay scattered to one side of the small table they sat at, but the game appeared to have lost their interest. Their grumbled conversation focused on the boredom inherent with pulling a shift on prison watch. She shook her head, moving across the room behind them, blending herself with the ascard in the air. Boredom would be such a luxury. Too bad one rarely felt that way when they had it.

Sneaking down the stairs that led to the prison cells, she unlocked the entrance gate with a touch of power, muffling the squeal of the rusty metal gate swinging open. Once inside she focused her power on Serivar, following the signature of his inner aspect to his cell. He sat on a small cot staring into the empty cell across from him. In this setting, after all that had happened, he no longer possessed any of the mystery and authority that had awed her when she first came to the academy. He looked frail and pathetic. She established a set of barriers around them to block sound and prevent anyone else from seeing her.

"Trouble sleeping, Headmaster?" she asked, infusing her tone and the air around them with disgust.

Serivar started when she allowed him to see her and stood, moving a few steps back.

"Going somewhere?"

"They allowed you down here?" His voice trembled.

She offered him a cruel smile. She hated this game, hated acting this way, but the man before her evoked such loathing that the performance was almost tolerable. "Do you really think they'd allow me in here? I'm still considered a traitor to the crown."

She felt a cold fear sweep out from him and he took another step back.

She took a quick moment to examine the barriers that kept Serivar from projecting his power out of the cell. As she suspected, the barrier was tuned to his inner aspect, which meant it would have no effect on her. Drawing on ascard, she used the trick she had learned from Sine, swapping herself with the ascard in the air next to him. She'd never tried moving beyond something solid like the prison bars between them, but it worked as intended and he backed into the rear wall, his eyes popping wide. Fear pounded off him now and she was almost ashamed at the satisfaction it brought her, but only almost. Images of Adran as she last saw him flickered through her mind, fueling her anger and strengthening her purpose.

"What do you want?"

She gave a sharp laugh. "As if you don't know. I want you to confess. Confess everything."

Serivar stood a little straighter, pulling on a cloak of confidence that her ability betrayed as false. "You can still come back to the academy and the King's Order, Indigo. Let Emperor Yiloch take the fall for this. I will stand behind you. Prince Caplin will stand behind you."

Perhaps he still hoped to intimidate her with his authority as headmaster and council member. Apparently, he didn't realize that the academy and the order were no longer the core of her life. Caithin was no longer the core of her life. She brushed back her hair, making the gesture seem casual, but it revealed her tattoo. Serivar narrowed his eyes, squinting at it in the dim light. Then his eyes widened again and she felt his nervousness grow to the verge of panic.

"I don't need you behind me anymore, Serivar. In fact, I'd prefer to keep you where I can see you," she added with a sour smirk. "I think you know what Myac did to Ian. I think you may have even played a part in that. Do you know what he did to Lord Adran? While you sat complacently in your little office, pretending innocence, telling yourself how righteous you are, Myac was in that room mutilating Adran. He tortured him until his heart gave out from shock and loss of blood."

Serivar shook his head. Fresh fear blossomed in his eyes. "No. I didn't know Adran was there. I didn't expect that to happen."

"But you didn't care, did you? Whatever Myac was doing in that room didn't matter to you, not then, but it does now."

Serivar shrank away, pressing back into the wall again. His eyes darted around the small cell, looking for some escape route to open up to him.

She drew on more ascard, pinning him in place and forcing him to meet her eyes. "You will confess everything. If you don't, I will hold you in place while Yiloch unleashes his pain on you. I'll make sure you suffer at least as much as Adran did. I promise. Myac's cruelty will seem kind by comparison."

Serivar whimpered and she decided that was as much of an agreement as she could expect. She released him and turned away, transporting herself back to the other side of the bars. "Remember, Serivar, you cannot hide from me and no one can keep me from you. With Myac gone, my power has no rival."

As she started to walk away, Serivar stepped up to the bars, emboldened by the distance between them. "I'm proud of you, Indigo. You've finally become the weapon I wanted you to be."

She had to catch herself, fighting the desire to strike out at him. Letting him get to her now, letting him see any flaw in her armor, would undermine everything she had done this night. Turning, she smiled, adding a subtle, unnatural shimmer to the copper in her eyes in the hopes of unnerving him further. His quick step back confirmed her success.

"Unfortunately for you, I'm not working for you anymore."

She turned her back on him again, gratified by the intense fear she felt blossoming within him. The gratification quickly dissolved into a sense of revulsion. Had she truly become the weapon he wanted to make her? His words, unwelcome as they were, rang true.

Was it too late to change that?

•

Back in the common area outside their rooms, she could feel that Yiloch was awake again. The thought of going back to her room to sit alone with her confused emotions appealed less than that of facing his misery. He needed an outlet, an explosion of rage that would break down the wall he'd built around his sorrow. Perhaps she could give him that. She couldn't stand leaving him the way he was and he wouldn't be any good to her before the king in his current state.

She tried the door, but it was still locked. She knocked. There was no response, but a surge of irritation from within the room confirmed that he had heard her.

"Yiloch, open the door."

She waited a few minutes before knocking softly again. When there was still no answer, she closed her eyes and scanned the room with ascard, making sure nothing had been moved since the Wakening Festival feast, when she had spent the night there in Yiloch's arms while Jayce lay in a drugged slumber in another room of the palace. It might be easier to manipulate the lock, but that was insufficient in its impact. He needed to be reminded who he was dealing with and the intrusion would force him to focus his attention on something outside himself.

Selecting a spot past the couch so that he would be looking at her when she appeared, she swapped herself with the ascard there.

When she appeared in front of him, he flinched ever so slightly, eyes widening a fraction in surprise. "You don't take a hint well," he snarled, quick to adjust.

"No. Not really." She met the hostility in his tone with flippancy.

"Then perhaps I should be blunt. I don't want you here."

She let out a sharp exhale with the pain of his curt rejection and focused past it. She wasn't about to give in that easily, not after all she had done for him.

"You really think you can chase me off so easily? I thought you a better judge of character."

Yiloch scowled at her, a dark fury rising in his pale eyes. "Don't provoke me right now."

"Why not? You're too busy bathing in your misery to be much of a threat," she hissed. His temper flared, black and dangerous, unpredictably strong. It wouldn't take much to drive him past his limits. She checked all of her protections, strengthening them as necessary and slipped a few tendrils of ascard into him, needling his rage closer to the breaking point with tiny manipulations.

"Do I disappoint you?" he growled. His pale eyes shimmered like daggers of ice as he glared at her. One hand dropped to the hilt of his sword. The muscles in his body tensed, prepared to move, and he started to draw on ascard.

Her nerves danced and she checked her many protections again, continuing her subtle ascard manipulation of him while she spoke. If she pushed him to the breaking point, they could pick up the pieces from there, but the wall he'd put up had to break first. The sooner it broke, the sooner he could face his grief and begin the healing process. "Frankly, yes. I had mistaken you for a stronger man. Maybe all the strength you ever had died in that room." The deliberate cruelty stung almost as much as the flash of anguish from him, but it worked.

Though she expected the retaliation, the speed with which he moved shocked her. It took all her will to stand steady when his blade swung at her. With her barriers protecting her from injury, she stopped the blade in the air and took hold of it with one hand. His eyes widened, staring at her hand. Maybe she should hate him for the attack, but she didn't. She had deliberately driven him to it and she loved him. She was probably the only one with the strength to love him the way he needed to be loved in that moment.

"You can't drive me away."

"Why are you doing this?" His voice trembled with pent up emotion, rage breaking before the weight of sorrow.

"Because I love you," she answered, making her voice gentle now, encouraging the fracturing of his defensive anger.

He released the hilt and turned away from her. "Haven't you noticed the trail of death I leave in my wake."

She dropped the weapon and he flinched when it hit the floor.

"I don't care," she whispered into the ensuing silence. When he said nothing she took a step closer. Her heart ached for the pain that radiated off him, leaching away his anger at speed now. She had helped force that pain to the surface. She wouldn't regret it, no matter how much it hurt. "I'm so sorry. I couldn't save him."

Yiloch sank to his knees, bowing over as if someone had dropped a great weight on his shoulders. She felt the pressure building within him and placed a sound barrier around them seconds before he threw his head back and a roar of fury and anguish burst from him. The torment encompassed in the sound sent a shudder through her and tears began to stream down her cheeks.

She walked up behind him then moved cautiously around to stand before him. His head hung so that his hair hid his face from her, but his body trembled. She touched his head, sliding her fingers into his silvery hair. He reached out then and pulled her against him, his face pressing against her chest, his tears dampening her dress. She wrapped her arms around him. His muscles were iron under her fingertips, taut and trembling with the force of the misery that filled him. She held him and waited.

"No empire is worth all of this," he murmured a while later. "So many have died because of me, because of my ambition."

Indigo closed her eyes and took a deep breath. To tell him that wasn't true would be lying to a degree. Still, she couldn't let it go at that.

"How many more would have suffered and died if you hadn't removed your father from the throne?" She gave the question a moment to sink in, not expecting an answer, then drove ahead. "You are a man of great status. Many will admire and adore you. Some will hate you and try to hurt you any way they can. A rare few will stand behind you regardless of what you do. One of those few is still here with you and she needs you." Her voice cracked and she fell silent, fighting back tears.

He moved her arms away and got to his feet. Gentle fingers brushed her hair back from her face and he stood staring at her for a minute as though seeing her for the first time in years.

"I know you tried," he murmured. "I know Ian and Adran weren't the only ones Myac made suffer in that room."

She drew back her power, blocking his emotions for fear that they would become something other than what she wanted them to be.

"I'm tired, Yiloch, and I am not the person I expected to be. I'm not sure how I feel about the person I am. I need to know that I haven't changed myself, my whole world, for nothing. Right now, I'm not so sure." Tears ran faster down her cheeks and he brushed a few away, but more followed.

"You're strong and beautiful and free to choose your future. If those things bring you no comfort in this moment, then as long as my love is something to you," he whispered, "you can be sure it wasn't for nothing."

She exhaled a mountain of tension, overcome by relief and the pleasure his words gave her. He leaned down and kissed her. Then he pulled her close and held her tight. She melted against him.

CHAPTER TWENTY EIGHT

Several hours later, they sat together on the couch, Indigo leaning against him. He had his arms around her. Her warmth against him was comforting. If only they could stay in this spot and forget everything else. He couldn't forget, though. Adran was gone and even though Myac was gone as well, his final blow left Yiloch feeling crippled. Even with Indigo there to ease the pain, he felt as though someone had cut away the core of his being, leaving him a shell of what he had been.

He breathed her in, seeking comfort in the scent of her. She shifted in his arms. A slender arm reached out, her fingertips touching the hilt of his sword where he had placed it on the table next to them. He watched as she traced the fine metalwork of the pommel.

"My mother had that made for me when I turned fourteen. It's created. It will never bear a scratch. The blade will never lose its edge."

Her hand stopped for a moment, and then moved down the hilt, caressing over the crossguard. He felt her shoulders and chest lift with a small sigh.

"It's beautiful, for a weapon."

Yiloch chuckled and kissed her head. She drew her arm back and turned slightly, looking toward the door. Her expression became distant, the look of an adept engaging their power in some way, then she nodded to herself and leaned back into him again. The power she had shown him in the time he had known her was unnerving. It was something he was going to have to get used to if he meant to keep her around. At this point, he would rather die than let her go.

"Ian's coming."

"I should unlock the door," Yiloch said, accepting her words as fact.

"I'll get it."

Before Yiloch could move to release her, the lock clicked and the door cracked open. She was finding practical applications for her powers. It showed that she was accepting what she was instead of denying the extent of her ability in fear of the possible darker applications. He continued to hold her for as long as she stayed there, her slight weight warm and welcome against him. When she moved to sit up, he released her reluctantly.

A soft knock sounded in the room and the door opened a touch more under the gentle pressure. She stood suddenly, gesturing for him to stay where he was. He moved enough to sit up then waited, trusting her. She was privy to much more information than he was.

She opened the door. Ian stepped into the room, his dragging feet attesting to a still weakened state. His eyes and nose were red. He had been crying. Indigo held her arms out to him and the young creator all but fell into her embrace. His shoulders shook as he wept in her arms. The door clicked shut, untouched, behind him.

"I saw Adran," he choked out.

Yiloch grimaced. To be fair, the healers wouldn't have known Adran was Ian's cousin, but there was no need to let anyone see such a thing. He got to his feet, but kept his distance, watching as Indigo soothed the young creator. He couldn't help wondering if she would use her power to help pacify him. Ultimately, it didn't matter, as long as her attentions eased his pain. It was a double standard, he knew, since he resented the fact that she had used it to manipulate him at least once, probably more than that, but that was simply the way he felt. He had a somewhat obsessive need to always be in control. Maybe she could help him with that too.

Several minutes passed and Ian finally stepped back from her. He wiped his face rather gracelessly with one sleeve then threw a wary glance at Yiloch.

He watched with a growing sense of unease as Ian took a deep, shaking breath and walked up to him. The creator stopped a few feet in front of him and dropped to his knees, bowing his head.

"My lord, I beg your forgiveness. I didn't expect…" his voice broke before he could finish and he knelt there trembling.

Yiloch clamped down on a sudden flare of anger in that part of him that still longed for someone to blame. If there was anyone to lay blame on, he was probably the most deserving, not the creator. Indigo placed a hand on Ian's shoulder and the youth steadied. Yiloch gave her a glance he hoped showed his gratitude then looked down at Ian.

"Ian, none of us expected what happened. We can see everything as clearly as we want to, looking back, but the future is still as much of a mystery now as it was then. You tried. We all tried." He stopped there, finding it hard to say anything more without his own sorrow getting the better of him.

Ian got unsteadily to his feet and looked at him, his eyes glistening pools of misery. Yiloch cursed inwardly and took hold of Ian's shoulders, pulling him in to a strong embrace. The young creator was the closest link he had left to his lost friend. Ian returned the embrace. Glancing past the youth in his arms, he saw Indigo nod, a faint smile of approval touching her lips.

Yiloch pushed him away after a few minutes. "You ought to rest. You look dreadful."

Ian smiled weakly, giving him a look that conveyed similar sentiments, then he nodded. Yiloch guided him to the bed with a hand on one shoulder. Ian shucked off his jacket and boots, falling onto the bed like a tossed sack of grain. His shoulders shook as he curled in on himself and Yiloch glanced at Indigo. She nodded, understanding the request behind his look. In seconds, Ian was asleep.

"You've done that to me a few times," he commented, watching Ian's steady breathing.

"Yes." She made no effort to deny it. "Only when you truly needed it."

He gave her a questioning look. "Like when you snuck out of Lyra this last time."

She shrugged, unwilling to argue with him about it now.

Are you coming back with me?

The words hung on the tip of his tongue, but he wouldn't ask. It was her decision where she went from here. It had always been her decision. She knew the offer was open. He could think of nothing better than to take her back to Lyra with him. She had so many skills that would be of great help to him and his country, not the least of which was that of keeping him sane. She could train healers, help Ian with the other adepts, even attend public audiences to alert him when someone lied or had ill intentions. With her apparent language skills, she might also be of help in dealing with the Grey Army. There were endless possibilities. All he cared about was that she would be close to him.

She was watching him with a shrewd expression now. "I don't imagine you want to go before the king in Caithin attire."

Yiloch glanced down at himself. The clothes he wore still bore Adran's blood, dried into the fabric in numerous places. His chest tightened at the realization, but she spoke the truth. He would rather go before the Caithin king covered in Adran's blood than wearing their clothes. Lyran blood ran pure through his veins. The history and pride in that blood were everything to his people, and they were still his people.

A small laugh drew his attention. She was shaking her head at him, smiling a weary, but fond smile. "Don't look so concerned. I think I can handle this."

In seconds, the blood was gone from his clothing. A small pile of red powder appeared on the ground before his feet. Yiloch knelt down and picked up a pinch of the dried blood. Some little bit of Adran that would disappear with time, the same way his memories would fade over time. He clenched his teeth, fighting the surge of emotion. Indigo's warm hand touched his face and he felt her sorrow through their link. He placed his hand over hers, closing his eyes as he pressed his face against the softness of her palm.

There was a knock on the door and he stood, glancing at Ian to make sure the sound hadn't woken him.

"Don't worry," Indigo reassured him as she moved to answer the door, "he won't wake for a while."

Yiloch nodded and followed her to the door. Caplin was waiting in the common area. He gave Yiloch's clothes a double take, recalling the state they had been in when he arrived, but he made no comment.

"King Gavin will see you both now, if you are ready."

Indigo glanced down at the dark dress she wore, her eyes wandering thoughtfully to the door of the next room.

"If you need a few minutes to change…"

She shook her head. "I can work with this."

In seconds, she had transformed the dress, changing the primary color to a rich, dark gold and the secondary color revealed at the bodice and through a split in the skirt, became a pale gold satin. Her hair, somewhat disheveled before, arranged into a rich caramel cascade of glossy waves.

Yiloch bit back a smile at Caplin's slack-jawed stare even as he wondered with a touch of unease what limits there were to her power.

"Well." Caplin started, at a loss for words. After a minute, he rediscovered some modicum of composure. "I suppose that will do. Shall we?"

Along the walk to the throne room, Yiloch observed that nothing had changed since King Gavin took his brother's place on the throne, at least not with any obvious sense of differing personal style. There were more guards than he remembered from his prior visit, a number of whom stood straighter as they passed, watching him with open mistrust. It didn't come as much of a surprise, considering what had happened to the prior royal family. Perhaps he would walk away from this audience with his innocence confirmed. If Indigo had any say, he certainly would. After she arrived in Yiroth with the Kudaness army at her back, he had little reason to doubt that she could make anything happen.

He remembered jovial King Jerrin from his first visit to Caithin. The man had been overly casual and a bit too absorbed with the finer aspects of rank. He had never struck Yiloch as a true leader, though he'd managed well enough and he was easy to deal with. What would King Gavin be like? He remembered the shrewd man from the King's High Council when he came to seek Caithin's alliance in overthrowing Emperor Rylan. Gavin would be more difficult than his brother had been. One rarely got so fortunate twice. Then again, they were siblings. Perhaps some of that welcoming disposition ran in the family.

At the double doors, Caplin left them, entering ahead to take up his proper place as prince. Indigo murmured something to the usher near the door who nodded and stepped in ahead of them. The man took up a spot to one side inside the door and nodded back to them, announcing them as they entered.

"Emperor Yiloch of Lyra and Lady Indigo Milan un Ani."

Yiloch was a little surprised at the title Indigo had given. That she distanced herself from her heritage here gave him hope that she didn't intend to stay when this was over.

The throne room, like the rest, was unchanged beyond the increased guard presence, four guardsmen for every two present on the previous visit. The throne room itself was understated, emphasizing in its simplicity the excessively ornate throne at its head. The man in the throne was heavyset like his brother, with the same dark eyes and thick nose. Beyond that, the resemblance vanished. The dark eyes were shrewd and calculating, quickly taking stock of Yiloch and Indigo, but holding all judgment inside. His dark beard and hair were well-trimmed, giving him a stern look that Yiloch could appreciate far more than the unkempt, bushy look his brother had favored. This man sitting on the throne looked like someone to be respected as ally or rival. The question remained as to which he would be.

King Gavin offered Yiloch a respectful nod, which Yiloch returned while Indigo offered a deep curtsy. She didn't wait for the king's acknowledgement, however, before rising from the curtsy, which won her an anxious look from Caplin who now stood to the right of the throne. King Gavin noted the gesture as well, with a tiny furrowing of his brow followed by what almost looked like a hint of a smile. Would he consider the Kudaness title she had given adequate explanation for her break from Caithin formality?

Oddly enough, Yiloch saw a brief flicker of approval in the king's eyes after a moment that was mirrored in the eyes of Lord Theron who now entered the room through a side door.

"Emperor Yiloch, I realize you came here under dire circumstances. Prince Caplin apprised me of your situation." He gave a slight nod in his son's direction. "However, it does surprise me that you came without more significant guard considering that you're wanted for regicide."

Yiloch felt his hackles rise, but Indigo took a step forward and curiosity stayed his tongue.

"Pardon me for speaking in your place, Emperor Yiloch." She looked at him long enough for him to give a nod of acknowledgement. "King Gavin, Emperor Yiloch has all of the protection he needs right here in this room." She gave a meaningful nod to each of the two guardsmen closest to the throne. "More protection, judging from the relative strength of your two adepts, than you have."

The guardsmen on either side of the throne, shifted ever so slightly and Yiloch smiled to himself. It truly was a pleasure to have her on his side.

King Gavin looked at the guardsman adept on his right who nodded once. He sat back in the throne and regarded her with a wary respect. His attention moved back to Yiloch after several minutes of silence.

"This is not easy for me, Emperor Yiloch. I have hated you with a passion I almost find frightening for the death of my brother and his family. Until a few hours ago, there was no one I could ever imagine hating more."

"Might I ask what changed a few hours ago, your majesty?" Yiloch asked, trying with little success to hide his surprise.

For just an instant, Indigo's expression turned cold enough to chill the room and he wondered what she knew of this, then the calm mask fell again.

"Someone I thought to be one of my most trusted council members opted to confess his guilt. Lord Serivar requested an audience with me this morning and explained that he and another man, a Lyran adept called Myac who was living here under an assumed identity, arranged the assassination of my brother and framed your adepts for it with the assistance of several recently removed members of the King's Order, two of whom have already acknowledged their guilt in exchange for some leniency in their sentences. Serivar went into considerable detail and Lord Theron's reports from his time in Lyra seem to back up his words. I'm not fond of being lied to. I'm uncertain why Lord Serivar was suddenly compelled to confess." Yiloch saw Caplin's eyes flicker to Indigo and away again. The prince suspected she played a part in Serivar's sudden compliance and he was willing to bet it was true. "Whatever the catalyst, he will die for his crimes."

Yiloch nodded. There was nothing to say. There was no way in which Serivar could pay enough for the people he had lost in this. It would have pleased him to spill the man's blood with his own hands, but King Gavin had suffered losses as well. This death was his to deal as much as Myac's death had been Yiloch's.

"It falls on me to acknowledge that you were wrongly accused along with several of your subjects, who, it shames me to say, are beyond my absolution. It would seem that you, that both of you..." he amended with a nod to Indigo, "...were misjudged and mistreated." Yiloch's jaw tensed as he bit back on his anger. He could feel Indigo's calming touch through their link. "The information I had led me to believe in your guilt. In light of this new information, I realize that we were all betrayed. I can only hope you will, in time, accept my apology. The alliance you built with King Jerrin is something we would like to see continue."

"I think..." Yiloch took a deep breath in an effort to hold his anger in check. Indigo's soothing contact, despite its manipulative nature, was suddenly a valuable asset. As much as he hated to admit it, Lyra needed this alliance right now. They were in a very vulnerable state. "My empire has seen much conflict of late. I have need to return to tend and heal its wounds and to see to those I have lost. Assistance with the stabilization of Lyra would be most welcome. Then when those affairs are in order, I would like to discuss our alliance further. And perhaps it might be time to open discussions regarding the slave trade."

King Gavin's jaw tightened, but then he released the tension with a heavy exhale. "Perhaps you are right. For now, I will offer an escort to see that you are not hindered in your departure. I have had little time to consider things since learning the truth of these ugly affairs. I am sure we can offer you assistance of some kind as you rebuild, but those discussions may need to take place at a later time."

Yiloch nodded, managing a gracious tone. "That would be deeply appreciated."

"Lady Indigo." Indigo met the king's eyes, standing a little straighter now that the attention had fallen on her. Yiloch fought a protective urge to move closer to her. She was capable of handling herself and of making her own decisions. "It seems we are in need of a new headmaster at the academy and head of the King's Order. Everything I have heard…" he glanced at Caplin who nodded, "…indicates that you would be well qualified for that position."

Indigo bowed her head. The link between them went silent and Yiloch struggled to maintain his calm as Caplin gazed down at her with unconcealed pleasure. The prince believed she would accept the offer, and why wouldn't she? They weren't only offering her welcome back into Caithin society, but as a person of considerable influence and prestige. He had lost so much. Would they take her from him too?

Indigo raised her eyes again. There was a strange mix of sorrow and pride in her expression. "Your highness, I am deeply honored. However, I cannot turn away from my duties in Lyra—"

"What duties?" Caplin interrupted, drawing a chastising look from his father for his outburst.

He frowned, staring at her with a hint of desperation in his gaze. Theron looked on with his unnerving serenity, considering all of them in thoughtful silence.

She met Caplin's eyes for a moment, her gaze tinged with sorrow. Then she turned her attention back to the king. A growing sense of victory filled Yiloch and he had to struggle to keep a smile at bay. It wouldn't gain him anything to provoke the prince.

"I have been asked to act as the ambassador for the Kudaness in Lyra. While I am there, I will also be training Lyran healers. I believe I am needed there right now more than I am here?" She spoke the last as a question and met his eyes.

"You are very much needed," Yiloch replied, not caring if they heard the relief and adoration in his voice.

A smile flickered across her lips before she faced Gavin. Caplin lowered his head, staring at the floor in resignation. Theron, oddly enough, smiled approval.

"If that is what you desire..." the King raised a questioning brow as he trailed off.

"Yes, King Gavin, it is." She punctuated the statement with a resolute nod.

"So be it."

CHAPTER TWENTY NINE

Dusk fell upon the docks as the boat turned out to sea, toward Lyra. A chill filled the air and Indigo wrapped her arms around herself. There was no reason to look back now. Caplin and Theron, who had accompanied them to the docks along with an escort of Caithin soldiers, still stood by the water watching the ship depart. She could feel them there, but there was nothing left to say, no reason to watch them disappear. Caithin was no longer her home. She would try to make a home on the other side of the Gilded Straight. In a letter she left with her uncle, she told him her roles there were what she wanted, her future assured.

Was this what she wanted? The thought of training other adepts truly appealed to her, as did working with Ian. The young creator reminded her of Caplin before they had grown apart, only he understood and accepted her ascard ability to a degree that Caplin never could. She smiled to herself. Yes, she would enjoy working with Ian. Yet, to be near Yiloch and never be able to have him as her own… Was she strong enough to stand that?

She drew upon more ascard to drive the ship a little faster. She had taken the time that morning to heal the wounds over Adran's body, something she would have done before Ian saw him had she not been too drained to think of such things. Now part of her ability remained focused on preserving the two bodies, Adran's on this ship and Myac's on board the one that followed with the two Caithin adepts keeping up its speed. Remembered tension lit a small fire within her, a shadow of the anger she'd felt earlier when she had asked the king's guardsmen to carry both bodies onto the ship.

Yiloch had refused to allow it. "I will not have that murderer and Adran carried in the same hold."

"Myac's body should be taken back to Lord Terral," she explained. "It is his right and his responsibility to deal with his son's body."

Indignation had rolled off Yiloch like a tidal wave, forcing her back a step. It was the underlying pain, however, that drove her to relent, throwing up a hand to stop his argument. He had clamped down on his rage, though it still blazed in his eyes.

"We will send Myac's body on another ship. I'll talk Caplin into sending a couple of adepts with us to speed that ship's passage, and I will speed this one."

Yiloch had agreed to the compromise. Looking back on the encounter, it wasn't hard to understand his position and the fact that he had managed to control his temper on the subject in his current state was a testament to how much he cared for her. It also strengthened her conviction that this was a bad idea. How could they possibly live in the presence of one another after he was married to Auryl? Such an arrangement would be torture. Perhaps she should have accepted King Gavin's offer and stayed in Caithin. She could have started over there and maybe found someone else in time.

The mere thought caused a twisting pain in her chest and she tightened her grip on her arms, her fingers pressing into her own flesh with near bruising force.

Sorrow, determination, and a remarkable strength of presence alerted her to Yiloch's approach. He glanced past her as he walked up to the railing, a dark anger bubbling to the surface when his icy gaze touched on the other ship. The anger drowned in a colorful palette of emotions when those beautiful eyes moved to her. She drew in her ability. It was too much like eavesdropping to be aware of so many feelings that weren't openly offered. She didn't want to know him that way.

"What now?" She forced the question out past a wall of apprehension. They needed to discuss the situation now, not later when the affairs of an empire might interfere. Here at least, he could do nothing but wait for the crossing to be over.

"Now?"

"For us? Will there be an *us* anymore?"

He leaned on the rail and she dared a glance, savoring the chiseled profile and the way his hair blew back in the wind. The muscles in his jaw tensed while he considered his reply and she had to struggle against the urge to read his emotions with her power.

"I have no interest in ever being without you again."

"But I can't be with you," she countered, yearning for some reassurance from him that made practical sense. Anything at all that would make their love feasible and finally put her fears to rest.

"I've told you before that none of my people would question your presence in the palace."

She took a deep breath, trying to ease the painful longing within. "I don't know that I can handle being second in your life."

He moved over behind her and wrapped his arms

around her, pulling her against him, then bent down so that his breath tickled her ear when he spoke and sent delicious shivers of desire through her. "You could never be second, Indigo. I couldn't bear to love anyone else this much."

"You know it isn't that easy—"

"You do love to make things difficult," he interrupted. "You're an unrivaled adept, a Kudaness priestess—"

"Priest," she corrected.

He chuckled and kissed her cheek. "A Kudaness *priest* and so many other remarkable things. I don't believe there are any limits to what you could be if you put your mind to it. What do *you* want to be?"

There was a slight tensing in his muscles when he asked. Could he actually be worried about her answer? She searched her mind. Of all the things she had been and had done, there was one thing that made her truly content, one place she was absolutely happy. She was there now.

"I want to be a teacher and a healer and someone people can respect and love. I want to be someone you respect and love," she murmured, pressing into him.

"You will always be that. We can figure out the rest," he whispered. She started to pull away and he added, "In a way that works for all three of us. I will not disregard Auryl's feelings in this. I promise."

Relaxing back into his arms, she closed her eyes to the salty wind and smiled. Somewhere along the way he had come to understand that, for her, disregarding Auryl's feelings wasn't satisfactory. Perhaps there was hope for him.

After a few minutes of silence, she turned in his arms and met his eyes. They still captivated her now as much as they had the first time she got lost in their pale depths. There was more pain in them now. A list of lost companions added to the still poignant sorrow of his mother's death. There was also love in those eyes, love he was willing to admit and fight for despite everything he had lost. He was a strong man, stronger than she had realized. She ran her fingers through his hair. Teaching in Lyra and acting as ambassador for the Kudaness were great honors and she could see herself coming to appreciate both roles as well as the ability to be where should could use her power to help and protect him, but this was what she wanted most.

"I believe we will work things out." Rising on the balls of her feet, she kissed him.

He pulled her closer, deepening the kiss, igniting desires only he could ignite. She wrapped them in a warm blanket of power that sheltered them from the wind. As their passion took hold of her, the ship moved faster still, pulling ahead of the other, driving toward home.

THE END

ACKNOWLEDGEMENTS

The people who have been most supportive in this journey don't change much, but there are sometimes those who come and go. As always, there are many people in my life who aren't mentioned here for brevity sake. All of you are still very important to me.

I want to offer specific thanks to the following people.

To my mom Linda for your loving support and for helping me brainstorm and refine my ideas.

To Michael for years of partnership and supporting my dreams.

To Rick and Ann for always being willing to read and give feedback on my books and for being the best of friends.

To my uncle Greg for being an avid fan of the series and a great editor on this book.

To Kai for sticking by me and helping keep me sane through an incredibly difficult time.

To my good friend and fellow author Eldritch Black for sharing long rides to the coffee shop full of cathartic rants and commiseration and for being an amazing writing companion. Also to the rest of that writing group, for making so many Thursdays productive and fun.

To Aradia for knowing I would succeed from the first time we met and being an inspiration in your dedication to your own art.

To my cover artist, Robert, and my interior designer, Brian, thank you both for your fantastic work and for your patience with me as I continue to learn this process.

I must also offer thanks to my sixth grade teacher, Mr. Johnson, for being so pleased and excited when I told you I was going to be an author and to my eighth grade algebra teacher, Mr. Siebenlist, for almost letting me flunk because you were so delighted that I was writing books in class rather than notes.

AUTHOR BIO

Nikki started writing her first novel at the age of 12, which she still has tucked in a briefcase in her home office. She now lives in the magnificent Pacific Northwest tending to her sweet horse, two manipulative cats, and a crazy dog. She feeds her imagination by sitting on the ocean in her kayak gazing out across the never-ending water or hanging from a rope in a cave, embraced by darkness and the sound of dripping water. She finds peace through practicing iaido or shooting her longbow.

•

Thank you for taking time to read this novel. Please leave a review if you enjoyed it.

•

For more about me and my work visit me at
http://nikkimccormack.com.

•

OTHER NOVELS BY NIKKI MCCORMACK

The Girl and the Clockwork Cat
A young adult steampunk adventure.

The Girl and the Clockwork Conspiracy
The adventure continues.

Forbidden Things, Book One: Dissidents
An epic, romantic fantasy.

Forbidden Things, Book Two: Exile
The fantasy becomes evermore complicated.